COWBOY MAGIC

THE TRIPLE C RANCH SERIES
BOOK ONE

JILL DOWNEY

BOOKS BY JILL DOWNEY

The Heartland Series:

More Than A Boss

More Than A Memory

More Than A Fling

The Carolina Series:

Seduced by a Billionaire

Secret Billionaire

Playboy Billionaire

A Billionaire's Christmas

The Triple C Series

Cowboy Magic

Cowboy Surprise

Cowboy Magic

The Triple C Ranch Series

Book 1

by
Jill Downey

This novel is a work of fiction. All places and locations are used fictitiously. The names of characters and places are figments of the author's imagination, and any resemblance to real people or real places are purely a coincidence and unintended. No part of this publication may be reproduced, stored in a retrieval system, copied, shared, or transmitted in any form or by any means without the prior written permission of the author. The only exception is brief quotations to be used in book reviews.

Cover Design Copyright © 2021 Maria @ Steamy Designs
Interior book design by Julie Hopkins
Editor April Bennett @ TheEditingSoprano.com

DEDICATION

In gratitude . . .
to my support team, my editor April, my interior book
designer Julie, and my book cover designer Maria. . .
and the three best cheerleaders ever . . .
Mom, Sandy and Julie

1

*G*unner Cane adjusted his mic as he looked out at the expectant faces in the crowd. Their contagious enthusiasm energized the band. The small venue, with a seating capacity of twenty-five hundred, had sold out in less than an hour. They were on the precipice of something big. He could almost taste it. He glanced around at his band, meeting their eyes, and nodded.

"Howdy folks. I'm Gunner Cane here with my band the Trailers. We're from Nashville and happy to be playing here in Atlanta. I wrote this song a couple months ago. We've never played it for a live audience and I hope y'all like it. One, two, three . . ."

"Destiny came calling on howling winds and I let you slip away . . . leaving me broken . . . all alone with my memories and whiskey laced dreams . . ."

The audience appeared spellbound as his song of heartbreak and regret weaved and wrapped its magic like a fine silk cloak. Gunner normally started the first set with an upbeat tune but he'd decided to try something different tonight. It paid off because the audience was eating it up.

"*I'll walk away . . .*" When the song ended there was a hush before the crowd cheered enthusiastically. It seemed they had a hit on their hands.

"Thanks y'all. We appreciate that. We're going to switch it up now and play an upbeat tune from our latest CD. You can buy it at the merch booth in the lobby and we've got some tee shirts for sale." Gunner switched out his acoustic guitar for an electric and they proceeded to rock the house.

Ninety minutes later they were backstage, soaking wet from sweat and high from their performance. Gunner grinned from ear to ear. "You guys were on fire!"

"You out did yourself tonight Gun," Randy the bass player said. "That slow burn of an encore gets 'em every time. You could mop the floor with your fangirls. I saw your favorite Nashville fan in the audience. She's obsessed."

Gunner rolled his eyes. "Yeah, I saw her."

Randy grinned. "She sure is a pretty little thing, young though."

Gunner blew out his breath. "That she is, and I'm definitely not into jailbait. Not interested."

"You can have your pick. You've got all the girls swooning. If I didn't like ya so much I'd have to kick your ass."

"Oh yeah, you and whose posse?" Gunner absently

watched as the roadies tore down, then snapped out of it and said, "Let's get out of here."

Jimmy, his drummer, walked up and slapped him on the back. "Let's party! I invited a few of the Nashville fans to meet us for some drinks. It's the least we can do for them coming all this way. Gotta keep 'em happy."

Gunner's jaw tightened. "You should have run it by me first. I'll just go on back to the hotel then. Have fun."

"Are you kidding me? Come on man, we've got to celebrate," Randy said.

Greg grabbed his arm as he abruptly turned to leave. "Where do you think you're going?" Gunner looked down at his hand and back up into Greg's eyes, his own glinting with suppressed anger. "Get your hand off me."

"You might not like this part but you've got an album to sell and fans to keep happy. Don't be the arrogant asshole that thinks your voice and looks alone will carry you. Do your job."

"Go to hell Greg." He jerked his arm free and stormed off.

"Gunner!" Randy called, following him. "Come on man, don't let that dick get under your skin. Let's go out for a couple drinks. He's right about keeping the fans happy."

"He doesn't give a shit about that. He's just trying to yank my chain."

"And it's working."

"You'll have to run interference for me."

"You know it bro."

"And keep that asshole Greg away from me."

"I'll make that my number one priority. I've got to call the wife then I'll be ready," Randy said.

"Tell Cindy I said hi," Gunner said. The rest of the band was already piled into the van. He squeezed into the back and after Randy finished his call the driver took off.

*H*ead pounding . . . heart thudding, body aching, *where am I?* Gunner cracked open one eye. He was in his hotel room. As he became conscious, he felt a warm naked body next to him and both eyes sprang open. *What the hell? Why can't I remember anything? I've never blacked out in my life.* Panicked, he sat up and the room began to spin so he laid back down, eyes squeezed tightly shut. *Shit, Harper. His obsessive fan.*

"You're awake," she whispered, stroking her finger down his bare chest. He snatched her hand and pushed it away. Sitting up again, he fought the waves of nausea that gripped him.

"What the hell are you doing in my bed?" he ground out, voice hoarse and gravelly.

"You don't remember?"

"Would I be asking if I remembered?"

Pouting, she sat up and tugged at the sheet to cover her naked breasts. "You invited me."

"There's no way."

"Then why am I here?"

"I don't know, but I sure as hell know that version isn't true."

"Why are you being so mean to me?"

Gunner peered under the covers, relieved to see that even though his chest was bare, he still had on underwear.

Harper eyed him coyly then slipped her hand under the covers. Gunner grabbed it, pushing it away. "No!"

"Then why did you invite me here?"

"I didn't. There's no way. I'm not going to say it again, I need you to leave now." He struggled to get out of bed. Finding her clothes on the floor, he threw them at her and stomped into the bathroom, locking the door behind him. *What the hell?* He felt like puking. Confused, he scrambled to remember anything about how he got back to the hotel last night. *Jesus.* He sat on the toilet waiting for the nausea to pass. After some time, he heard the hotel door click shut and checked to make sure that she'd actually left. *Good. She's gone. A hot shower, round up some aspirin and then I'm going to find out what went down last night.*

He let the jets pound against his shoulders, the water almost scalding him. He felt like shit and his head throbbed so hard he'd have sworn he'd been on the losin' end of a buckin' bull ride. He'd never in his life had a hangover like this one and he was no saint. He worked hard and played even harder. He'd done enough partying to know the difference. This was unlike anything he'd ever experienced before. He'd been drugged. He'd bet his last dollar on it. But who and why?

After he toweled off, he texted Randy.

Gunner: WTF dude.

His cell pinged almost immediately.

Randy: What the hell happened last night?

Gunner: You tell me! I don't know what happened. I woke up in bed with Fangirl. No idea how I got here, let alone how she did.

Randy: Seriously? Dude when me and Jimmy put you to bed you were alone. Bro, you were trashed. I've never seen you like that.

Gunner: You've never seen me like that because I don't get like that.

Randy: What about Fangirl, was it that Harper chick? What'd she say?

Gunner: Yeah her. She says that I invited her. It's BS.

Randy: Not good! See ya in five."

*G*unner sat on the edge of the bed and scrubbed his hands over his face. *What the hell happened to me last night?*

He opened the door at Randy's light knock. He strode in, eyes widening when he saw Gunner. "You look like shit!"

"Gee I hadn't noticed," Gunner countered.

"Talk to me bro."

Gunner sat back down on the unmade bed. "Last thing I remember is sitting at the table and suddenly feeling dizzy. The rest is gone. Total blank. Randy, you know me. I can hold my liquor. I've never blacked out in my life."

"I've gotta say, you have been burning the candle at

both ends and you've been stressed out about leaving our record label not to mention our prick manager."

"I know all that, but that isn't it. Someone doped me."

"That's a pretty heavy accusation. Why would anyone do that?"

Gunner buried his face in his palms and blew out a breath. "I have no idea and no way to prove it."

"Wow, if that's true it's pretty dark."

"Yeah, tell me about it."

"Simplest explanation, it was your number one fangirl, Harper. She's been after ya for a long time."

"Could be, but if she was hoping to get laid, she went about it all wrong. It's kind of hard to get it up when you're passed out cold."

"Dude, I don't know what to tell you."

"Got any aspirin?"

"Yeah." Randy pulled a bottle out of his overnight bag and shook two into Gunner's palm. He swallowed them without water.

"I guess you'll have to chalk this up to experience. Good lesson to keep our eyes on our drinks. Could happen to anyone. Happens to girls all the time. Really sucks."

"The way I'm feeling, I may never drink again."

"Let's get something in your stomach. The hotel offers free breakfast." He glanced at his watch. "We've got a half hour before they quit serving."

"All I want is coffee. I just have to throw my toothbrush and shampoo in my tote and I'm good to go. Listen, I need you to spot for me. If you see any signs of Harper, I'll cut out."

"Got it. Let's go eat."

"Thanks for believing me Randy."

"We've been around the block together a time or two. You're like my brother. I've got your back. You've got about ten hours to sober up before the next show."

Gunner's throat tightened. "I know. Not sure I'll make it."

"The show must go on as they say."

Gunner took one last look around the room or more accurately, the scene of the crime, then slammed the door behind him.

2

Sophia Russo pulled off her apron and stomped to her locker for the last time. Grabbing her bag, she raced out the door to hail a cab. The weather cooperated for the perfect sendoff . . . gray skies and a sloppy wintery mix of sleet and snow. As she tried to wave a taxi over, a passing car doused her with cold slushy water.

With her hair dripping wet and chilled to the bone, she huddled in the cab and fumed. *I got fired because of that jackass celebrity chef? I can't believe this! I thought the manager was my friend.* In one fell swoop she'd not only lost her job but she'd also lost someone she'd thought of as a friend. *This is so unfair. How dare they choose a known womanizer over me. I don't care how good a chef he is!*

Sophia could barely contain her anger by the time the cab pulled up to the luxurious River North condo she shared with her fiancé Scott. She usually felt a moment of wonder when she arrived home, but not today. When they'd bought it three years ago, they'd been ecstatic to find the perfect home in the most sought-after area of Chicago. The location suited them perfectly—close to work for both of them, and the river walk was a stone's throw away. But today all of that felt empty and insignificant.

She tipped the taxi driver then hurriedly escaped inside the lobby. Her hands shook as she pressed the up-arrow button which would take her to the twenty-third-floor penthouse. The doors slid quietly open and she sent a silent prayer of thanks that she had the elevator to herself. Slumping against the back wall, she deflated. Her thin veneer of anger gave way to despair.

In a daze, she robotically stepped out when the doors swished open. Mechanically entering her key combination, it beeped and the door unlocked. She stumbled inside and removed her coat, kicked off her shoes, tossed her bag aside then threw herself onto the couch.

Staring blankly at the ceiling, the shock offered temporary relief from the devastating events. She heard a loud bump coming from the back of the condo. *Did I just hear Scott? What would he be doing home in the middle of the afternoon?* She heard another bang. *Scott is home! Thank God!*

She ran down the hallway and pushed open their bedroom door, reeling back as if she'd been struck. Her fiancé was in *their* bed with his secretary. She grabbed the door frame to keep from falling, suddenly dizzy, her body clammy with sweat. They hadn't heard her. She turned and stumbled back down the hall toward the kitchen. Like a wounded animal, her rational mind had shut down and she operated from instinct. Yanking open the refrigerator door, her eyes frantically surveyed the shelves. Spying the Boston cream pie she'd baked the day before, she grabbed it and pried off the plastic lid, tossing it over her shoulder. Pie in hand, she stomped back towards the bedroom.

Her head felt ready to explode. As she approached the bed, an indignant roar erupted from deep inside. "You dirty cheating bastard! How could you?" Her shrill words were deafening. She lifted the pie and threw it at the shocked couple now cowering on the bed. They tried to duck beneath the sheets but she had the advantage of surprise. It gave her some satisfaction to see them dripping in goo.

As she stormed out of the room, she threw over her shoulder, "Don't bother trying to contact me. I never want to see you again."

On her way out she swept all of their pictures off the fireplace mantel, sending them smashing to the floor. Her anger carried her all the way to her parent's bakery. When she saw her dad, the pain of the betrayal let loose and he caught her as she slumped to the ground. He joined her on the floor and held her, rocking as her body racked with sobs. He didn't ask any questions, he just let her cry it out.

When her tears subsided, she haltingly told her dad the entire story. When she finished, she whispered, "Oh Dad, what am I going to do?"

He squeezed her tight and said, "You'll be alright. Your mom and I are right here by your side. You don't need any of them. You're strong and capable. You'll get through this, I promise."

3

"*D*id you think this day would ever get here?" Sophia asked Amelia, as they disembarked from the plane. She and Amelia, her bestie and current travel companion, had been planning this trip for almost a year.

Since her break-up she'd been living with her parents above their bakery and coffee shop, filling in for her mom and taking her to her doctor's appointments. Her mom had been receiving chemo and radiation treatments for early-stage breast cancer. Thankfully she'd received a clean bill of health and Sophia was no longer needed. As of last week, she was officially unemployed, single and digging into her nest egg to take this dream vacation.

"Holy hell. Did you just see what I saw?" Amelia said, grabbing Sophia's arm. "Our first real live cowboy!"

"Yes, and a gorgeous one at that," Sophia said, eyes glued to the man in question.

Amelia took one look at her friend and giggled. "Close your mouth and quit staring."

Fanning herself Sophia said, "I can't help it. I think he's looking right at me. Oh my God! He's walking this way."

Amelia rolled her large hazel eyes. "I can't believe Ms. Independent with a fortress guarding her heart is acting like she has a schoolgirl crush over some random cowboy. Maybe there's hope for you after all."

"This is no random guy, he is hot! Plus, I'm on vacation and I haven't felt this light in a long time. I'm actually beginning to see that getting fired and breaking up may have been the best things that ever happened to me. I got to spend time with my parents, help Mom through her treatments, go to a couple plays and symphonies, eat at restaurants where other chefs cooked for me—you know, what regular people do." She snuck another glance at the cowboy. "Yep, he's coming straight towards us."

"Yikes. Do I still have lipstick on?" Amelia said, becoming flustered. "Wait! OMG . . . that's Gunner Cane!"

"Who is Gunner Cane?"

"Do you live under a rock? He's a Nashville singer-songwriter or shall I say was. He was just making it big when he up and quit. Big ass mystery. Duh . . . I just thought of something. Gunner Cane!"

Sophia's nose crinkled. "So?"

"As in Cane . . . Triple C Ranch . . . get it? Cane . . . C . . . plus I read somewhere that his family were ranchers. This could be the big break I've been waiting for. My nose is twitching."

"Oh no you don't." Sophia hissed. "This is our vacation."

"Chillax. I can do both. It's been way too long since I've had a breaking story."

"Forget it. I know what you're like when you're into your journalistic mode."

"Shh." Amelia plastered a smile on her face.

The corners of Gunner's dreamy brown eyes crinkled as he smiled, "I think you may have dropped something." Holding a patent-leather pink clutch in one hand and her wallet in the other, he presented them to Sophia with a wink.

Embarrassed, Sophia snatched them from his hands. She didn't dare meet his eyes. She mumbled, "Thank you . . . it must have fallen out."

"You might want to be more careful next time," he said, in a slow sexy drawl.

Her cheeks were on fire and she cursed her propensity for blushing.

"Ladies," he said as he tipped his cowboy hat. "Have a good day." They both watched him saunter off, mesmerized by his confident stride and gorgeous ass in his faded Levi's.

Her cheeks still warm Sophia said, "Now that was humiliating, damn him. I probably came off like some fangirl. He smirked at me, then had the nerve to wink."

"I can think of a thousand things worse than him winking at me," Amelia said. "Besides that, he's used to it."

"You're not helping. That was embarrassing. Geesh,

my wallet of all things. He must have thought I was a real airhead."

"Get over it. It can happen to anyone and so what if he saw you drooling, it's a compliment."

Sophia glared. "Again, not helpful." She straightened, then puffed out her chest comically mimicking him in an exaggerated drawl, 'You might want to be more careful next time!'"

It made Amelia laugh. "Come on, let's go get our luggage and then see about our rental car." She tugged on her best friend's hand. "We didn't fly all the way out here to Wyoming to let some arrogant country singer rain on our parade. Plus, I may have just received a gift from the gods."

Sophia glared at her friend. "I'm warning you, no work."

"A girl has to make a living. Being a freelance journalist means you take whatever you can get wherever you can get it. I need this so badly right now I can almost taste it. Please say you'll help me."

"Absolutely not. Its unethical. We'd be here on false pretenses. Keep me out of it."

"It wasn't intentional . . . We didn't look for this. It was fate. Can I help it if the perfect scoop landed in my lap?"

Sophia looked heavenward as they linked arms and headed to the baggage claim area. She knew her friend well and she was like a bloodhound when she caught a scent. It was going to be next to impossible to convince Amelia to back off. They joined the other passengers gathered around the carousel waiting to grab their luggage.

Sophia spied one of her bags . . . the extra-large hot pink suitcase came toward her and she stepped up to retrieve it. As she struggled to hoist the heavy burden off the conveyer, a large tanned hand reached for it and easily lifted it, parking it next to Sophia's high heeled feet.

Startled, she looked up and fell right into the same velvety brown eyes from before. Gunner Cane, that drop dead gorgeous, arrogant cowboy.

Her lips pressed together. "Are you always in the habit of sneaking up on complete strangers?"

"Not always," he drawled, his eyes raking across her face, lingering on her lips.

"Well thanks," Sophia said. Feeling the familiar heat in her cheeks she bowed her head. *I will not make the same mistake of looking him in the eyes.*

"I take it you're moving here?"

Surprised she looked up, her eye's widening, then she noticed his teasing smirk. "Aren't we funny, a real comedian. Aren't you wasting your talent out here in the middle of nowhere?" Sophia asked, giving him an obvious fake smile.

"Could be. Actually, I'm not that funny, music's my thing. By the way, that pink monstrosity weighs a ton."

Sophia rolled her eyes. "I've been told. That's why they invented wheels."

Eyes twinkling, he said, "So that's the reason. I've always wondered about that. I'm Gunner."

She ignored him and watched for her second bag.

"Hi, I'm Amelia and the one moving here is my friend Sophia," Amelia said, smiling, revealing dimples and a small gap between her two front teeth.

"Where y'all coming from?" Gunner asked.

"Chicago," Amelia said.

"You wouldn't by chance happen to be here for a stay at the Triple C Ranch, would you?"

Sophia glanced up through narrowed eyes. "Why do you ask?"

"I came to fetch a group of nine that came in on this flight. I knew there were a couple of folks coming from Illinois that declined our pick-up service. I just made an educated guess."

"Is it too late to hitch a ride?" Amelia asked.

"I have plenty of room," he said.

Sophia jabbed her elbow sharply into her friend's side. "Don't you remember we thought we might want to explore a little on our own."

"I don't know about you, but I'd love a chauffeur right about now," Amelia said, shooting a warning glare at Sophia.

"You won't really need your own car anyhow. We offer excursions and sightseeing, not much of a reason to rent a car." He looked at Sophia and said, "You might be safer if you have someone to look after you, all things considered. We don't see a lot of pink in these parts, it could draw unwanted attention." He gave her a wide-open grin which set her teeth on edge.

She mumbled under her breath, *"Such as yourself?"* She busied herself looking for a pretend something in her clutch. Glancing up through her lashes she saw that he was staring at her.

"What?" she said.

"What?" he responded.

"Don't you have something more interesting to do besides stare at me?"

"Not really," he said.

"Use your imagination," she said primly.

"Oh I am."

Sophia spying her second bag, grabbed it from the carousel and plopped it down beside the other one. The rest of the group had retrieved their luggage and were waiting expectantly. You could feel the excitement in the air.

"Don't you think your bags clash a little?" he said, flashing that irritatingly charming grin.

"Is that any of your business?"

His lips twitched. "Seems to me like ya got a bee in your bonnet." His gaze scanned the group and he said, "Looks like the gang's all here, follow me."

Sophia slung the strap from bag two over her shoulder and extended the handle of her humongous pink suitcase until she heard it click. She struggled to keep up as she grappled with her luggage . . . *the heels certainly don't help.*

Amelia was already way ahead of her. Her practical friend was used to traveling light and leaving at the last minute to follow a story. She had on tennis shoes; hence she had no trouble keeping pace with the rest of the group. Amelia wore her dark brown hair in a short shag cut; she was a no fuss no frill kind of girl. She had struck up a conversation with the enemy, otherwise known as Gunner, and seemed to be flirting. *Grrr . . . Fairweather friend!*

"Don't mind me, I'm just along for the ride," Sophia

muttered to herself, her heels click-clacking loudly on the tiled airport floor.

Gunner looked back and stopped until she caught up. "Do ya need some help with that buffalo you're hauling?"

"No, thank you."

Gunner shrugged. "Suit yourself."

"I will."

A good-looking guy separated from their group and walked back to join them, grabbing the handle of Sophia's suitcase right out of her hand. "Here allow me. I can't stand to see a beautiful woman doing hard labor. I'm Ben, by the way."

Sophia batted her dark brown eyes at him. "Why thank you, Ben. I really appreciate it."

"Don't mention it."

She looked at Gunner and tilted her chin up. Gunner shook his head and rolled his eyes at her. "Okay folks, y'all wait here while I run ahead to get the van, I'll meet you out front."

"Oopsy, already on the bad side of our cowboy, I see," Amelia whispered.

"It was his fault."

"I'm pretty sure he was flirting with you. Play nice, you could end up being my ace in the hole."

"Leave me out of your scheming."

"I can tell. He's already into you."

Sophia scoffed. "Into me? Is that what you call it?"

Gunner pulled up to the curb in the black SUV limo and hopped out.

"Times a wastin'," he said cheerfully, as he loaded their luggage into the back. "Let's get y'all back to the ranch and settled in. We've got about an hour ride to get there. I'm sure you're hungry and Mama has a grand spread planned for your welcoming dinner."

Sophia and Amelia exchanged a glance. Grinning, Amelia silently mouthed "Mama?" Sophia shrugged.

A tall blond guy reached out to Sophia to give her a hand up, but Ben beat him to it. She smiled at them both, thanking them demurely. Gunner watched her with narrowed eyes. *Take that Mr. Hot Shot country star I've never even heard of!*

A middle-aged couple took the two front seats right behind the driver's seat and the woman couldn't stop her excited chattering. "Oh my God! Is this luxurious or what? White leather seats . . . have you *ever*?" A young and cute twenty-something girl hastily claimed the front seat next to the driver.

"I've got both of your CDs. I can't believe I'm sitting here next to Gunner Cane! Will you be the one taking us out on horseback?" she gushed as Gunner climbed in.

"Might be, could be me or one of my brothers, or one of the other wranglers that work on the ranch," he said. "I'm glad you like the CDs. Who do I have the pleasure of sitting next to?"

"I'm Megan. Those are my parents sitting right behind us."

Her mom then turned in her seat to address the rest of the group seated in a lounge type set-up in the back. "I'm Margaret and this is my husband Bruce, and our beautiful daughter Megan's in the front seat."

Everyone seemed warm and friendly, tossing out greetings and names.

Gunner called out, "Help yourselves to the beverages of your choice, we have a fully stocked fridge back there. Beer, wine, vodka and mixers, anything your heart desires."

Since Sophia was closest to the fridge, she became the designated bartender. "I draw the line at fancy drinks," she said.

"Damn, I wanted a martini, lightly shaken, with a twist of lemon," this coming from a grinning Ben, her helper, who like her had city slicker written all over him. Sophia wondered why he'd booked this trip. Probably hoping for a true cowboy experience.

"I'm Sophia, by the way. Thanks for your help with my suitcase; I've never learned the art of packing light," she said, grinning.

He stared at her wistfully. "When I booked this trip, I hadn't even considered the possibility that I might meet the love of my life. Did you just walk off the set of a movie or what?" he said.

Sophia beamed at him, her ego partially assuaged from her brief exchange with that annoying cowboy in the driver's seat. "What's the next best thing to a martini?"

"Gin and tonic would be great, still want that twist of lemon though."

"I think I can handle that."

The rest of the group opted for beer, and Sophia passed them out. Gunner had turned up the stereo and country tunes streamed through the surround-sound speakers, adding to the celebratory vibe.

Sophia couldn't keep her mouth from gaping at the magnificent scenery. The endless sky, the mountains,

the wide-open ranges, the wildflowers, the sheer vastness of the territory was spellbinding and oddly
comforting, like somehow, her worries were all insignificant by comparison.

She happened to glance towards the front and met
Gunner's piercing eyes glinting from his rearview
mirror. Her heart fluttered in her chest. *What is wrong
with me?*

"You're awfully quiet all of a sudden, is everything
alright?" Amelia asked.

"Yes, just taking it all in. It's incredible isn't it?"

"Yes, and then some."

"It's like all of my troubles are a speck of dust," she
admitted.

"I know, right?" Amelia said, nodding towards the
front and winking.

Sophia ignored the implication and said, "Just look
at those mountains."

Ben chimed in, "Is this your first time visiting
Wyoming?"

"Yes. How about you?" Sophia said.

"I've been out west several times. Not here to
Wyoming, but Montana and New Mexico. I love it. It's a
come-to-Jesus moment every time."

"I can see why," Amelia agreed.

"Me and Scooter are here mostly for the fly fishing," Doug, the tall blond, chimed in. "We'll do a little
horseback riding and maybe even some floating down
the river, but I'd be content to fish and eat the entire
time."

Scooter added, "This is our third vacation with the
Triple C. They go all out. The food is fantastic, and they

have square dancing and campfires, and there is always the pool and a good book if you feel lazy."

"They also have a bar. Maybe you'd let me buy you both a drink sometime?" Doug said, as he eyed Amelia and Sophia appreciatively.

Amelia smiled warmly. "I'm sure that can be arranged."

Sophia looked at the group of three women who appeared to be traveling together and asked, "What about you guys, what's on your vacation bucket list?"

"Horses and cowboys!" Renee admitted cheerfully.

The other two women nodded their agreement. "Yeah, we're here to relax and ride, and hopefully flirt a little," Angie added.

Renee nodded towards the front of the van, "The menu isn't too shabby."

Amelia and Sophia exchanged a glance.

"Hey, what are we chopped liver?" Ben groused.

Renee laughed. "Who said you weren't part of the menu?"

"Good save," he said.

"Look! I think we're here!" Sophia said, as they drove through two imposing wood pillars with a rustic Triple C logo burned into the wooden cross beam.

They wound around the gravel lane until the grand lodge came into view. Sophia gasped. "It's beautiful!"

"Wow. It looks like a Swiss chalet," Amelia said.

"Everybody hop on out. We'll tend to your luggage and deposit it in your cabins, oh except for you, Red," Gunner said, grinning at Sophia. "Since you didn't want any help."

She sent him daggers, hoping it would pierce his huge ego. "No problem."

"Come along Sophia. As irresistible as you are, we'd better follow the others and head on over to the main lodge. We have a little welcoming intro to the place to tell y'all how things work around here. After that we'll take you to your cabins and you can freshen up before supper." Sophia stared straight ahead and marched haughtily towards the lodge, her stiletto heels unsteady on the gravel. She heard Gunner chuckling softly and wanted to scream. Two hound dogs were baying, tails wagging enthusiastically. Sophia stopped to pet them. "And who are you two beauties?" she cooed.

"These two mutts are our official greeters. Lenny and Clifford. Ya gotta love a hound." Gunner grinned. "They take their jobs very seriously."

"They're adorable." She crouched down to pet them and laughed when one of them swiped her face with his big tongue.

She followed Gunner and they stepped onto the large veranda then followed the group into the main lodge.

"Wow! This place is gorgeous. Look at those massive log beams, and the humongous stone fireplace," Amelia said, pointing as Sophia walked up. The foyer was huge and had inviting club chairs and couches forming a U-shaped area to gather around the fireplace with a big screen TV perched above it. A wagon wheel chandelier dangled from the wooden crossbeam directly over seating area.

Amelia whispered, "What were you and my subject talking about?"

"Trust me, nothing of importance, except I did get to meet Lenny and Clifford. Much humbler than our cowboy."

"Oh really? Is that why your cheeks are flushed?"

"No, it's called irritation. He is so full of himself."

"This is going better than I could have dreamed of. Is it possible that you're fighting an attraction to him?"

"Ha! Is he good looking? Yes. Am I interested? No! I like my men kind and considerate, not sarcastic and big-headed!"

"Whatever you say. He's the complete opposite of Scott . . . which I might add, is a very good thing. Scott was an uptight snob and you were way too good for him. Gunner seems laid back and fun. You can have a great vacation flirtation while helping your friend solve the best kept mystery in Nashville. Why did Gunner Cane leave the industry when he was on the precipice of stardom? And while we're at it, I myself am interested in that handsome bartender back there," Amelia said. She pointed to an archway leading to a dimly lit bar complete with the requisite horseshoe logo burned into the wooden sign over the door.

"You're impossible. The bartender does look pretty cute though. You have two weeks to pursue. Maybe that will take your mind off of this spy nonsense."

"Doubtful. I'm good at multitasking."

Ben approached, eyeing them speculatively. "You ladies want to meet up for a drink later?"

"I'm sure we'll have loads of opportunities for that in the next couple of weeks," Sophia said. "We'll probably crash early tonight." Her eyes were drawn against her will to the irritating Gunner Cane, who was raking his hand through his thick tousled hair. Those brown eyes crowned by thick dark lashes and brows that matched were too much. He glanced over and caught her staring. *Dang him!* He winked, gazing at her lips for several seconds too long. Something stirred deep inside and she felt her body tingle with excitement.

"I'll turn y'all all over to my sister Becca; she's way better with words than me. She'll give you the low down."

A young woman with a bright smile and her dark hair tied up in a ponytail stepped up and said, "Gather round, and welcome to the Triple C, I'm Becca, the youngest of the Cane tribe . . . except for my nephew Clayton. We're proud to say that the ranch has been in our family for four generations. All of the cabins are what we like to call rustic luxury. Each one has a gas fireplace, hot tub and all the amenities to make your stay comfortable. The cabins have great views of the mountains and walking trails right outside your door. We keep our guest numbers to twenty-five a week so we can make sure you have the ultimate dude ranch experience. There's a little something for everyone. Archery, cattle drives, skeet shooting, hiking, dancing, campfires, there will be something to suit your fancy. I'm the host, concierge, you name it, I do it around here. Don't hesitate to ask me about anything, that's what I'm here for. My cell phone is on the info sheet in your cabin."

Sophia raised her hand tentatively. "Are there bears or mountain lions that we should be worried about?"

"Unfortunately for the grizzlies their population is way down and they're listed as threatened. We haven't had any encounters or sighting here for years. The mountain lions tend to be shy so groups are better. We recommend that you never hike alone." Becca smiled. "You'll be safe here. Just don't wander off too far and take a pal."

Sophia liked Becca already. She had a warm demeanor and seemed gentle and kind . . . *unlike* her brother.

Becca resumed her introduction. "The dining hall is to your left and you can see the bar entrance toward the back," she said, motioning with her hands. "We have cocktail hour every evening from seven to eight with drink specials. Friday is the outdoor BBQ. We serve breakfast, lunch and dinner here at the main lodge dining room and our mama along with Chef James do all the cookin'. You won't be disappointed I promise you." She continued, "We offer ranch raised beef and chicken, farm fresh eggs, locally grown produce and all our meals are made from fresh ingredients. Don't worry, you can work off the calories if you want to."

Renee said, "What about river rafting?"

"Yep, I forgot to mention that. We partner with an outdoor adventure group that can fix you up. For those of you here to ride, tomorrow Gunner will assign you to a horse according to your experience level. You will ride the same horse for your entire stay. Trail rides, cattle drives, and you'll be responsible for your horse's care . . . stalls, grooming . . . but the boys will lead you through all of that."

Sophia whispered to Amelia, "I can't wait to ride."

"Me either," Amelia whispered back.

"We offer expert guides for hiking and fly fishing, which is practically out your front door, and I teach a two-step dance class before our big dance night. Camp-fires, floating excursions, you definitely won't get bored."

Another tall cowboy with dark hair, chiseled cheeks, and piercing dark eyes appeared. "This is my oldest brother Luke. He'll take you two guys to your cabins now," she said, nodding at Scooter and Doug.

"Eli, come on over here and show these ladies to their cabin." Becca said, motioning towards Renee and her two friends. "This handsome cowboy is my brother Elijah, and our family's rodeo star. We've been gifted with his presence in the height of rodeo season due to injuries from a bucking bronco. He's off for a few weeks recuperating after chewin' some gravel."

Sophia's eyes widened when she got a good look at Eli. Lean sinewy muscles and strikingly good looking. Dark hair like the rest of the family and laugh lines fanning out around his hazel eyes as he said hello to the group. Drop dead gorgeous!

Sophia almost laughed out loud at Amelia's expression. She whispered, "Close your mouth, you're catching flies."

Eli stopped beside Sophia and Amelia and said, "Ladies I look forward to showing you around the ranch. I'll make sure your stay here at the Triple C is a memorable one." His gaze felt like a caress and Sophia's heart raced. Then he turned to lead the other group of women to their cabin.

Sophia said softly on a moan, "Why can't he be the one taking us to our room?"

Becca motioned to Gunner who was talking with a young woman by the bar entrance. He ended the conversation and sauntered over. "Gunner, will you show Sophia and Amelia to their cabin?"

"My pleasure. Ladies, follow me."

Of course, we'd get stuck with the hot shot. Sophia rolled her eyes at Amelia who stuck her thumb up, smiling like she'd just won the lottery.

4

*G*unner's boots sounded loud on the wooden front porch. He unlocked and opened the door to their cabin and stepped back for them to enter.

"Oh my God! It's delightful," Sophia said, breathlessly as she entered. The small but open living area was rustic yet lavish, with a small kitchenette and a cozy couch and club chair in front of the fireplace. They peeked into their shared bedroom, which was right off the main room. There were two full-sized beds with frames made of cedar logs, covered with red plaid quilts and overstuffed pillows. Very inviting.

"I love it!" Amelia said.

Sophia peered out the front window. "That view alone is worth the price of the ticket . . . it's amazing!"

"You just wait until you get out on your horse. It'll blow your mind," Gunner said. "Had to leave it all and come back again to fully appreciate it. I took it for granted 'cause it was all I knew, born and raised here. I can tell ya, that scene right there," he nodded toward the window, "it never gets old."

She glanced at Gunner as he stood gazing out the window and felt her heart fluttering again at his raw animal magnetism. Despite her annoyance with his overconfidence, there was no denying that he was one gorgeous man. His dark hair curled softly just below his ears. The sun had left his skin a golden tan, *Geesh . . . those laugh lines fanning out around his eyes, lips made for kissing . . . STOP,* she abruptly pulled her thoughts away from that dangerous territory and onto a safer topic.

"What horse will I get to ride?"

"Are you completely green?"

"By green you mean no experience?"

"Yep."

"Then I'm as green as it gets. City girl born and raised. I've never been on a horse, but I've wanted to since I was a little girl."

"I imagine I'll put you on either Scout or Pirate. We have some great beginner horses, but those are two of my personal favorites."

"What color are they?"

"Scout is a tan buckskin and Pirate's a black and white Pinto."

"What about me? I had lessons for a few years in my teens, but only in dressage," Amelia said. "And, I've taken trail rides on my vacations."

"I'll probably give you an intermediate ride, maybe Dale or Cash or even Bonnie."

"I like the idea of riding a horse named Bonnie," she said, laughing.

"She's spirited but has a good head on her shoulders," Gunner said.

"Perfect," Amelia replied.

"Well, I'll let you two get settled. Supper is served anywhere between five and six, family style with your meat cooked to order."

"I'm starving, we'll be there at five," Sophia said.

"See ya then," Gunner paused and gave Sophia a penetrating stare before leaving.

"He is totally into you," Amelia said. "Winning!"

Sophia frowned and tucked her hair behind her ears. "Really Amelia. I wish you'd drop it. I'm a terrible liar and he has a right to his privacy. Plus, it's not that he's into me, he's doing his job."

"Wrong. It's so obvious, but enough about him for now. Sophia can you believe it, we're here!" she twirled around.

"No. I can't believe it. It's like a dream. What are you wearing to dinner . . . or should I say supper?" She giggled.

"I'm changing into shorts and a fresh tee shirt."

"I'm wearing my flouncy flowered sundress and my red leather cowboy boots."

"Of course, you are! That will be sure to make a statement," Amelia said. "Cowgirl fashionista who has never seen the back end of a horse."

"Whatever, you can't dissuade me, I'm going for it."

"You'll look hot no matter what you wear. Every guy here is already half in love with you."

"It's a curse," Sophia said, grinning.

"Good thing I love you so much or I'd be jealous,

but since we've been friends since middle school, I'm used to it."

"You have your own share of admirers. I don't feel the least bit sorry for you. You sneak up on them and pow, before they know what hit them, they're gaga. Now I'm going to change. I need food!"

*T*wenty minutes later they were walking back to the main lodge. There was something about her red cowboy boots that made Sophia feel sexy. Her dress hit about mid-thigh and swirled around her shapely thighs as she walked. The spaghetti straps left her slim arms and shoulders bare and the outfit displayed her curves and long legs to their best advantage. She had tied up her hair in a high ponytail that trailed in waves down her back. Her eyes glittered with excitement.

Sophia saw Gunner do a double-take when they entered the dining room and Amelia shot her a look which said *I told you so*. He sat at a table with his family; Becca was there, the brothers and a young boy of about three or four years. An older man with steely gray hair sat at the head of the table, and a lovely sixty-something woman sat to his right. Due to the strong resemblance, Sophia thought it was a safe assumption that the older man was the patriarch of the Cane family.

She and Amelia took a seat at a long table with Ben, Scooter and Doug. Sophia was glad they'd decided to ride in with the group. It was nice to already have made a few acquaintances.

Ben was a real flirt and Sophia found herself relaxing, enjoying the friendly banter. "You girls sure do take my mind off of the fishing I've been dreaming about. Maybe we can talk you into some casting on the river?"

"No way. First off, I couldn't stand to see that poor little fish dangling off my line and secondly, I'm here for the horses," Sophia said.

"Don't worry, we catch and release," Doug said.

Amelia said, "I'd consider it."

"Count me out. But if you want to try don't worry about me," Sophia said to Amelia.

Amelia patted her friend on the back. "Don't take it personal guys, my friend here is a girly girl. I can't wait to see her muck stalls. Soph and horse manure . . . now that's worth its weight in gold."

Sophia's eyes went round. "What? Muck? What does that mean?"

Eli took that moment to appear and, leaning down, he rested both hands on the table. "Ladies, don't let them scare ya off."

"Means cleaning the stalls," Ben said, grinning from ear to ear.

"Who said we'd have to clean the stalls?" Sophia's voice came out in a squeak.

"It's part of the ranch experience. Becca did mention stalls in her little spiel. You must have blocked it," Ben said, laughing at her shocked expression. "If I'm not out fishing, I'll muck your stalls for you. But you'll get used to it. It builds character."

"I already have enough character. I'll have to pass," Sophia said determinedly.

"Good luck with that," Scooter said. "You won't get to ride if you don't plan on taking care of your horse."

"I'm on vacation, and horse poop stinks and its gross," she replied.

Elijah looked at Sophia's shocked expression his eyes glinting with humor. "It's Sophia, right?" At her nod he continued. "You don't have to do anything you don't want to do. If anyone tells ya otherwise just come to me."

She smiled, suddenly feeling shy. "Thanks . . . ah . . . Elijah." Her heart beat a mile a minute. *Geesh! How old am I?*

"Our mom makes some mean mashed potatoes. The secret is loads of garlic, butter and sour cream. Don't tell her I told you." He winked.

Sophia took a big mouthful of the mashed potatoes that were drowning in gravy and looked heavenward. "I'm dying here, this tastes incredible!"

"Every meal is this good!" Scooter said. "Just one of the reasons we keep coming back."

Eli straightened. "I'll leave y'all to your supper." He walked back to his table as she and Amelia watched, wondering if they'd just arrived in heaven.

She happened to look over and caught the gaze of Gunner who stared at her with narrowed eyes, looking like she was his next meal. Her face heated and she quickly looked away. *Oh my* . . . she reflexively touched her lips. He was one hot cowboy. She couldn't decide who was the sexier between the two brothers, Eli or Gunner. Overconfidence must run in the family or was a requisite of being a cowboy, because these boys had it in spades. Then there was Luke. He seemed a little too dark and brooding for her taste but those other two . . . *mmm.*

She surreptitiously stole glances at the Cane brothers throughout dinner. Her body was energized and all tingly and alarm bells were going off in her head. She wasn't here for a fling. She was here to figure out the mess that was currently her life. It had been six months almost to the day since her world had imploded. She needed to make some decisions . . . she couldn't allow herself to get distracted by the sinfully gorgeous charmers and she was not going to help her friend get any scoop. *Nope . . . not going there . . . I mean it! End of story.*

5

*I*t was all Gunner could do to stop himself from staring at Sophia Russo as she entered the dining hall. He watched as she brushed an escaped lock of hair behind one ear. The rest of her wild red mane was secured in a ponytail and fell in warm soft curls to her mid-back. She was stunning . . . body to die for, smooth creamy skin, eyes a dark coffee-bean brown. He would have his work cut out for him keeping a lid on his desire. She made him want to whisk her away on Amitola, keeping her tucked away from the rest of the world and all to himself.

Elbowing him in the side, his sister Becca whispered, "You're staring."

"No, I wasn't."

"Whatever, you can lie to yourself but from where I'm sitting it's obvious. She is a beauty that's for sure."

"Just my type," Elijah piped in.

Gunner snorted. "Every woman's your type."

"She may be stunning but she is a guest. You know the policy," his father said sternly.

"Yes, we don't want to forget that now, do we?" Gunner said.

"Now Bill, they're all grown up, I think we can trust their judgement on who they can date or not date," their mom Abby inserted.

Gunner had to force himself to concentrate on his meal, which tonight featured beef tenderloin with garlic served with carrots, broccoli and a side salad. His mom Abby was the head chef for breakfast and lunch, but several years ago they'd hired Chef James to take over the dinner menu, all except for desserts and the freshly baked breads she made daily.

The ranch hosted about twenty-five at full capacity and his mama had several cooks that assisted in food prep. After four generations, they had the ranch operating, most of the time, like a well-oiled machine.

Unfortunately for Gunner, Sophia took a seat right in his line of vision. He drew in a long breath. Damn but she was fine. When she glanced up and saw him staring at her, she'd quickly looked away . . . but he wasn't alone, he'd caught her looking his way a time or two. He knew he was playing with fire, but he had full intentions of being her designated wrangler during her stay at the Triple C, even if it meant fighting his brother for it. Some things were non-negotiable.

He might not be able to touch but that wouldn't stop him from looking. Hell, a light flirtation was part of the package as far as many of the female guests were concerned. He wouldn't want to disappoint anyone. They paid big bucks to vacation at the Triple C. He looked forward to the next couple of weeks keeping the guests happy. One fiery red head in particular. Things were looking up.

6

*A*fter dinner had settled, Sophia and Amelia explored the grounds. They saw Renee and a small group standing around the outdoor riding arena and decided to check it out. She waved and Renee gave her a thumbs up. They climbed onto the fence rail to see what the fuss was about. A horse and rider raced around the ring at breakneck speed, kicking up dust. There were blue barrels placed at either end and they were doing figure eights, circling at a gallop.

The rider was shirtless and tanned, his arms and back muscles strong, straining with exertion. His abs looked like a washboard, not an ounce of fat anywhere on his lean body. He and the horse appeared to move as one. It was breathtaking to watch and Sophia's heart was in her throat.

As he flew by them, Sophia's eyes widened. "That's Eli."

"Wow, you're right! If I wasn't crushing before, I sure am now," Amelia said. "I guess he really is a rodeo star."

After several minutes Eli transitioned to a slower pace to cool down. As he trotted by, he smiled at them and said, "Evening, Ladies."

Sophia had never experienced the feeling before now, but she finally understood the definition of the word swoon.

"Hi," they both gushed at the same time.

"Be still my beating heart," she whispered to Amelia, pretending to fan herself. They weren't the only members of the Elijah Cane fan club. Renee and her friends at the other end of the ring were gawking just like them.

"Damn, he's certainly got the wow factor," Amelia said. "Sorry, not sorry, he's home recuperating."

"Looks like he's ready to get back to it fairly soon."

"I'm sure he's practicing to gain his strength back."

"I could watch him ride all day long," Sophia said.

Elijah jumped easily off his horse, grabbed the reins then headed straight towards them. "How do I look?" Sophia asked, hastily brushing her fingers through her hair.

"Honestly? Gob smacked."

"Huh? You!" She glared. "That's not what I meant. And what about you? You look like you just met Harry Styles," Sophia said, shoving her playfully. Amelia giggled as she lost her footing, ending up with her feet on the ground.

"Ta da. Landed on my feet. I'll get you for that."

"Have y'all had a chance to look around the barn yet?" Eli asked, stopping next to them.

"No, we were just starting out and saw you practicing. That's as far as we got."

"I'm heading that way myself. Why don't you follow me?"

"Okay."

Eli's body was slick with sweat and his horse's coat was wet from the workout. It hadn't rained for a few weeks and they kicked up dust as they went along; the rhythmic clip-clopping of hooves on the hard ground was oddly satisfying.

"How would you gals like to go to a rodeo sometime? Maybe we can squeeze that in before you leave. What do you think?"

"Yes," they both said in unison.

He grinned, laugh lines fanning out around his gorgeous hazel eyes. "Well, that was easy enough. I hope it works out."

Arriving at the barn entrance, Eli said, "I'm going to keep on walking Rusty until he cools off. You can check out the barn." He pointed them in the right direction and walked on.

As they mosied down the aisle, Sophia's breath caught as she eyed the beautiful black horse poking its head out of the stall. "Em, over here!"

She touched the velvet nose and the horse nuzzled her palm. "Why are you all alone in here?" She cooed.

She was startled when a male voice responded. "She came up lame so she's on stall rest."

"Oh," Sophia said. Turning, she met the gaze of a handsome cowboy with sparkling green eyes and blond hair peeking out from beneath his cowboy hat.

"I'm Beau, you'll be seeing me around. I'm a ranch hand."

"Nice to meet you. We just got here this afternoon. This is Amelia and I'm Sophia."

"Nice meetin' ya. Where y'all from?"

"Chicago."

"If there's anything ya need just ask me. I can give you a short tour of the barn now if you'd like."

"That would be fabulous! What's this horse's name?" Sophia inquired.

"Amitola. It's a Native American name that means rainbow."

"That's a beautiful name," Amelia said.

"She's one of Gunner's favorite mares."

"My ears were burning," Gunner said as he approached, expression brooding, with Lenny and Clifford at his heels.

"I was just introducing them to Amitola."

Gunner turned to meet Sophia's gaze directly, his eyes burning a hole through her. "How was your supper?"

"It was really great." She was embarrassed to hear how breathy her voice sounded.

"I see you've met Beau. He's worth his weight in gold around here. He knows how to run the ranch better than I do. My right hand man." Beau smiled shyly and tipped his hat towards Gunner.

"I noticed you both swooning over my brother Elijah. I wouldn't take him too seriously. He's a notorious bang tail. I'm giving you fair warning."

Sophia's brows drew together. "Bang tail?"

"That's a wild untamed horse, you know, a mustang," Beau said.

"Oh. That's a new one. We'll keep that in mind. And what about you? Are you trying to tell us that you're settled down and all domesticated?" Sophia said, arching one brow.

His eyes scorched her lips. "Difference between me and Elijah is, when I find something I like, I play for keeps."

Her breath caught in her throat. "Oh, um . . . well . . . so you say. This is your horse?"

"Yeah."

"She's gorgeous."

He continued to stare at her and said softly, "Yes she is."

Gulp.

"I'm happily stuffed to the gills," Amelia said, breaking the tension. "If we eat like this every day, we're going to have to buy new clothes in a bigger size."

"You'll work it off with your barn chores," he replied, eying Sophia lazily.

"Ch . . . ch-chores?" Sophia said.

He suddenly grinned, flashing his gorgeous white teeth. "Yes ma'am. Chores. Nobody gets out of that. It's part of the wild west experience."

"Oh. But your brother said we have a choice about that."

"Not really. Don't look so worried, Red. I'll teach you."

Through gritted teeth she replied, "My name is Sophia."

"I reckon I already knew that *Sophia*. I happen to think Red suits you better."

"Hardly original," she said. Her pulse had quickened hearing the way he had said her name . . . he'd somehow made it sound like a caress. *Maybe it would be better if he did stick to Red.*

"Didn't claim that it was," he said.

She abruptly turned her back to him and sweetly asked Beau to give them the tour he'd promised.

"Sure thing," Beau said. "Without a doubt it will be my pleasure."

Gunner leaned in real close to her ear, she could smell a hint of mint and felt his breath stir her hair. "Looks like you've already got all the men eating out of your hand. Not going to get you out of your chores though." He grinned wickedly.

Sophia gave him a dirty look. "Are you sure about that?"

"Yep. I'm the boss."

"This is my vacation you know."

"Didn't you read the description of our ranch before you signed up?"

"Kind of. I must have missed the part about paying big money to work my butt off."

He laughed out loud. "That's a good one. I'll leave you to it Beau. I'm going to soak Amitola's foot. Ladies, I'll see you both bright and early tomorrow morning. Be prepared, you'll be getting plenty dirty. Adios."

"Dirty? What? But . . . I . . . I . . ." He'd already turned and walked away.

Amelia laughed at her friends shocked expression. "What part didn't you get about horses and dude ranch? Barns, poop and dirt go together. Wake-up, you're not in the city anymore."

"I know but . . ."

"No buts. Look on the bright side, not only are we in the most beautiful place I've ever seen, the eye-candy is beyond. It'll be fun."

Sophia's nose crinkled. "I guess."

Beau said, "Ready for that tour?"

"Yep."

"Follow me ladies."

7

*A*fter their tour, Amelia suggested they check out the bar. "Let's go introduce ourselves to my next conquest and grab a drink while we're at it."

"Sounds good to me," Sophia said.

Like the rest of the lodge, the bar was rustic chic, with exposed beams, scarred wooden floors and low lighting providing a cozy, wild west ambience. There were several booths lining the back wall and tables scattered around. A fire was roaring in the stone fire-place at the far end of the room and the pool table was in full use. The west-facing wall was comprised of windows that offered a view of the mountains and a back deck with extra seating.

They sidled up to the bar and waited while the bartender served another customer. The back of the bar was lined with fancy liquor bottles illuminated by dimly lit sconces, but the show-stopper was an exquisite painting of a wild horse smack in the center.

She bumped Amelia with her elbow. They were in luck; the bartender was the same cutie Amelia had been hoping to meet. He wore a white dress shirt and black apron and a million-watt smile. "Good evening ladies, what'll you have?" he asked.

"I'll take a glass of Chardonnay," Sophia said.

"Same," Amelia said, staring unashamedly.

He opened a fresh bottle of wine and poured out two generous portions of the amber liquid, his efficiency revealing his experience.

"I take it you two just arrived? I'm Hank by the way." His expression open and friendly.

"I'm Amelia and this is Sophia."

"Where y'all from?"

"Chicago," they said in unison. Laughing Amelia said, "That seems to be the most popular question around here."

"Yeah, people come from all over the country."

Sophia closed her eyes at the first sip of wine, savoring the taste of the dry blend. There were several groups seated at tables close by and she listened to snippets of their conversations, enjoying the stories of adventures they had experienced at the Cane ranch. She smiled taking it all in.

"What d'ya think so far?" Hank asked.

"It's amazing," Amelia said.

"Wine suit ya?"

"I love it. Nice oak finish," Sophia replied.

"Do you want the whole bottle? It's cheaper that way and you can always take it back to your cabin if you don't finish it."

They both nodded their heads yes.

"I'll put it in a wine cooler for you."

"Thanks Hank," Amelia said, giving him a flirtatious smile. "So, have you worked here long?"

"Yeah, since I reached drinking age." He placed their bottle in the clay cylinder.

"Do you work here full time?" Amelia asked.

"Pretty much. Five nights a week from five to close, which varies according to the guests."

Poker faced, Amelia asked, "You must know the Canes fairly well then."

"They're pretty much family. Gunner and I have been best friends since we were little kids."

Amelia's eyes lit up and Sophia shot her a warning look.

Sophia startled when Gunner plopped down on the stool right next to hers. He gave her a once-over and said, "Hank treating ya right?"

"Yes," she said, slightly breathless. *Damn him anyway.*

"You ready for tomorrow? We get started around ten on the first day, nine thereafter except on your flex days. You'll meet your horse and get a crash course on where everything is kept . . . the wheel barrel . . . the rake, the horse bedding . . ."

"Oh, I almost forgot about the 'chores'," Sophia said, rolling her eyes before taking another sip of her wine.

"That's the spirit. A hard worker . . . already mentally preparing herself. Gave me goose bumps just now. Give me a beer Hank, the usual."

Sophia watched as Gunner took a long swig from the frosty mug, lazily wiping the foam from his lips with his tanned forearm. She peered at him from the corner of her eye, irritated by this unwelcome attraction. He had a sensual way of moving that made everything he did seem sexy. Too bad he was so damned arrogant and sure of himself.

Gunner suddenly swiveled around, now facing her, legs straddling her bar stool. His gaze swept over her face, lingering on her lips a touch too long. Her skin felt seared. The intensity of his brooding stare made her want to squirm in her seat. She clasped her hands in her lap, forcing herself to stay still.

The long look felt like it lasted minutes when in fact it was probably seconds. She only knew that for those few seconds time stood still. She found herself more aroused than she had ever been in her life, aware of a tingling between her thighs that she couldn't ignore.

"Um . . . so . . . was that your dad and mom sitting at your table tonight?"

He took his time answering, "Yeah, that's my father, Bill Cane and my mom Abby. He's as tough as old shoe leather and my mom's the complete opposite. Don't get me wrong, when it comes to her children, she is something fierce and she has a way of working my dad without him knowing it."

"You look a lot like your dad," she offered.

"Yeah, I suppose so, with variations," he said.

"And the little boy?"

"My nephew Clayton; he just turned four."

"He's adorable," Sophia said.

"Yes, he is that and he gets away with murder. His mom died before he was three years old, so his grandparents and aunt and uncles, me included, spoil the shit out of him. We're all trying to compensate. He is still a great kid despite us."

"Oh no! How sad for him."

"Yeah, Lauren, Luke's wife, died of cancer, only thirty-eight years old."

Sophia put her hand to her heart. "That's terrible. I'm so sorry Gunner."

"Yeah, me too. I miss her, we all do. Best sister-in-law you could ask for. She and Luke were high school sweethearts."

Maybe he's not as bad as I thought. It would be safer to assume the worst; with his looks and charm, not to mention the fact that he was an almost-famous country singer, she was pretty sure her original assessment was accurate . . . yet still her heart warmed and she softened a fraction of an inch.

"I can't even imagine how one goes on after a loss like that."

"Got to, for Clay, for Lauren, she wouldn't have it any other way, and she was a force to be reckoned with. Was quiet and sweet till ya crossed her. She'd come after us from the grave. He's actually a special little kid. I think he's a child prodigy or something like that, he's already playing the piano. It's unbelievable how quickly he catches on to stuff . . . almost scary."

Sophia laid her hand on Gunner's strong forearm and he looked down then back up to meet her eyes. Like putting a match to dry kindling, they both felt instant heat. *Not good.* She jerked her hand away as if she'd been burned. His eyes smoldered as they bored into hers.

He stood abruptly and said, "I'd better turn in. We

have a big day tomorrow." Chugging down the last of his beer he banged the mug on the counter and left a twenty on the bar. As he walked away, he threw over his shoulder, "Amelia, Sophia, see you in the morning. Breakfast is served family style."

"Goodnight," Sophia said.

Amelia stood and stretched her arms overhead, "See you tomorrow, Gunner."

"Night Gunner, thanks for the tip," Hank called after Gunner as he strode out of the bar without another word.

"Well then, that was sudden, kind of like his exit from Nashville. Was it hard for him when he first came back?" Amelia asked.

"Not for me to say," Hank said, turning his back to them.

Sophia rolled her eyes at Amelia and shook her head.

"We should call it a night as well," Sophia said. "I'm ready for bed."

"Me too. Thanks Hank. You'll definitely be seeing me around."

"I'm counting on it," he said, corking the unfinished bottle and handing it to her.

Leaving a generous tip, the women left and made their way back to the cabin. The minute they escaped the bar Sophia hissed, "Way to go Captain Obvious! That went over well."

Amelia grinned, "I'm just warming up."

"That was about as subtle as a bull in a china shop."

"I guess I'll have to work on my charm."

When they got to the cabin, the first thing Sophia

did was to pull off her boots. "Freedom. My tootsies are thankful."

"Let's sit on the front porch and listen to the crickets. We can finish our wine out there," Amelia said.

"I'll get the glasses," Sophia said.

They both plopped down on the porch swing and propped their feet up on the split railing.

"Is this a little bit of heaven or what?" Amelia said, sighing deeply.

"Just a little bit. It's so peaceful."

"Except for all the testosterone. I'm not sure my heart can take it," Amelia said.

Laughing Sophia agreed, "I know, it's almost painful."

"Isn't Hank sexy as hell? Added bonus . . . he's an intimate friend to Gunner Cane. I can kill two birds with one stone."

"You're relentless. Will you just give it up already? You're stressing me out!"

"I know, but you'll adjust once you surrender to my demands. Back to our topic . . . I know who your type is," Amelia said, smirking.

"You do huh?"

"Starts with a G and ends with an R."

"And you're delusional my friend. First off, I don't really have a 'type' and he'd most definitely not be it if I had one. Way too cocky for my taste. I could never be with someone I had to compete for. Not to mention, I'm certain they have rules and it's a safe bet that dalliances with the guests would be on the list of 'Do Nots,'" she said.

"Yeah, except if my short-term memory serves me, I

think we just agreed to go to the rodeo with Elijah Cane."

"Does a rodeo count as a dalliance?"

"I'll pretend I didn't hear that. I know my friend Soph has a firmer grasp on reality than that . . . at least most of the time. Now more importantly, do you think Hank would be allowed to date the guests?" Amelia asked, staring at the ceiling dreamily.

"I'm sure you'll find out sooner or later. He's definitely into you."

"Yeah, this is shaping up to be the best vacation ever."

"I'm so glad we did this, even if I am jobless and soon to be broke," Sophia said.

"You'll find a job in no time. The worst-case scenario, you can keep working at your parent's bakery. They would love for you to stay on. They are in heaven now that their favorite pastry chef is back."

"I know, but it would literally feel like I was going backwards not forward. I love them to pieces, but I don't want to stay there forever."

"But you do love baking. You seem so happy when you're covered in flour."

Sophia's smile lit up her face, laughing she said, "You've got a point there, I do love it. We'll just have to see what happens. I'm not sure what I'll do next," Sophia said.

"You can't throw away all the blood, sweat, tears and training over something that wasn't even your fault. Who cares what people think? The truth always comes out eventually."

"Meanwhile my culinary reputation is in shambles."

"You're much better off. You always had to watch your back around that miserable chef anyway, not to mention that your supposed friend and manager sold you out."

"Just think, six months ago I was at the top of my career game and now I'm back at my parent's bakery, vacationing in the wild west, and crossing dude ranch off my bucket list."

"Life is so weird."

"I know," Sophia agreed. Yawning loudly, she said, "I can barely keep my eyes open. Will you take care of turning things off and locking up pretty please?"

"Sure thing."

"I'm dying to jump into that comfy looking bed."

"I'm not going to be far behind you. Night Red."

"Don't you even . . ."

Laughing Amelia lightly pushed her foot against Sophia's butt as she headed to bed.

8

*S*ince returning from Nashville, Gunner was
doing his damnedest to convince his father
and himself that he was back to stay. He'd finally
managed to pull himself out of his depression. But as
far as his father was concerned, Gunner wasn't sure
that he'd made much progress. The clipped retort that
guests were off limits had been a reminder of why he
had left in the first place . . . Control.

His father kept a tight rein on everything connected
with the Triple C. Gunner had felt suffocated as a
young man learning about life and himself. He'd never
failed to remind his children of their duty and privilege.
Being born into four generations of ranching didn't
leave a kid many choices. It was expected that he and
his brothers and sister would carry on the family business and traditions.

The fact that he and Eli had chosen different paths
and even Becca for a short while, had never sat well

with his father. To him, their dreams had simply been a rebellion and a slap in the face, signifying their selfishness and ungratefulness for the blood and sweat of past generations. Gunner and Eli had dared to want something different for themselves . . . had needed to break out on their own. An unforgivable sin in their father's eyes.

It didn't help that in the end, his father had been right about him all along. He had to find out the hard way that this was his home and where he belonged. The music scene and city life, playing bars until two sometimes three in the morning, waking up hung-over, the endless partying . . . it had been fun until it wasn't. He had a fallout with his manager Greg over Greg's sister and his record label had failed to make good on their promises. His contract had been about to expire anyway, which at the time he'd thought was just as well, since some bigger labels had been sniffing around to recruit him. The final blow had been the drugged hotel set-up followed by incriminating photographs delivered anonymously via text. After that he didn't know who to trust. That had been a deep cut into his sense of reality and the end of his dream. The timing seemed as good as any to throw in the towel.

The dark path he'd been traveling wasn't going to change itself. His music career was over. Nothing more had ever surfaced about the photographs and Gunner assumed it was because they'd accomplished what they wanted . . . him leaving Nashville.

He'd already hung in there for ten years and he was tired of the scene. After all that time with only one big break, an opening-act gig for Miranda Lambert, he had finally realized that it was far more likely he'd kill himself with drinking than that he'd ever make it in the tough and competitive music industry. He had returned home. Now six months later, he was still trying to prove himself to his father and figure out his life.

It'd been a long time since he'd had felt as drawn to a woman as he was to Sophia Russo, maybe never, almost like a spell had been cast. He should listen to his better judgement and stay as far away as possible from her, but then again, why not allow himself a little fun? *Who am I kidding? I'm not into playing around anymore. Where can it go anyway . . . she's only here for a couple of weeks, then what?* Even so, at the moment his common sense was losing. He didn't think he could pass on this opportunity for a tantalizing distraction. He knew he'd be playing with fire but right now he just didn't give a damn. He blew out his breath. *My life has become a bit too tame . . . from one extreme to another.*

He reached over and turned off the bedside lamp. Fluffing his pillow, he turned on his side and forced himself to shut down his thoughts. He had a full day ahead of him and he already knew that it would include an undeniable temptation . . . in the form of one stunning red head with eyes the color of espresso beans.

*A*fter a restless night of tossing and turning, Gunner was surprised that he felt energized as he walked around checking the progress of his guests. He stifled a laugh when he stepped beside Sophia, he couldn't help himself. She had just taken a tumble trying to clean out her horse's hoof. While squatting behind the back leg she had awkwardly tried to hang on as the horse pulled away, causing her to fall backward right onto her gorgeous jean-clad ass. Gunner reached out to give her a hand up. Standing, she dusted off her backside and knelt to try again.

"Here let me show you," Gunner said, grabbing the hoof pick from her tight grip. He crouched down beside her and tapped Pirate's leg; the horse immediately lifted it. Their shoulders touched as he demonstrated and he could swear he caught a flash of desire before she narrowed her eyes into a glare. It was all he could do to concentrate on the hoof planted firmly across his thigh. *Focus!*

Clearing his throat, he said, "Now, Pirate has been around the block a time or two, so he knows when someone is a greenhorn. You have to act like you know what you're doing."

"And how am I supposed to do that when I haven't a clue?"

"Watch closely and learn," he said. He bit back a smile when he saw her luscious lips tighten. "You can't learn anything with a closed mind."

"I'm all ears."

"See you have to face the back and cradle him against your knee. Bend your legs like this—kneeling is fine for church but in this situation, you have to squat. Dig your heels in for balance and pick out the dirt and debris like this," he said. "Now you try."

She blew out a breath and held out her hand. "Gimmee."

"Have at it," he said grinning. He could tell she was

irritated and he didn't know why it pleased him to get under her skin so easily.

"Do you have to stare at me? It's annoying," she said.

"I need to supervise, and I have to admit, the view is pretty good."

"Are you intentionally trying to irritate me or is it just in your nature?"

"A bit of both I suspect."

She had shown up right on time this morning, all decked out in her red cowboy boots, designer jeans, and red sleeveless tank top. The crowning effect was the navy bandana tied around her neck. It cracked him up. City girl goes rogue. He was shocked that she didn't have on a cowboy hat and leather chaps.

She wore her hair swept up in a high ponytail with long tendrils already escaping and feathering around her delicate features. Biting her lip and wearing an adorably serious expression, he watched as she maneuvered the pick while stabilizing herself and the horse. He noticed the swell of her breasts and forced his gaze away. *What a babe!* All woman. Slim hips, rounded ass, perfectly lush breasts, long legs . . . mmm. *Maybe volunteering for the beginners' group wasn't the brightest idea after all.* He'd had a hell of a fight with his brother Eli over it. In the end they'd tossed a coin and he'd won.

"See, you're getting the hang of it," he said.

"Don't sound so surprised."

"I'm not; you're not my first greenie. You're catching on fast though, that's all I'm saying."

"Thanks." He saw her suppress a smile, appearing pleased by his compliment.

Reluctantly he moved on to check up with the others. He did have an excuse to spend more time with Sophia since she was the only one in the group of six with zero experience. The rest either had some exposure or they hadn't ridden since they were kids, all novices to varying degrees. They had already moved on from the hooves and grooming and were ready to fetch their saddles.

"Let's wait until Red over there is done, she's struggling to figure out which end of the horse is up. We'll head to the tack room together," Gunner said.

This produced a few chuckles from the guys, and a glare from Amelia.

"I'm kidding," he said. Amelia turned her back to him, displaying her loyalty to Sophia.

Megan was in this group and Gunner could tell that she was high maintenance. Her demands had started the minute she saw him. She had a question for everything and was quite obvious in her attempts to gain his undivided attention.

"Gunner," Megan called out in a sing-song voice, "I need you."

Blowing out his breath, he walked over to her and her mount Dale, "What can I do for ya?"

"What's this thingy for?"

"That 'thingy' is a curry comb and it is used to loosen dirt and mud from the horse's coat."

She giggled. "Oh, I was just wondering."

Sophia finished and stood with the rest of the group waiting for Gunner to lead them.

"Follow me, gang." They lined up like little ducks and followed their leader to the tack room. After a brief introduction about where things were located and what they would need, he instructed everyone to grab their designated bridle and saddle and carry them out to their horses.

"You can just sling the saddle over the wood railing until I can demonstrate with Dolly, then I'll supervise the novices." Sophia glared at him. *Novices? Really? GRRR, why does every word that he says get under my skin?*

"Now first watch how I tack up Dolly, then I'll help you both with your horses," he said, nodding at Sophia and Megan.

They watched intently as he hoisted the saddle over Dolly's back, tucking and threading the cinch into the round ring. Then he demonstrated putting the bridle on.

"Alright, now y'all try it," Gunner said.

Sophia seemed to have no trouble placing the saddle on Pirate's back, but the cinch caused her problems. Gunner stepped up beside her to help and the electricity between them was tangible. Gunner caught a whiff of her scent, like a field of flowers. He leaned in a little closer, breathing deeply.

She turned and they practically bumped noses. Quietly he said, "You smell pretty damn good city slicker."

Her eyes flashed. "Better than being a hayseed."

He chuckled, amused at how easy it was to get under her skin. "Are you always this prickly?"

Gritting her teeth, she said, "Actually no, so it's probably you!"

"If that makes you feel better . . ." He grinned wickedly at her, enjoying the sparring.

Megan interrupted, calling him over for help with her bridle. Lips pursed in a pout, she said, "This horse doesn't like me."

"She doesn't know ya yet. Too soon to tell. She'll reserve her judgement until you've been tested." Gunner secretly thought that Megan was probably right. Horses were pretty good judges of character.

"Tested?"

"Yeah, she'll be checking you out for the next few days, assessing your skill level and trying to gain the upper hand. But she's a good horse. Not a mean bone in her body."

"Is that supposed to comfort me?" she said nervously.

"Yep." Turning to the group he said, "I'll go around and check everyone's cinches and after I give it the okay, you can go over to the mounting block and get on." He saved Sophia for last. She watched, biting her bottom lip as he tightened her cinch. "You best quit looking at me like that or I won't be responsible for what happens next."

Her eyes widened as her breath hissed, and he bit back a smile as she sputtered. *She's way too easy.*

Holding the stirrup steady, he instructed her to slip her foot in. Reaching her leg up, she grabbed ahold of the saddle horn at the same time. "Now hold tight and I'll hoist you up," Gunner directed. He placed his hands around her waist and easily lifted her off the ground as she slung her leg over the horse's barrel. She looked down at him, her lips tugging up at the corners. "Thanks."

"Just doing my job. Some parts of it are more satisfying than others."

She rolled her eyes heavenward as he winked.

He quickly mounted Dolly and trotted to the front of the group. "Everyone lineup behind me. Megan and Sophia, you're in front of the line, right behind me."

Sophia called out, "I can't get Pirate to budge."

Gunner turned in his saddle and looked over his shoulder, "Put a little leg on him and click your tongue. Just squeeze your legs together."

Her horse completely ignored her.

"Give him a gentle tap on his side with your heel; Pirate's a little barn sour," Gunner said.

"What does that mean?"

"It means he's a homebody. He'd rather be out in the pasture or at the barn eatin' his fill than working."

"I'm afraid I'll hurt him."

"I keep forgetting that you're a tender-footed city girl. I promise, you won't hurt him none. If you don't show him who's boss, he's going to keep testing you. Now take a deep breath and tell yourself you've got this and try again."

His teasing mood unexpectantly turned to tenderness as he saw Sophia close her eyes and take in a deep breath. He heard her as she gave herself a pep talk and realized that she was nervous.

"You can do this . . ." she said, as she gave a gentle kick. Pirate immediately moved forward. "It worked!" she said, her eye's sparkling, almost childlike in her excitement.

"That-a-girl." Gunner said. He felt a strange ache in his chest as he straightened in his saddle, urging his own mount forward. They followed him in single file. He was unsettled by that stirring in his heart, a feeling that he hadn't had for a long time. *Just who is getting under whose skin, slick?* He shook his head to clear his thoughts and refocused on the trail ride. Best to remember his father's admonitions and keep his mind from wandering back to what it would feel like to have that soft creamy skin naked against his.

9

*S*ophia sank into her saddle as Gunner had instructed and tried to connect her body with Pirate's. Her hips swayed with the movement of her horse's gait. It had a soothing effect and she felt her previous irritation melt away.

The scenery was breathtaking. Sophia had never been this moved by her surroundings. Gunner's broad shoulders and confident seat, his body relaxed and one with his horse, stirred something deep inside of her. His hair was an unruly mop beneath the Texas Rangers baseball cap he wore backwards. She had a funny feeling that after this vacation she would never be the same.

Sophia decided to ignore the butterflies in her belly. Earlier when he'd tightened her cinch, he'd been so close that she'd caught his scent, earthy, some kind of soap, and her pulse had quickened as a wave of heat had coursed through her body. Pure cowboy.

He turned his head and caught her gawking and his eyes burned straight through her. She bit her bottom lip and his lips tilted up before he turned to face the front again.

"Everyone doing alright back there?" He called over his shoulder.

Snap out of it. Shaking off her lustful thoughts, she focused on the beauty of her surroundings.

"Yes." They all responded. Everyone seemed to be as awestruck as she felt. Surely the electricity she felt deep inside her core was due as much to her surroundings and the sense of adventure . . . most definitely *not* because of the seductive cowboy riding in front of her.

*B*eau greeted the group when they returned from their ride. He grabbed the reins from Sophia while she dismounted, then loosened her horse's cinch before unfastening the bridle and replacing it with Pirate's halter. When he removed the saddle for her, Sophia glanced around furtively. "Are you sure you should be helping me? Aren't you afraid you'll get in trouble?" She jerked her head towards Gunner.

Beau grinned. "He don't scare me none."

Out of the corner of her eye she saw that Gunner was busy with the others and not paying any attention to them. Breathing a sigh of relief, she followed Beau to the tack room, carrying the bridle.

"Thanks Beau."

"No problem."

"Thanks for what?" A smooth as silk, irritatingly familiar voice said.

"Oh nothing. He was just giving me some pointers."

"Like showing you how to get out of doing all the work?" Gunner said dryly.

"Now Gunner, in all fairness she didn't ask for no help. I just took it upon myself."

"From now on don't."

Sophia put both hands on her slim hips, and lifted a perfectly sculpted eyebrow. "Don't you think you're being a bit too bossy?"

"I am the boss."

"And obviously on a power trip."

"You'll never learn how to do it yourself if everyone does it for you. I can't say as I'm blaming Beau here, I'm struggling to leave you alone myself."

Her eyes snapped wide open in surprise. "You are?" She said, her voice coming out in a squeak.

His eyes swept her face lingering on her lips. "Don't look so surprised Red. I can't believe you aren't used to it. You're almost from another planet. A 'make a guy go crazy' kind of beautiful."

Her jaw dropped.

Beau chuckled. "Don't take no mind to this snake charmer. He was a big shot country singer awhile back. He knows how to make the ladies swoon."

"Thanks for the help, bro." Gunner punched his friend's shoulder good naturedly. "Whose side are you on?"

"Mine," Beau replied.

Flustered Sophia hurried out of the tack room and back to safety. *Oh my, a charmer indeed.*

10

*T*heir third full day ended with a campfire and smores, perfect weather, and clear skies. Sophia felt pleasantly tired. She stared dreamily into the flames, the smell of smoke and pine evoking childhood memories. She could feel muscles in her body that she'd never noticed before now. Her inner thighs felt sore and she could see why the ranchers were so muscular and ripped. She smiled. She'd actually mucked stalls three days in a row and it wasn't that bad. In fact, she didn't even mind the smell of horse manure . . . she kind of liked it.

"What ya thinking about Red?" Gunner's low warm voice penetrated her thoughts and she glanced up. He sat down on the log right next to her and stretched his legs out in front of him. She watched as he took a bite of his smores, white teeth sinking into the oozing concoction of cracker, marshmallow and chocolate. She was hypnotized by how he licked the chocolate from his lips.

Shaking off her thoughts, she replied, "How tired and sore I am and how good it feels. My body is like mush, all relaxed." She hugged herself and looked at him from the corner of her eye. "I had a really good time today. I'm glad you paired me with Pirate. I'm in love."

"You did real good."

His praise warmed her from the inside out and she felt her toes curl. "Thanks."

He squinted at her and said, "Is it my imagination or are you softening towards me?"

Her lips tugged up at the corners. "Let's just say you're growing on me."

He put his hand over his heart and leaned away from her. "Are you trying to sweet-talk me?"

She laughed. "Who me? No nothing like that. I'm just grateful is all. I needed an escape from my thoughts and I haven't picked up my troubles all day long, same for yesterday. It's as good as therapy."

His hand reached towards her face then, as if having second thoughts, he pulled it back, sticking it in his pocket. She realized she'd been holding her breath and it escaped in a sigh.

Eli and Becca came out carrying coolers and a guitar. Elijah placed the guitar case right next to Gunner.

"I told you I wasn't playing," Gunner said, jaw set.

"Come on Gun, what would a campfire be without a little music? And you're the best guy I know for the job!" Becca cajoled.

"What do you think everybody? Shouldn't Gunner play a few tunes for us?" Eli said.

The twenty plus guests scattered around the fire all began to chant, "Gunner, Gunner, Gunner..."

He blew out a breath and scrubbed his face with both palms before raking his fingers through his hair in exasperation. "Eli, you've put me on the spot. What part of no don't you understand?"

Eli snorted. "It's a cryin' shame to let all that talent go to waste. Time to quit licking your wounds and pick up your guitar again. You've been hiding out way too long," Elijah said.

"You sure do like to hear yourself talk," Gunner grumbled.

Sophia narrowed her eyes and shook her head at Amelia when she saw her friend's ears perking up . . . *bloodhound.*

Megan said, "Please. I'll feel like I died and went to heaven. You just *have* to play for us Gunner."

Renee and her two friends both chimed in as well. "Yeah. How many people get to say that they had a famous country singer play for them around a camp fire?" Renee added.

Megan looked at Gunner dreamily, her crush evident. "Yeah, my friends will die from envy."

Am I the only one that never heard of Gunner Cane until this trip? He looked so distraught that Sophia felt a tug on her heartstrings. She leaned in and said softly, so that only he could hear, "Don't do it."

He looked into her eyes and something flickered for a moment before being extinguished. He looked back down at his guitar and bent over opening the case. In slow motion he pulled out the instrument, handling it like he was afraid to touch it.

Subdued, he began tentatively twisting the tuning pegs as he plucked the strings until he was satisfied. To Sophia he looked devastatingly vulnerable and she wondered what his story was . . . not for Amelia's scoop but for more personal reasons. *Am I developing feelings for this man already? Did I get him all wrong?*

He began to hum and picked out notes on the strings, his worn cowboy boot tapping out the beat against the dusty earth. Without looking up he said, "This is a friend of mine's song. You may know it, 'Here Tonight,' a Brett Young tune, one of my favorites."

It was obvious from the moment he began to sing that he was not just an ordinary singer . . . his voice was sorcery! Extraordinary really. Buttery, smooth, low with perfect pitch, and unique, nobody else sounded like him. He weaved a spell around the campfire that had Sophia mesmerized. The melody, the words, sexy, romantic, swoon worthy . . . *God help me!* The words swirled around her . . . *One kiss away from heaven*? She almost touched her lips. She watched the firelight dance across his face, lending a haunting quality to his performance. She looked around at the others and saw her own bemused expression reflected back, all equally captivated.

He glanced up and their eyes locked, his burning with the intensity of some emotion only he knew as he sang. It sent desire darting through her. She swallowed . . . hard. *Talk about getting lost in someone's eyes . . . cowboy magic.*

When he finished the song there was a hush as

everyone tried to absorb what they'd just heard. . . *a star*. Then the whooping and hollering commenced.

"Wow dude! That was awesome. Can we make requests?" Ben asked.

"All depends," Gunner said. "Throw one at me."

"How about Eagles, 'Peaceful Easy Feeling?'"

"Sure, good one but only if y'all sing along with the chorus."

He morphed into a performer so quickly that Sophia began to think that the doubt she'd witnessed was merely a figment of her imagination. The guitar had become an extension of him. It was obvious he was gifted beyond mere talent, he was born to sing and play. *Why had he quit?*

Amelia who'd been sitting across the fire moved over to sit beside her. She leaned in and whispered, "Don't let me down. He is totally into you."

Everyone happily sang along to the classic . . . *I mean even if you weren't into country you had to know this tune.*

"I'll play one more then I'm turning in. How about 'Forever and Ever, Amen' by Randy Travis?"

Both of Megan's parents clapped their hands enthusiastically. "Bruce used to sing that to me," Margaret said. "I may cry."

Gunner flashed a dazzling smile and said, "That'd be a mighty fine compliment Margaret." She beamed like a schoolgirl. Bruce slung his arm across his wife's shoulders and hugged her.

As Gunner began to sing the timeless song about forever love, Sophia suddenly felt like she was hyperventilating, fighting a full-blown anxiety attack. *Did anyone have the right to be so damn beautiful? What am I going to do? I don't want any part of Amelia's plan . . .* Panicking she jumped to her feet, startling Amelia and earning a wide-eyed look from Gunner.

She turned quickly, fighting her urge to run, barely managing to hold it together. When she reached a safe distance from the camp circle, she bolted back to the cabin like the devil was on her heels.

She closed the door behind her and sank slowly to the floor. Wrapping her arms around her bent legs she rested her forehead against her knees. Her breath rapid and shallow, she forced herself to take deep slow breaths. *Did I just go and make a fool of myself?* Squeezing her eyes tightly shut, she willed her heart to quit racing. *Calm down. Maybe nobody noticed.* She stomped her boots and groaned. *I looked like an idiot, I'm sure everyone knew exactly what was going on. I'm sure I looked ridiculous, practically swooning. I'll never be able to show my face again!*

She remained huddled until the anxiety loosened its grip, then hauled herself up and into the bathroom to brush her teeth and get ready for bed. *Yeah, like sleep is going to happen.* She crawled under the covers and pulled out her cell, googling Gunner Cane. Scrolling through the headlines her jaw dropped. "Gunner Cane leaves Nashville, is it for good?" "Gunner Cane ready to sign on with Wide World Records." "Gunner Cane the rising star of Nashville." "Gunner Cane and Natalie Storm announce their engagement." She was dumbfounded. *What? I guess I have been living under a rock.*

She read several of the articles in a daze. She glanced at the bedside clock and saw that thirty minutes had passed . . . not good because she wanted lights out before her roomie returned. Even if she hadn't given it away to the entire group, she'd never get past Amelia's hawk eyes, not to mention the fact that her friend would take full advantage of the situation. She didn't need Amelia's prying tonight.

*T*wenty minutes later, she'd just turned off her bedside lamp when Amelia quietly tiptoed in. "Are you asleep?" Amelia whispered.

Sophia kept her breathing soft and even, feigning sleep . . . apparently convincingly because Amelia didn't say any more. She heard her get ready then crawl into bed, within minutes she was snoring. *Lucky her.*

11

*S*ophia sipped her coffee, tired from a night of tossing and turning. When Amelia sat on the stool next to her, she held up a hand. "I don't want to talk about it."

Playing it cool, Amelia sipped her coffee. "Talk about what?"

Sophia sat up straight. *Really? This is too good to be true. Maybe I wasn't as obvious as I had thought. Maybe Amelia has given up on her half-baked plan.* She sneaked a peek at Amelia, her relief short-lived. Her friend's eyes were sparkling with curiosity. *Dang it*!

"I mean it."

Amelia put a hand to her chest, eyes rounding innocently. "What? I didn't say a word."

"At least seventy percent of all communication is non-verbal."

She waved her hand. "Don't worry, you weren't the only fangirl there last night. We can use this to our advantage. He'll never suspect that you have ulterior motives."

"That's because I don't!" Sophia stuck her fingers into her ears to drown out her friend. She slumped in her chair and whined, "Lalala—I can never show my face again. I'll have to sit in the cabin for the next two weeks and you'll have to deliver all my meals. I actually googled him last night and there were gazillions of articles about him. Gunner Cane this and Gunner Cane that, I'm mortified. He probably thinks I'm some groupie. And furthermore, I will *not* be a part of your strategy."

"Even if it saves your best friend's career? Wow, some friend you're turning out to be. It's not like you'll ever see him again after this trip. And about last night, well, I wouldn't worry about it. It's not as if you fainted or screamed out his name," Amelia teased.

"That's not in the least bit funny. Your best friend is mortified and you don't have an ounce of empathy."

"You were adorable."

Her face heated and burying it in her palms she moaned. "Could this be any worse?"

"Just say you had gas."

"I mean it!"

"Relax. Nobody noticed but Gunner and me."

"Great. I feel so much better now."

"As I told you at the airport, he's probably used to it. Why be embarrassed? Sexual obsession is nothing to be ashamed about."

"Shut up before I kill you!"

"Listen, it wasn't a big deal. The only evidence of

your crush was you stumbling blindly away from the campfire."

"That's it, you're dead to me now." Sophia elbowed her friend in the side.

"Okay, I give, I'm sorry, I'm just kidding . . ."

"I do *not* have a crush! I got carried away by the music and the atmosphere."

"Of course," Amelia said, patting her on the shoulder.

"He's too big for his boot's . . . he's self-important, he's . . . he's . . ." her voice trailed off as she realized her opinion of him had changed rather drastically and she no longer saw him that way.

"Let me finish for you . . . handsome, warm, talented, charming, sexy . . . As I see it here are your choices . . . hide for two weeks or take the bull by the horns, hold your head up and own it."

"Own what?" she managed to croak out.

"Your sexual fantasy . . . Ha! I meant to say your confidence, your womanhood, your sensuality."

"You're the worst."

"I'm trying to get you to lighten up. No crime was committed. It was nothing I swear! It just seemed as if you were in a hurry to get to bed."

"Really?"

"Really. Well . . . kind of. I mean, I knew something was up but nobody else noticed, I'm ninety-nine-point-nine percent sure of it."

"What about Gunner?" Her eyes narrowed. "You said he seemed surprised."

"You were sitting right next to him. If he asks, just

tell him you didn't feel good . . . your stomach was upset or something."

"Will he believe it?"

"You'll find out. Now get dressed. It's time for breakfast. You can do this." She held up two fists and pumped her arms. "Go Sophia."

Glaring, Sophia disappeared into the bathroom to get ready to face her humiliation head on. *No pain no glory as the saying goes.*

*S*ophia searched carefully for the best outfit to hide behind. She pulled out her navy blue, oversized, peasant-style smock top and paired it with baggy boyfriend jeans, effectively concealing any hint of her curves. She'd tamed her hair back into a severely tight ponytail, slipping it through the back of a ball cap. The crowning touch, was a pair of large tortoise-framed fake glasses. . . *genius if I do say so myself*. Satisfied, she pulled the visor low and went to meet her friend, who did a double-take when Sophia stepped into the living room, then burst out laughing.

"You've got to be kidding me. You know this makes you stand out more, don't you? You look like a movie star trying to go incognito."

"I don't want to hear it. This is more for me than anything. I need a shield and this is it. Otherwise, I have nothing." Her mouth was stubbornly set, brooking no argument.

"If you say so. I've got your back sista."

They linked arms and headed to the lodge for breakfast, her earlier irritation with Amelia gone.

Sophia kept her head lowered and avoided any eye contact. Only after sitting with her back to the Cane family's table did she take a breath. She anxiously chewed on her bottom lip, relieved that they were the only ones at the table so far.

There was a large stainless-steel warmer full of cheesy scrambled eggs, another with bacon and sausage, a pitcher of OJ and a mound of toast at their table. Sophia spooned a small portion of the eggs onto her plate and poured herself a glass of juice. She had zero appetite and her stomach roiled at the smell of the bacon. She picked at the food in front of her.

"You have to eat something. It's a long time between now and lunch."

Still keeping her head down, she said quietly, "Is he here yet?"

"No."

"Tell me the second he shows up."

"I will. Eli and Luke, the dad and mom, Becca and the kid are already eating. Relax, you're blowing this out of proportion."

"I know, but I can't help it."

"Can't help what?" Ben said, plopping down across from Sophia.

"Oh . . . um . . . that I'm not very hungry."

"Why'd you leave so abruptly last night?" Ben asked.

Sophia's head jerked up and she flashed daggers at Amelia. "What do you mean? I was tired so I went to bed."

He bit back a laugh. "You looked like you'd seen a ghost. We were all worried. What's with the glasses?"

"They're fake," Amelia said suppressing a grin.

Sophia felt her cheeks flame and she wished she'd just be sucked up into another dimension, she didn't care where.

"I didn't feel well last night. My stomach was upset."

"Probably gas," Amelia said, biting her lip to keep from laughing.

Sophia pushed her plate away and said, "I still don't feel quite up to par, I think I'm going to take the day to relax in my cabin. Amelia, please let Gunner know for me." She jumped to her feet and rushed out before her friend could stop her. Keeping her eyes glued to the ground, she hurriedly walked to the exit. She flew outside and ran smack into something warm and solid. She gasped as her face smooshed against a broad muscular chest and a pair of strong arms wrapped around her saving her from falling. The white cotton tee shirt smelled very familiar. She groaned.

"Hey, Red. Rushing off again?" he whispered seductively in her ear.

Mortified, she kept her face buried against his chest. Voice muffled, she said, "I'm sick."

"You sure about that?"

She could hear the laughter in his voice and wanted to scream. Instead, she pushed against his chest, but he held on tight.

"Let me go."

"What if I don't want to? You feel pretty damn good and I've been wanting to do this since I first set eyes on you."

"You have?" she mumbled.

"Yeah, I have."

She dared a glance up and met a pair of gleaming dark eyes sparkling with humor. She bit her bottom lip. "Sophia, you're making it damn near impossible for me to resist."

"I'm . . . I . . . I can't do this right now."

He tilted her chin up with his fingers and rubbed his thumb across her bottom lip. "Do what?"

"You know what."

"You're thinking way too much. You're supposed to be on vacation. Quit worrying. What's with the glasses?"

"It's called fashion."

He stuck his face next to hers and studied them closely. "They're fake?" he asked incredulously. She stiffened and he quickly added, "You do look pretty damn cute in them." She glared. "Well, you do! Truce? I promise to behave myself. Scout's honor." Grinning, he held up his palm.

She bit back a smile. "You're bad."

"You weren't planning on playing hooky today, were you?"

"Um . . . yeah . . . as a matter of fact I'm heading back to the cabin to lay down. I didn't get a minute of sleep last night." She put her hand over her mouth realizing what she'd just confessed to. Talking fast she said, "Sometimes I can't sleep, especially if I'm in a strange bed or I'm over tired, sometimes I just get up or read a book or . . ." her voice trailed off as he continued to watch her, his eyes now locked on her lips.

"Red, you're killing me. You're not really thinking of leaving me to fend for myself with Megan, are you? Not to mention, giving up on Pirate. Besides I've been looking forward to showing you my special place today and Pirate will be mighty disappointed . . . because it's his favorite too."

He released her and she felt oddly bereft. "Well . . ."

"Pretty please," he said.

"I guess . . . I'll take something to settle my stomach and if it works, I'll be there."

"Don't even make me pull my Tarzan costume out. I'd hate to have to physically drag you out of there."

She smiled weakly. "You win, I'll be there."

"That's good then. You in those glasses . . . makes me think of those librarian scenes . . . you know the ones . . . you let your hair down, take off the glasses . . . but you might want to ditch the disguise so Pirate will recognize you." He tweaked her nose then left.

Grrr. I'd like to strangle that man.

12

The first thing that struck Sophia was the peacefulness and quiet. They reached the mountain stream and everyone dismounted. All she could hear was the horses blowing out their breath, the babble of water flowing over rocks and her own heartbeat. Everyone was silent, as if they were in a sacred chapel, all taking in the beauty of their surroundings. It was so vast. Thank God she hadn't skipped out on this ride. Land, land and more land . . . views for miles. The lush wilderness in every shade of green from emerald to turquoise, the smell of sagebrush . . . heavenly.

"If y'all look in your saddle bags you'll find your box lunches," Gunner said. "Also, a thermos of iced tea. I packed some water if anyone prefers it. I have some carrots and apple slices for your horses. I'll set them out."

Sophia avoided looking at Gunner and busied

herself pulling out her sandwich and gulping down some sweet tea."

"This is the most beautiful place I've ever been," Amelia said, sighing.

"I feel like we've stepped back in time or we've been transported to another universe," Sophia said.

She and Amelia perched on a huge rock and Sophia noticed that Megan watched and waited until Gunner sat before sidling up next to him.

"Maybe I should pick Megan's brain about Gunner, since she seems like a super fan," Amelia whispered.

Sophia polished off her peanut butter and jelly sandwich then absently nibbled on a carrot, staring out at the horizon. The warm sun on her back was making her sleepy. She leaned her head on Amelia's shoulder and closed her eyes. "I'm about to fall asleep," she said yawning.

She drifted, suspended somewhere between wakefulness and sleep. She was vaguely aware of quiet conversations, the stream babbling, the distant sound of a hawk shrieking, her friend's bony shoulder and Gunner. There had been a new awareness between them when she'd shown up at the barn that morning. It was if they were connected by some invisible thread. Gunner was careful to keep things professional but she had felt his gaze following her all day.

Eyes still closed, half asleep, her nerve endings tingled as she sensed him approach. He sat down next to her and her sleepiness vanished, replaced by a racing pulse now on full alert. Still, she kept her eyes shut.

"Are you glad you came?" he asked quietly.

He knows. No use faking it. "Yes." She opened her

eyes and stretched her arms overhead. "It's beyond lovely. Thanks for talking me into it."

"This is one of my favorite spots. I didn't want you to miss it."

She glanced at him from the corner of her eye. "Do you miss Nashville? I mean more the singing and playing. I had no idea how talented you were."

"Yeah, I do. I had big dreams. It's getting easier though."

"Why'd you quit?" She felt Amelia perk up next to her and wanted to kill her.

"Long story. A little bit of bad luck and loads of stupidity. In the end there wasn't much of a choice."

"I'm sorry."

"Me too. But hey, I'm not complaining. Look where I landed."

Sophia smiled. "Not too shabby."

"What about you? What do you do back in Chicago?"

"Well, that's another long story but suffice to say, currently I'm an unemployed, classically trained pastry chef. Lately I've been helping my parents out at their bakery."

His eyebrows rose. "Well, aren't you full of surprises. I'd have never guessed."

"Don't let her fool you. She worked in a highly competitive industry for one of the top restaurant groups in Chicago. Trained in France, sought after by many. She had quite the reputation," Amelia said.

"Probably the best dressed and most beautiful as well," he said.

"Bingo. Which unfortunately didn't do her any

favors. Having to deal with huge male egos who wanted her and wouldn't take no for an answer, the underbelly of the restaurant biz." Amelia said.

Sophia quickly tried changing the subject. "Well, that's all in the past now. I'm waiting to see what comes next."

"Why, are you giving up on it?" Gunner asked, his brow furrowed.

"You could say that I've burned some bridges. If I do pursue it again, it won't be in Chicago."

"Now it's my turn to say I'm sorry."

Sophia shrugged her slim shoulders. "It was a blow for sure. The whole thing made me question every-thing—love and trust, integrity . . . frankly, my whole life."

Gunner stood and said, "I probably understand that more than you might think. I'll look forward to hearing more if you ever want to share." He raised his voice to address everyone and said, "Time to head back."

She looked at him closely, "I'd like that . . . I mean the sharing. I'd like to hear your story." As their eyes met, she felt confused and a twinge of guilt. On the one hand she had been sincere, but a nagging voice in the back of her head was questioning everything . . . her loyalty to her friend . . . her growing attraction to Gunner. *Just who am I serving?*

His eyes flickered before he turned and strode away.

Gunner waited to make sure everyone was mounted before jumping onto his own horse and leading them back to the ranch.

13

*G*unner paced the floor of his cabin, restless enough to climb the walls. He had half a mind to walk on over to Sophia's cabin and ask her if she wanted to go grab a drink from the bar. Now that would be just plain stupid. He decided for the one-thousandth time that day to back off, lay low and forget about having any sort of relationship with Sophia Russo. Yet . . . *Okay that's it.* A little horse time was the cure for just about anything. He needed to soak Amitola's hoof anyway. He headed for the barn.

"Hey girl. Won't be long now and you can get turned out with your comrades," he said. She nickered softly. Patting her neck, he gave her an oat treat as a reward for keeping her foot in the tub of warm Epsom salt water. Sitting on a bale of hay next to her, he let his thoughts wander.

The early years in Nashville had been full of beautiful women and one-night stands. Hell, he'd been a kid, twenty-one and away from home for the first time. But a couple of years of that had been plenty, it had left him lonely and cynical . . . until Natalie.

When he met her, he'd been ready to settle down. She'd shown up at the audition for fiddle and back-up singer and for him it'd been love at first sight. They'd jumped right into a relationship and were engaged by the end of their first year together. There'd been lots of ups and downs. Fights, drinking, both of them passionate and ambitious. When she'd walked out, he'd been broken up. The only woman he been with since was his manager's sister Amber. He'd been pressured into dating her but he'd gone along, knowing from the git-go that it was a big mistake. He'd paid a heavy price for not being true to himself and so had Amber.

Now, here he was, a year later, drawn to a woman who was unquestionably one of the most beautiful he'd ever laid eyes on. But what was it about Sophia that made him wish for something more? Exquisite yes, but it was more than that . . . she was feminine, comical without trying . . . fiery, stubborn, yet vulnerable and soft. She wore her heart on her sleeve and would be devastated to know that. She thought she was sealed up tighter than a drum, but to him she was an open book. He knew she was attracted to him and the other night by the fire had made it that much harder for him to ignore his own needs. He wanted her . . . forbidden fruit. Old as time.

"How's she doing?"

As if he'd conjured her up, there she was.

Her hair was loose and wild, cascading around her shoulders and down her back, eyes soft and warm.

"Hi."

"Hi," she answered shyly. "I hope it's okay for me to be here. I left Amelia at the bar but was too restless to go back to the cabin. I thought I'd explore a little."

"*Mi casa es tu casa* . . . or in this case my barn is your barn."

"Thanks."

"She's healing up nicely. Another day or two she'll be turned out with the rest of the herd. I won't ride her for a couple more weeks."

"She's so beautiful," she said, as she reached into the stall to stroke her.

Gunner studied Sophia, watching an array of emotions dance across her face. "Sophia . . ." He stopped himself.

She tilted her head and looked at him. "Yes?"

"Um . . . do ya think you'd like to go for a full-moon walk with me?"

She seemed surprised and laughed softly, the warm sound stoking his internal fire. "That sounds lovely."

"Let me finish up here and we'll do that. I'm feeling a bit restless myself."

The bright moon illuminated their path as they strolled across the grounds. "So, can I ask you some questions?" he said.

"Of course," she said.

"Any boyfriends back home?"

"Nope."

"Are you pining for anyone . . . nursing a broken heart?"

She paused before responding, then shook her head and said, "Nope. All healed up."

"Good. Did you grow up in the Windy City?"

"Yes. My parents had the bakery before I was born. Have you been?"

"Yeah, I was on tour and we hit Chicago. Lots of great restaurants, so much to do there. Nice city."

"I already know where you grew up but what drew you to music?"

"Don't know exactly. Born that way. Mom says I came out singing. She encouraged it and I got my first guitar when I was nine."

"How sweet. No one special in your life?"

"Nope. It's been a while." He took her hand in his. "Here, come this way, I want to show you another special place." She hesitated. "I'll only bite if you want me too." She smiled and he felt her relax.

Her hand was so soft and small in his and the jolt of electricity ran up his arm and straight to the ache in his chest. The full moon cast a glow over everything lending a sense of fantasy to the night. He stopped when they reached a split rail fence line at the precipice overlooking a valley now bathed in moonlight. It looked mysterious.

"Let's stop here," he suggested. They stepped onto the bottom rail and he began to hum the song from the other night. He bumped his shoulder against hers play-fully and she bumped him back. "*Please just let me stay . . .*" he sang softly.

"You sure know how to get to a girl," she said gently. "You're not playing fair."

"Nothing fair about it. You were the last thing I expected to find when I showed up at the airport." He studied the outline of her delicate features caressed by the moonlight, her jawline, her slender neck; he saw her swallow.

"Oh," she said breathlessly.

"But here we are. Ahh, Sophia," he said on a sigh. "What am I going to do about you? Huh?"

She glanced up at him and he took one look into her bright eyes and was lost. He tipped her chin up and leaned down, softly kissing her lips. She sighed against his mouth as his hand slid slowly down her smooth bare arm to grasp her hand.

Reluctantly he lifted his head. "One kiss away from heaven . . . was I right?"

She smiled, her expression soft. "Yes."

"Sophia, you're a real sweetheart. I want you. Pretty much consumed by you, truth be told."

"I leave in eight days, then what? I'm not sure I'm capable of a fling; just walking away and chalking it up as a lovely experience isn't really my style." She pulled her hand from his grasp.

"I didn't think it was. Not really mine either. I haven't lived the life of a saint, but those days of skimming the surface are long gone for me."

"I wish I could just go for it, enjoy the moment, carpe diem, but it scares me to open up like that. I'm afraid I won't be able to turn it back off once I leave here."

He studied her earnest face, her bewitching dark eyes, the worried line between her brows, and realized he had no answers. He only knew he felt protective of her and wouldn't put his own needs before her best interests.

"I would never want to hurt you, Red. You're way too special for that." Giving her one last peck on the lips he jumped off the rail and said, "Let's head back."

He saw her disappointment mixed with something unfathomable, but knew it was for the best—at least that was what he told himself at the moment. He wasn't sure if his chivalry would stand the test of time, but for now it was best to put the brakes on until they were on surer footing.

14

*S*ophia opened one eye and looked at the clock. Seven AM. She flopped onto her stomach and punched her pillow before covering her head with the blanket. *Why? The one day I get to sleep in and I can't.* Since today was a flex day everyone got to do whatever they wanted and the horses got a break. They had plenty of choices for filling their day off: shooting skeet, fly fishing, guided hikes, a day on the river, a two-step dance class led by Becca, a bread baking class with Abby, braiding horses' manes, or no schedule at all. Tonight was the ranch dance party so she and Amelia had decided to sign up for Becca's two-step class. The only other thing on their agenda was to laze around the pool.

Gunner. Dang it! Remembering his soft lips against hers and his intense liquid gaze had her squirming with desire. She felt tingly inside. She groaned and kicked her feet against the mattress. *What am I going to do?* One thing for sure, sleep was an impossibility now. May as well get up. She slipped on a pair of loose boxer shorts under her oversized tee shirt and went to find coffee.

She found Amelia sitting on the front porch, her bare feet propped on the railing, drinking her morning java and munching on a breakfast bar. "I'm skipping the country breakfast today. My jeans are getting tight," she said.

Sophia sat down next to her friend holding her steaming mug of coffee. "I'm skipping it too. At home I rarely eat breakfast. Anyway, we'll be getting exercise with the dance lesson today and on a positive note, maybe your jeans are tight because you're building muscle. We've certainly been working off any extra calories at the barn."

"Hopefully. Let's go for a hike this morning."

"Okay, a hike sounds great. Gunner is right, this view never gets old." Looking at the panoramic view of the mountains, Sophia could feel the peace and calm of her environment seeping into her bones. A soft breeze stirred her hair and she brushed away a strand tickling her cheek. Her feet hung over the railing and the sun warmed her toes. The worry that'd been niggling the back of her mind had eased, replaced with a jittery excitement in her core. She wouldn't name it and refused to give much attention to its source. She'd credit it to the fact that she hadn't had a real vacation in over three years.

"This place is working its magic," Amelia said.

"It is for me too. By the way, how did it go with Hank after I left last night?"

"Dreamy. I really like him. A vacation fling is just what the doctor ordered. However, as a source for information about Gunner he sucks. His lips are tighter than a drum. How about you? Did you go straight to bed after you left?"

"No. I was restless and took a walk. I ran into Gunner at the barn. We went for a moonlight stroll."

"Rot-roh. Sounds romantic. Well? Were you able to gather any intel?"

Sophia sighed. "Not really. We mostly talked about me."

"Soph," Amelia whined. "You couldn't even get in a couple of questions?"

"I'm not comfortable with it, besides I'm terrible at subterfuge . . . you know that. Find out yourself. Count me out."

Amelia frowned. "Hank is pretty much a dead end too. If there is any mystery to be had, it will go with him to his grave. After my third question he started to look suspicious."

"He's loyal. That's how friends are supposed to be."

"Maybe, but it's thwarting my mission. Not to change the subject but seems like there's been a shift between you and Gunner. You really like him, don't you?"

"Maybe, but he's so out of my league. I'd never feel secure being with someone like him . . . besides that, I've only been with two guys my entire life. The chances of me shedding my inhibitions enough to enjoy a fling are practically zilch."

Amelia snorted. "Out of your league? No way. You never know, maybe a fling would do you some good."

"As tempting as it may be, I'll pass. I'm keeping it in the flirtation zone."

"That's fun too, but I've learned to never say never." Amelia took the last gulp of her coffee and stood. "I'm going to grab a quick shower. Take your time and enjoy this glorious view."

"Okay," Sophia said. After Amelia left, Sophia leaned back and closed her eyes, her senses taking in the smells and sounds of nature. At first it had seemed so quiet after living in the bustling city of Chicago, but if she really listened, it was full of soothing sounds . . . she could hear the stream behind their cabin, birds calling, the wind stirring the leaves of the trees, soft music drifting from another cabin . . . boots crunching on the gravel path. *Boots?* Her eyes flew open.

"Good morning Sunshine. Aren't you a sight for sore eyes," Elijah said, his warm gaze giving her goosebumps.

"Morning Eli." She could feel her cheeks heating.

"What are you up to today?"

"We thought we'd take a hike then we signed up for Becca's dance class. Other than that, the pool is calling us."

"Maybe I'll see you around. If not, save a dance for me tonight."

"Oh . . . um okay, I'll do that."

"I'll have something to look forward to then." He smiled, his white teeth gleaming against his tanned face. Tipping his cowboy hat, he nodded then left her sitting there with a racing pulse, fanning herself.

Whoa! So much male attention at one time . . . especially from guys this hot. Time for that walk. I need to blow off some steam.

*A*fter taking a long hike they ate a light lunch then headed for their dance lesson. "I'm so excited. I've always wanted to learn some fancy two-step moves," Amelia said. "Hank said he'd take a break and dance with me tonight if he isn't too busy."

"I promised Elijah a dance."

Amelia's eyes widened. "Wait . . . what? I thought you were into Gunner."

"Variety is the spice of life, best to keep my options open," Sophia said, steering her away from Gunner. "They're both delicious."

They entered the dance hall and saw Becca talking with some guests off in a corner. Sophia had thrown on a pair of old faded jean shorts with a white vee-neck tee shirt tucked in and her cowboy boots. Amelia was similarly decked out sans boots. She'd opted for tennis shoes instead. Ben, Doug and Scooter were there as well as Megan and her parents. There were some guests she hadn't met yet but everyone looked excited to be there. *This should be fun.*

Becca's eyes were twinkling with humor as she gathered everyone together. "First things first. This is for fun. No perfectionism allowed. It's okay to step on each other's feet. We're learning. Looks like we're pretty evened out with men to women so that helps. We'll learn the basic steps without music then we'll add music. After you're comfortable with the basics I'll teach you some turns and twirls. It's really fun. Laughing at yourself is encouraged."

Ben came over and tapped Sophia on the shoulder. "Be my partner?'

"Sure. Thanks."

Becca said, "Everyone grab a body. Scooter can you come up front and be my demo partner?"

He grinned, "At your own peril. Did ya wear steel-toe boots?"

"I can handle you, no worries." Everyone laughed. "Everybody, face your partner. We'll start just facing one another and holding hands . . . then I'll teach you the holds after we've got the steps down. Now it's two quick steps and two slow. Remember the guy steps forward with his left and the woman steps back with her right. If you forget, just remember the woman is always right. Ha ha. We always move counter-clockwise and the faster couples to the outside. Two quick, two slow, two quick, two slow."

Becca stopped and watched them go around. "Good job. Now we'll add the proper hold position. Girls put your left hand on his right shoulder, guys you'll put your right arm around her with your hand just below her shoulder blade. Then you'll hold your other hands loosely, palm to palm." She put Scooter in position. "Step together and walk, same thing . . . two quick two slow." They all moved in a circle, some more gracefully than others. There was lots of laughter and stops and starts.

They practiced until everyone had the hang of it then Becca said, "Now I'll add the music. It's kind of like juggling. Every time we add something, things get harder. Remember what the key word is?"

Everyone shouted "Fun!"

"You're very quick learners." She went over to her phone and hit play and suddenly country music streamed through speakers positioned for maximum sound.

"Here we go. Get your holds. Guys step forward with your left, girls step back with your right, one two, one two."

Sophia looked into Ben's eyes, his glinting with humor and interest. "Hell of a view. I hope I can concentrate."

"You'd better. My toes are very sensitive."

"I'll keep that in mind."

"You're actually a natural Ben. I'm glad you're my partner."

"Hold your judgement until we get to the turns and twirls," he said smiling down at her.

An hour later Sophia was hot and sweaty and euphoric from the dancing. She and Ben had paired beautifully together and had mastered the turns and twirls much to her delight. Becca had even used them to demonstrate.

"Well twinkle toes, who knew?" Amelia said.

"Jealous much?"

She pinched her fingers together, "Just a wee bit."

"You caught on pretty quick, too," Sophia said.

"It's a blast."

"I know. I love it!"

Ben walked up as they were leaving. "See you tonight then?"

"Yes. We can warm up together."

He squeezed her shoulder. "I was hoping you'd say that."

"Later then. Thanks Ben. I had a great time."

"Me too."

She and Amelia linked arms and slowly walked back to their cabin. "You'd better be careful," Amelia warned. "I think Ben has it bad for you."

"Oh, it's nothing like that. We're just friends."

"You may feel that way but he doesn't."

"I'll keep that in mind. Thanks." Sophia suddenly stopped and stepped in front of Amelia, a big grin on her face, she held out her arms and put her friend in the two-step hold. "Let's go. One two, one two." Amelia's hazel eye's twinkled back at her. They synced immediately and continued on toward their cabin two-step style. "Let's practice some fancy moves," Sophia said, both giggling as they rotated, pivoted and twirled. "Fast slow fast slow, spin, twirl."

They both missed their step when they heard a wolf whistle and applause.

"Beauty in motion."

"Gunner!" Sophia said.

"Looks like you're ready to keep up with me tonight."

Flushing, she said, "I can hardly wait until the dance."

"If I wasn't excited before, I'm about to boil over now."

"How did the archery lessons go?"

"Great fun. I missed you though. Next time I'm signing you up for some skeet shooting. You'll like it. See you on the dance floor."

"Oh . . . I . . ." Flustered she became totally tongue-tied.

She met Amelia's amused glance. "Looks like your dance card is full with a waiting list," Amelia commented.

"Just so I'm wedged in there. See you both later then," Gunner said.

After he'd disappeared into the barn, Sophia jumped up and down. "I've never had this much fun in my whole life! I'm so glad we're here."

"Me too." Amelia held her arms out, "Shall we?" And they two-stepped all the way back to their cabin.

15

*G*unner hadn't been kidding when he'd told Sophia he'd missed her today. She was all he had thought about. Usually when he was busy, he got into the task, but not today. He'd been distracted as hell. Seeing her just now, eyes sparkling with joy and wild red hair in total disarray as she danced that two-step, well . . . his heart had just about leapt out of his chest. *Have I ever felt this way before? No, not like this. I hope her dance card isn't too full or I may have to empty it.* It was going to be a long wait between now and eight o'clock tonight.

His cell phone rang and he studied the number frowning. Nashville area code. The record label again.

"Hello, this is Gunner."

"Gunner! You're a hard man to pin down these days. It's Phillip Krauss."

"Hey Phillip. I thought it was you. I surely do appreciate your interest, but my answer hasn't changed. I'm not interested."

"Listen, I think you should at least let me fly you down here to listen to our proposition. I know we can do better for you than your old label. You've got what it takes. You were hitting your stride; I have a sixth sense about these things. I know a superstar when I hear him. You have to give it another shot."

"Look I gave it ten years. My last album barely made it out of the starting gate."

"It was a great album. It was your label's fault that it sputtered out."

"Maybe, but I'm all settled in here at my parents' ranch. Getting used to the slower pace again. I don't think my heart could withstand another rejection. The music industry is brutal. My record label screwed me, my manager screwed me, I was burned."

"I know you were. Hard to know who to trust. When you fly down here, I'll get some of my big acts to meet with ya, tell you what I'm like . . . what our label stands for. We put the musicians first. Ethical practices come before profit."

"I'll think about it. That's the best I can tell ya right now."

"Hey, its progress anyway. I'm sensing a crack in your armor. I'll try not to get my hopes up too high."

Gunner laughed. "Yeah, good idea. Look, seriously, I will think about it but I'm pretty settled in here. It's been six months since I left and I'm not missing it."

"Your talent is being wasted there. I'll look forward to hearing from you."

"Hey, thanks for your faith in me. Even if I hang up

my guitar for good, I'm glad to know my music was decent. You're the best out there so it's the highest compliment I could ask for."

"I'm not just blowing smoke Gunner. Please, meet with us."

"I'll give it a good going over. Thanks again." He hung up thoughtfully. *Could I give it another shot? Should I? What about those pictures? Weird that nothing more had ever come of it.* It was hard to ignore the excited feeling in the pit of his stomach. He'd thought he'd buried that dream for good and now here he was, with that proverbial carrot dangling temptingly in front of him again. *Damn!*

*T*he dance was in full swing by the time Gunner entered the hall. He was late because he'd had to round up some cattle that had wandered through a broken fence line. He'd done a half-ass repair job, but it'd need tending to as soon as possible. He scanned the room and waved to Hank who was serving from a portable bar set up in the corner of the room. He continued his search until he spotted Sophia. *Ahh, there she is.* She'd left her hair loose, a wide headband keeping it away from her face, the rest cascading around her shoulders and down her back. She had on a pair of tight low rider blue jeans and a black sleeveless crop top that left her waist and creamy arms bare. And she was dancing with his brother Elijah, laughing up at something he'd said. He had his arms around her body, holding her a little too closely for Gunner's liking. His stomach coiled. He'd see about that. He strode briskly across the wooden floor and tapped Eli on the shoulder.

Eli looked at him challengingly. "I don't think so bro."

"Be a good boy and play nice with others. Didn't Mama teach you manners?"

"We've only had two dances together."

"That's two more than me." He raised an eyebrow at Sophia and held out his hand. She looked slightly dazed as she slipped her hand into his. He pulled her away from Eli and into his arms. Rather than the two-step hold, he held her against his body and buried his nose in her hair. "I've been waiting all day for this moment," he said. Smoothing his palms down her back he rested them in the low curve below her waist, his fingers splayed around her soft skin.

Breathless she said, "You're late, is everything alright?"

"Yeah, glad you noticed."

She leaned away and stared up at him, her hands cupping his shoulders. "I'm glad you're here."

"No place I'd rather be," he replied. She rested her cheek against his chest and he wondered with amusement if she could hear his heart pounding. *How old am I? I feel about fourteen right now.* "You make me wish for things I'd about given up on." In response, she slipped her arms around his waist and hugged him tight. He had to strain to hear her soft reply, but he thought she said something like *me too.* He smiled.

A Chris Stapleton tune came on, one he liked to cover. "I play this one," he said. "*You can be my four-leaf clover,*" he sang along.

"I like it."

"Will you? Be my four-leafed clover?"

She missed a step and he tightened his arms around her. His insides heated up like the sun was shining straight through him. His groin tightened. Tipping her chin up with his knuckles, she smiled sweetly, biting her bottom lip. It made him half-crazy with desire.

"I'd like to bite that bottom lip myself. When you smile at me that way, it makes me want to throw you over my shoulder and carry you off like a damn caveman. I want you all to myself."

"Did you go to charm school or something?" she asked.

Grinning he said, "You bring out the beast in me."

Another tune came on and he said, "Show me what you got; perfect two-step tune." He put her hand on his shoulder and stepped forward as she stepped back. They two-stepped several times around the floor then he said, "Ready for something fancy?"

She threw back her head and laughed. "Why not. We'll make Becca proud."

They were in perfect sync as he guided her around the floor counter-clockwise. Some of the people from class joined in the procession. They stayed toward the outside since they were moving fairly fast. He started in a promenade position, then turned her into a wrap, then she spiraled out. Away from each other, then together again. Twirling, spiraling, quick stepping. *Damn she is good.*

The song came to an end and they stopped in the middle of the dance floor to catch their breath. "That was fun! Where'd you learn to dance like that?" she asked.

"You can't hardly call yourself a cowboy if you can't dance the two-step."

"That was beyond a two-step."

Her eyes looked like shiny black sapphires, her lips rosy and ripe; before he could stop himself, he leaned down and softly kissed her lips. Her sharp intake of breath and wide-eyed expression brought him back to reality with a jolt.

"I'm sorry. I couldn't help myself. My body had a mind of its own there for a second." He watched as she touched her lips, seemingly thrown off balance. "Let's get ourselves a drink. Sound good to you?"

"Yes, I'm ready for a cold one. And Gunner?" He raised his brow. "I didn't mind . . . um . . . the kiss that is. I liked it."

He smiled in relief. "I'm glad to hear you say that. Makes my heart pitter patter." He grabbed her hand and held the palm against his chest. "Feel that?" She nodded as her lips tugged up at the corners. "That's the beat of my own personal love song."

She laughed and playfully shoved him. "You are a habitual flirt!"

"Don't say that, you're breaking my heart."

"Sure I am."

"Let's go get those drinks. All this dancing made me thirsty." He didn't release her hand as they walked to the bar together.

Hank clapped as they approached. "You two look like professionals out there."

"Yeah, sure we do," Gunner said.

"I'll have an IPA," Sophia said.

"Make that two."

Amelia and Ben came off the dance floor and joined them. Amelia smiled at Hank and he winked at her.

"Hey, partner," Ben said to Sophia.

Sophia nodded her head towards Ben and explained to Gunner. "He was my dancing partner in class today. We were Becca's star students."

"Listen twinkle toes—her new nickname," Amelia explained, "—anyhow that's only because Becca missed Doug and me gliding around the circle. We busted some moves."

"I'm sure that's true," Sophia said, eyes dancing with light.

Eli strolled over and narrowed his eyes at Gunner. "Weren't you the one who insisted on playing well together? Seems like you're hogging this lady's dance card."

Gunner punched his arm lightly, "No hard feelings. We were on a roll. Isn't that right Sophia?"

"Yes . . . um . . ." she looked down at the floor.

Megan rushed up and grabbed Gunner's arm pulling. "You promised you'd dance with me."

"Let me down this beer then you're on," he guzzled it, setting the empty bottle on the bar. "Let's go."

He felt empty when he put his arms around Megan. It wasn't near the same. It was like riding a horse you didn't know, meaningless. He could fake it though. He didn't want to hurt her feelings. "Did you enjoy the dance class today?" he asked.

"I loved it! Gunner, I've been dying to ask . . . um . . . I hope I'm not being rude. Are you seeing anyone? I know you were engaged with your fiddle player, but I read you guys broke up and that you were dating someone else, but then they said that one ended too."

"Let's just say, I'm interested in someone. Rule number one, don't believe everything you read. Those tabloids make shit up. Too much trouble to correct their lies."

"Well . . . I know for fact you were with Natalie Storm. I saw you guys playing on You-tube and it was pretty obvious. She's really beautiful."

She stepped on his foot and he said, "Lets concentrate on the steps; my life's not that interesting."

"Okay, if you say so. I just want you to know that I'm a huge fan. I hope you start playing again."

"Thanks for that," he said, then swung her around, making her laugh.

As he scanned the room, he saw that Sophia was back in his brother's arms and was surprised at the fire of jealously that ripped through him. Eli was a player pure and simple. He wanted her nowhere near him. She was way too sweet a girl. He'd have to have a little talk and set him straight. Sophia happened to look over and catch his eye. She smiled warmly and his jaw relaxed. She was into him . . . she had to be. This much chemistry surely couldn't be one-sided.

He tuned back in to what Megan was saying, counting the beats until he could return to Sophia's side. Good thing Pops wasn't around to see his sons ignoring the Cane Rule book . . . and for the same girl. This could get interesting.

16

"*I* can't believe we're over halfway through our vacation already; really if we count travel time, we only have five full days left!" Amelia said.

Sophia sighed. The thought of leaving broke her heart. A flash of Gunner's dazzling smile flitted across her mind and she hugged herself. In six days, she'd be leaving. Her mind told her to put some distance between herself and Gunner, but her heart said enjoy it while you can.

"I know. I don't want this to ever end. I love it here."

"You and Gunner on the dance floor," she fanned herself, "smokin' hot!"

Sophia flushed. "Was it that obvious?"

"You guys were in your own little world! I saw Elijah watching you and daggers were shooting from his eyes."

"You're exaggerating."

"Hank noticed it, too."

"He did?"

"Yep. I hope it doesn't come to a showdown," Amelia grinned, displaying her delightful dimples. "I'd hate to see either of those gorgeous men with bloodied noses."

Sophia shrieked, "Stop it, you're freaking me out. They're two grown men. We're all just having a little flirty fun."

"I'm teasing, but I do think there's some sibling rivalry going on. Don't say I didn't warn you. Let's head on over to the dining room. I'm ready for some of Abby's cheesy potato casserole."

"Mmm, and her biscuits and gravy."

"Race ya," Amelia said, running out the door with Sophia right on her heels.

"No fair, you got a head start!" Sophia yelled.

They were doubled over laughing and out of breath by the time they reached the dining room. "You cheated!" Sophia said.

A husky male voice said, "Who's cheating?" Sophia looked up into Gunner's smoldering dark eyes. "Good morning Amelia . . . Soph. How'd y'all sleep?"

Her heart fluttered erratically. "I didn't sleep, it was more like I slipped into a coma." He chuckled, his eyes crinkling at the corners as he opened the door for them.

"Eat hardy," he said, then left them to join his family.

Sophia watched him walk away . . . *his butt in those faded Levi's . . . oh my*. She loved his broad shoulders . . .

his long easy stride, hair curling softly around the nape of his neck.

"Sophia, get a grip, you're gawking."

Sophia blinked like an owl and shook her head. "Oops." Amelia grabbed her arm and tugged her along to their table.

"What am I going to do with you?" Amelia said. "You have to at least pretend to be nonchalant."

"I'm cool," Sophia said, feeling her cheeks heat.

Ben sat down, followed shortly after by Doug and Scooter. Ben cleared his throat and said, "I guess I'm out of the running with both of those Cane brothers in pursuit."

"Ben, don't be silly. They're doing their jobs and part of it is entertaining the guests. Besides, I'm not interested in a vacation tryst, and you and I are friends."

Doug and Scooter snorted with laughter. Scooter said, "Oh no! Delegated to the friend-zone. Ouch."

Just then they heard a crash coming from the kitchen followed by someone crying out. Sophia watched as Gunner jumped to his feet and ran toward the canteen.

The entire room hushed, everything suspended . . . waiting to see what had happened. Seconds later, Becca came running out looking pale and frightened and bent down to whisper something to her father. He stood abruptly and rushed to the kitchen.

Becca faced the diners and made an announcement. "Sorry for the interruption. Please continue with your breakfast. There was a little accident in the kitchen. Abby took a tumble from the step ladder and injured her wrist. We're taking her to the hospital to have it checked out. We appreciate your understanding." Becca returned to the kitchen and everyone in the dining hall erupted into conversation.

Bill Cane rushed out, presumably to get the car. Minutes later Gunner came out with his arm around his mother who wore a makeshift sling, Becca on the other side patting her on the back comfortingly.

Amelia and Sophia looked at each other. Amelia said, "Not good. Poor Abby. I hope it's not serious."

"I know. What the hell will they do without her?" Ben said. "She has this mess hall functioning like a military facility."

"At least they have a large family and competent employees. Hopefully the assistants can handle it without her," Amelia said.

"I'm going to volunteer to help," Sophia said.

"What? Soph, it's your vacation! I'm sure they have back up."

"Amelia, it's a small family-run business, I know if this happened to my mom and dad they'd be screwed."

"You're right, it's just I know how badly you needed this vacation. With all you've been through."

"Maybe Abby is okay and won't need my help. If not, I'll offer."

"You're such a good person," Amelia said.

Sophia waved her hand. "It's no big deal. I've got the experience, it's nothing special and it's the right thing to do."

They finished eating in relative silence, everyone worried about Abby. Sophia got up her nerve and approached Luke. *Why did he have to be so intimidating? He was always so serious.*

"Um, Luke, I'm so sorry. I hope I'm not intruding; I don't know if you remember, I'm . . ."

He interrupted and said, "Sophia Russo."

She smiled, "Yes. Is there anything I can do to help? Dishes maybe? My mom and dad own a bakery with a small coffee bar, so I grew up washing dishes and cleaning up. I'd really like to help."

"I'm waiting to hear back from my father; we don't know if we're dealing with a sprain or a break. We'll know more after they've x-rayed her. I appreciate the offer but you're a guest. I hope you won't let this disturb you too much," he said, his lips actually turning up at the corners.

"It's no bother . . . really. I want to help. I'm also a pastry chef, so I can fill in if you need me."

She noticed Clayton staring at her and she smiled. *He looks so solemn for such a little boy.* Her heart melted. He must miss his mother so much. "Hi, Clayton, I'm Sophia. Your Uncle Gunner told me how good you are with music. He said you can already play the piano. That's really cool!"

"I'm no good. Not like he is." His soft brown eyes were so much like his Uncle Gunner's.

"You're just beginning. Not many four-year-olds I know can play piano at all. He also said you can beat him at hide-and-seek, too."

His little face scrunched up, "We-e-e-l-l, maybe."

"Maybe we can play sometime before I leave."

He looked up at her, finally engaged. "Do you know how?"

"Yes. Do you play Red Light Green Light?" He

slowly shook his head. "Well, it's a lot of fun. I'll teach you, if it's alright with your dad."

"We'll see," Luke said. She watched as Clayton's lips quivered.

Boldly she pushed ahead. "Luke, really, I'd love to play with Clayton. Since we have a free day, let me take him for a couple of hours this morning and you can check on your mom. Please."

He looked down at his son's hopeful expression and blew out his breath. "I suppose. You promise to behave yourself?"

Clayton bowed his head. "Yes father."

"Great. Let's shake on it, Clayton," Sophia said, holding out her hand. At Clayton's perplexed look she explained. "It means we're sealing the deal . . . we're making a promise to play together."

He grinned for the first time, revealing tiny teeth with a gap between his two front ones. "Okay." He slipped his tiny hand into hers and she was in love already. She wanted to pick him up and squeeze him.

"Is ten alright?"

Luke nodded. "Yes, that will work. It will give us time to eat breakfast and digest. I should hear something about Mom by then. Are you sure you want to do this?"

"I will be devastated if you say no." At his doubtful expression, she said, "Really, I love kids, it's no trouble at all." Clayton beamed up at her.

"See you soon," she said, ruffling his hair. She left to find some willing bodies to join them. The more the merrier.

17

*S*ophia braided her hair into two pigtails and rubbed sunscreen onto her face. She had changed out of her skirt and donned her cut-off jean shorts and a tee shirt. "Cowboy boots or Converse?"

"Definitely your pink tennies. You've about worn out your boots."

She slipped into her tennis shoes over bare feet and tied the laces. "Ready. Can't be late for my date. He really pulls my heart strings. Wait until you see how serious he is. We have to make him laugh."

"Kids are my specialty. And since we're both basically still kids ourselves, I am confident in meeting our objective."

"Doug and Ben said they'd play, and Megan, and even Renee's group."

"Come along comrade. Mission . . . to make one four-year-old's day."

Sophia saluted. "Aye-aye captain. Onward."

*L*uke sat perched on the front entrance railing of the lodge and Clayton stood solemnly beside him. "We're here!" Sophia called out cheerfully. "This is my best friend Amelia. Amelia this is Clayton."

Amelia bowed theatrically at the waist. "Queen of fun, at your service."

Luke's lips twitched.

"Any news?" Sophia asked.

"She broke it. It's going to require surgery, a plate and a few screws."

Sophia covered her mouth. "Oh no!"

"You got that right."

"Grandma bwoke her arm," Clayton said.

"Scary huh?"

He nodded, looking so worried that Sophia crouched down to his level. Putting a hand on each shoulder she looked into his eyes. "Hey, I broke my arm when I was five. I had to wear a cast and everything. It's not the end of the world, trust me."

He looked at her, his brow furrowed. "Did it hurt?"

"Yes, but not for long. They'll give her medicine to help." He nodded thoughtfully. She could only imagine after losing his mom what was going through his head right now. Luke reached down and patted his son on the back.

"She'll be fine. Your grandma wouldn't like it if she knew you were worrying."

Sophia said, "We won't tell her . . . but you know what? She'd understand. Don't bottle it up inside."

Luke got the hint and crouched down beside them. "She's right buddy, but I promise your Nana will be as good as new before you know it. Okay?"

"Pwomise?"

"Promise."

Clay swiped his arm across his eyes and Luke ruffled his hair.

Sophia took Clayton's hand and pulled him along to meet the others.

A half hour later the teams and rules for Red Light Green Light were established and they were on their third round. Ben was the traffic light this time and Sophia and Clayton held hands waiting for Ben to turn his back to them so they could scamper ahead.

He turned away then called, "Green light."

Sophia and Clayton made a run for it, stopping just in time. They were safe. But Ben had caught two more, Amelia and Megan were out, leaving only three left in the game.

Sophia nudged Clay. "It's between us and Scooter now. We'll have to really go for it."

"We have to beat him!"

"Green light."

They went for it and as Scooter passed them Sophia grabbed a hold on his shirt and pulled him down; unfortunately, she stumbled and fell beside him. "Run Clayton run!"

He put his head down and ran as fast as he could while Sophia held on to Scooter's leg so he couldn't get up.

Laughing, Scooter cried foul. "No fair!"

She punched him. "You are really going to take a four-year-old's win away?"

"Yep."

Sophia dove on top of him and held him down. "Not on my watch."

Scooter was laughing so hard he couldn't get up if he tried. "Okay, you win."

Clayton jumped up and down in his excitement as he reached Ben and tagged him. Sophia got up and ran over, picking him up and twirling him around. "The champ."

The family SUV pulled up and Gunner hopped out. Sophia froze in mid-turn when she caught sight of him. His gaze roved over her from head to toe, his expression unreadable, and her throat tightened.

"Uncle Gunner!" She put Clayton down and he ran to his uncle, who scooped him up into a bear hug. "How's Nana?"

"She's doing great buddy. She's out of surgery and Aunt Becca and Grandpa are with her. She'll be home later today."

"I won Red Light Green Light."

"That's great. Did Sophia teach you that one?"

"Yeah." He whispered something into Gunner's ear which made him chuckle.

Her heart melted seeing him hold his nephew so lovingly. He would make a great dad. She felt an unfamiliar yearning in the pit of her stomach and pressed her hands against her belly. Gunner put Clay down and slowly walked over to her as his gaze took a slow journey from her face all the way to her pink converse tennis shoes. Her skin felt branded as he paused on his way back up to stare at her bare thighs, which suddenly made her aware of just how cut-off her shorts were.

"Where are your boots?" His glittering eyes were glued to hers and she couldn't breathe.

"My dear friend told me that she's tired of my boots and to give them a day off."

He grinned. "I'm not saying whether I agree or disagree but . . ."

Sophia pouted. "You don't like my boots?"

"I love your boots . . . nobody and I mean *nobody* looks as good in a pair of boots as Sophia Russo. You take my breath away."

"Oh, um . . ."

Clayton interrupted them excitedly, calling for another game. "Uncle Gunner you can play too."

"Not today. I've got to get some work done before I go back to pick up your Grams."

He reached out and tugged on one of Sophia's pigtails, smiling. "I like the braids too. You look like a real country girl now."

Flushing under his penetrating gaze, she looked down at her feet. He leaned in so close she could smell him . . . all man, a hint of soap and Old Spice. His lips skimmed her ear as he whispered, "My nephew told me he was going to marry you when he gets big."

Her hand flew to her heart and she said, "That's the sweetest thing I've ever heard."

"I've got some stiff competition."

"That you do. Really no contest." She glanced up at him through her lashes.

"Is that so?" His smoldering look made her hiccup and he laughed.

Luke joined them on the front lawn and broke it to Clayton that it was time to wash up for lunch. After a little grumbling, he followed his dad after extracting promises from everyone that they'd play with him another day.

"Thanks, you guys. You made Clay's day," Gunner said.

"No worries. We're just a bunch of kids in grown-up bodies," Amelia said.

"Gunner can I talk with you privately for a minute?" Sophia said.

"Yeah. You can walk me to the barn."

They strolled slowly towards the barn. Sophia didn't know how to broach the subject so she dove right in. "Don't say a word until I'm finished talking. You can think about it and get back with me later."

Curious, his eyebrows rose. "Okay, I'm all ears."

"I want to help. You know I'm a baker, and I'm also trained as a chef. I can sub for you this week until you find a temporary replacement."

He started to speak and she held her palm up, "I said no talking. I've worked in a busy restaurant for the last several years, I grew up working for my parents in their bakery and I'm good. It's the perfect solution. I'm here for six more days. By then, you should be able to find someone to help. Talk it over with your family and let me know. I can start immediately. And I'm cheap. I'll do it for free."

"It's . . ."

"I'm leaving now. Goodbye." She pivoted and walked briskly away before he could respond, leaving him scratching his head.

18

*G*unner dried the last pot and threw the towel over his shoulder as he looked around at his mom's spotless kitchen. They'd managed to get through yesterday's lunch and breakfast this morning without any major catastrophes, but it had been harried. Sophia had pitched in with breakfast prep and he'd been impressed. She was a real badass in the kitchen and she made it fun. Gunner liked the idea of Sophia Russo becoming part of the Triple C team.

In fact, an idea had popped into his head as he'd watched her that he couldn't let go of. Maybe she could stay on for the next six weeks, until his mom was healed and ready to go back to work. Seemed like a win/win to him. Sophia was currently unemployed; they needed a chef. One plus one equaled two.

First, he'd have to run it by the family, but he couldn't imagine why anyone would object. The thought of her staying on for another six weeks made him very happy. He whistled a tune as he grabbed the trash bag and hauled it to the outside dumpster. Things were looking up.

"What are you so happy about?" Eli asked.

He abruptly quit whistling. "Where were you this morning?"

"I finished repairing that fence line."

"Oh. Thanks. That was on my list. Good thing you have an excuse. Have you talked to Ma yet today?"

"Not yet."

"Becca said she's in pain but resting. I want to have a family meeting today about hiring Sophia as a temp, to fill in for Mom until she can return to the kitchen."

"Hell yeah! Do you think she'd do it?"

"She's in between jobs and seems to like it here . . . there's hope."

Eli squinted as he rubbed his jaw. "If she isn't a guest then I can really go for it. Great idea, bro."

"I don't think so. I've had my eye on her since day one. If anyone is going for it, it'll be me." Gunner glared at his brother, challenging him to disagree.

"Maybe we should let her decide. What do ya think little brother? All's fair in love and all that. She already agreed to go to the rodeo with me anyway. That counts as a date." He grinned rakishly.

"Sophia's a sweetheart. She's not the kind of woman to casually mess around with."

"Oh really? She seems to like to have a good time. And who says I'm not serious?"

"Eli, back off. You'll be heading back to the rodeo circuit soon anyway. You have your pick of the buckle bunnies, isn't that what you call your rodeo groupies?"

Eli crossed his arms. "I'm impressed with your command of the rodeo lingo, little brother. Sophia is in a class all her own . . . you can hardly compare her to anyone else. Can't seem to get her off my mind."

Gunner gritted his teeth and bit back a reply. "I'm heading over to check on Mom. See you later."

"Later."

*H*is brow furrowed when he saw how pale his mom looked. She sat in the recliner, working on a crossword puzzle. "Hey, Ma. How are you feeling?"

"Madder than a wet hen. How dumb could I get? Toppled right off that damn stool."

Gunner smiled. His Ma rarely cursed and he felt relieved that she hadn't lost her sass. She was quite the banty rooster and he loved her for it. You always knew where you stood with her.

"We all make stupid mistakes and that's a fact. It could have been a whole lot worse." She glared at him and he got the hint. Now was not the time for positivity. She was still too pissed.

"How did breakfast go?" she asked.

"In apple pie order as you like to say. Thanks to our guest Sophia Russo."

"Isn't that the beautiful redhead you and Eli are fighting over?"

"Now Ma, we aren't fighting over her. You know Eli doesn't stand a chance against me." He grinned broadly. "But yeah, that's the one. Her parents own a bakery slash coffee shop and she grew up helping.

Liked it so much she went on to culinary school to become a pastry chef."

"Oh!"

"She's agreed to help out until she leaves or we find a temporary replacement."

"That would solve our problems for a few days but then what? It won't be easy to find someone who is willing to work for two months then be jobless again."

"We'll figure it out. I want to talk with the rest of the family, but what if we ask her to stay on? She did say she's currently between jobs. What do you think?"

"I think I'd like you to bring her on over right now so we can have a little chat."

"I'm sure I can arrange that."

"Since it is *my* kitchen, I'll make the decision. We won't need a family discussion over the matter."

"Well then, since we have that settled, I'll go round her up for ya."

"I'll be here. And son?" Gunner turned back and raised his brows.

"Let me do the talking."

"Yes ma'am."

*H*e knocked and listened through the screen door for any sounds of activity. "Anybody home?"

Sophia appeared and pushed the door open smiling warmly. "Hi. What brings you to my doorstep?" Barefoot and wearing a short cotton sundress, her flawless skin tempted him to trail his fingers down the length of her bare arms. Her hair was piled up on top of her head in a messy swirl of chaos.

"First off I want to thank you for your help with breakfast this morning. You saved our asses."

"It was fun. I told you I'm glad to help out. Cooking is my happy place."

"Yeah, you say that, but you are on vacation after all. I want you to know it really means a lot." He tried to meet her eyes, but she kept her gaze lowered as if uncomfortable with the praise.

"Please don't make a big deal about it." She finally looked up and he had the almost unbearable urge to kiss her. Her dark eyes were so warm and sympathetic that he found himself getting lost.

"Soph, my ma asked me to bring you over so that she could personally thank you. Can you spare a few minutes now?"

She put her hand to her throat, eyes wide. "There's no need for that. I'd be embarrassed."

"She won't take no for an answer. She'll be fit to be tied if I don't show up with you."

"That sweetheart? I have a hard time believing that."

"That's because you don't know her."

"I guess I'll have to go then. I have to protect my cowboy from his big bad mama, don't I?"

His stomach clenched at the casual endearment. *Did she just say 'My cowboy'?*

He cleared his throat, then said, "Are you ready then?"

"Let me slip on some shoes and let Amelia know where I'm off to."

"I'll wait on the porch."

*S*he opened the screen door and stepped out. She'd added some pink lip gloss and traded the bun for a high ponytail. She looked fetching, her pink converse tennis shoes a charming contrast to her short cotton dress. Her long bare legs made him heat up. *Down boy, we're off to meet with Mama.*

"Let's go," she said and she linked her arm through his as if they'd been doing it forever. He bit back a satisfied grin.

19

*S*ophia loved the feel of Gunner's strong biceps flexed beneath her fingertips. A bolt of electricity had run through her body when she'd grabbed ahold of him, but it'd be too obvious to pull her arm away now. She'd just have to deal with her quivering nerves. Acutely aware of his hip brushing against hers, she kept catching the scent of his freshly laundered tee shirt. He had on his signature Rangers ball cap worn backwards, which did her in every time. Those chocolate brown eyes and the laugh lines fanning out . . . *Honestly, could he be any sexier?*

She didn't know why she was nervous about meeting with Gunner's mom. Up until now they'd only exchanged greetings, so in some ways she felt this would be there first official introduction. She wanted his mom to like her. Best not to examine that for the moment. Her nerves were already frayed enough as it was.

Gunner unlinked their arms and held her hand when they reached the large wraparound front porch. Interlacing their fingers, he called out through the screen door. "We're here."

They stepped into a massive foyer. A wide curving staircase with an ornate wooden bannister led to the second-floor landing which overlooked the welcoming living room where Abby waited for them. Her metal gray hair was pinned into a neat bun and she had on sweats and a button-down cotton shirt.

"Your home is beautiful!" Sophia said earnestly.

"Thank you my dear. Please have a seat. Don't be shy. Gunner, get our Sophia some sweet tea please."

"Yes Ma, I'll do that. Can I get anything for you?"

"I'm fine, I've got my water here."

Sophia sat on the loveseat closest to Abby and clasped her hands in her lap to keep herself from fidgeting.

"Nice to finally meet you Mrs. Cane. I wondered how you all fit in one house. No need to wonder anymore. This place is massive."

Abby's lips tugged up at the corners. "Call me Abby, please. It is big. Two bedrooms on the main floor and four upstairs."

"It's lovely. Despite its size, you've made it feel cozy. I already feel at home."

Abby laughed warmly and Sophia relaxed. Gunner returned with her tea and sat next to Sophia, draping his arm along the back of the couch. She felt his warm thigh brushing against hers, sending tingles up her spine. Tongue tied she searched for something to fill in the silence. "How are you feeling, Mrs. Ca—Abby?"

"I'm frustrated that I'm stuck to this chair and in a bit of pain, but this too shall pass. You have certainly made an impression on my boys," Abby said.

Sophia felt her cheeks warm. Wringing her hands, she stammered, "I . . . um . . ."

Chuckling Abby said, "No need to be embarrassed. My sons have good taste."

"Now Ma! See Soph, I tried to warn you."

His mom narrowed her eyes, "Warn her about what?"

"I warned her that you can be a real pistol. She was under the impression that you were sweet."

Abby's hearty laughter filled the room. "I've never been accused of being sweet, just ask my husband. Let me get to the point. Gunner tells me that you're a chef and you're between jobs. Is that true?"

"Um . . . yes, I am. This vacation came on the heels of my mom's clean bill of health. I've been helping out at my parent's bakery while she went through chemo treatments for breast cancer."

Abby's brown eyes, so much like Gunner's, glowed with compassion. "I'm so sorry to hear that your mom's been ill."

"Thank you. I'm grateful that she caught it early and is now cancer free."

"Sophia you don't need to give me an answer immediately, but I'd like to offer you a temporary position here as our head chef and baker for breakfast and lunch until I can work again. We have a chef that prepares our dinner menu. It would probably be for two months or so. We'd compensate you for the inconvenience, and you'd have free lodging. Not to pull on your heart strings but we're desperate. We're fully booked through October. You'd have two assistants and of course the family to help out."

"I don't know what to say," Sophia said.

Gunner said, "Say yes. Don't think too hard about it."

"We'd be forever grateful to you Sophia. I hope you'll consider it."

Sophia sipped her tea then set the glass on a coaster. "It's a huge compliment that you'd entrust your kitchen to me. I will think about it and get back with you soon. I know you'll need an answer as soon as possible. But no matter what, I'm more than happy to work until I leave."

"Not without compensation you won't," Abby said firmly. "And since you're on vacation you won't be responsible for lunch. We always keep that meal pretty simple and light anyway."

"I'm happy to cover both Abby."

"Lunch is a lot of fast order fare like burgers and garlic frites as well as soups and sandwiches, salads. Nothing too fancy. Gunner told me you've worked in busy restaurants so it shouldn't be too overwhelming for you."

"I'm not at all intimidated. Serving twenty-five is a piece of cake."

Gunner picked up her glass and stood. "Mom you should rest now. You look like you're in pain. I'll work on convincing Sophia."

"Nice to finally get a chance to talk with you Sophia. I hope you'll say yes, but no hard feelings if you don't."

Sophia stood up to leave. "I'll give it some serious thought. I hope you feel better soon."

"Pop in and say hello anytime. I'll be climbing the walls after a few more days of this inactivity."

"I will."

There was sudden commotion as Clayton barreled through the front door. "Nana, I got to ride on the tracker with Uncle Eli!" He stopped in his tracks, surprised to see Sophia and Gunner standing there.

"Hi, Uncle Gunner . . . and Miss Sophia."

"Hi, Clayton. Did you tell your Nana about the new game you learned to play the other day?" Sophia asked him.

He grinned and nodded his head.

"He caught on so fast."

"My grandson is a very quick learner. I'm so proud of him."

Already moving on he said, "Gran can I watch a cartoon?"

"Of course. I'll probably take a snooze right here with you."

"Well, I won't keep you. Thanks again," Sophia said bowing slightly. Gunner took her hand to lead her out of the room.

"Why is Uncle Gunner holding Miss Sophia's hand?" Clayton said.

Sophia tried to jerk her hand away but Gunner held on tight. He turned to respond. "Because I'm trying to win her over. What do you think?"

Eyes sparkling, he said, "Yes. And then you should marry her until I'm big enough."

"Ha! Great idea."

"Gunner, get going before Sophia passes out from embarrassment," Abby said.

Gunner laughed and pulled her toward the front door. "Bye Ma."

"Bye, Abby. See you around, Clayton." Under her breath, *impish little squirt.*

When they reached the door, Sophia stopped and turned around. "Yes, I'll do it."

Abby's face brightened; the worry she'd worn now replaced with a warm smile of relief. "Really?" At Sophia's nod she said, "Thank God! You don't know how happy you've just made me. Feels like a thousand pounds have been lifted."

"I'm excited. I've never been able to be that spontaneous. Up until I lost my job, my life had been planned out meticulously. It's a great opportunity to try something new."

Gunner stared deeply into her eyes, his velvety brown gaze doing a number on her pulse. "Are you sure?" he asked softly.

She nodded and he swooped her up in a bear hug and swung her around.

"Put me down!" she said, giggling.

When her feet were planted firmly on the ground, he hugged her tightly against his chest and whispered, "Thank you Soph. I'll make sure you don't regret this."

The sound of the wooden screen door slamming shut followed by Eli's sarcastic drawl broke the spell. "What are we celebrating?"

"Soph has agreed to stay on and manage the kitchen until Mom can get back to work."

Eli raked his eyes across Sophia's flushed face and said, "Now that is something to celebrate."

"It's good for me too. I'm happy—maybe I'll have my life figured out by the end of it," Sophia said.

"And have some fun while you're at it," Eli said. "I'll be able to take you to that rodeo I promised."

"We were heading out. Come on Sophia. Later." Gunner took her hand and hauled her out the door under the watchful eye of his brother. Sophia felt the rivalry between the brothers, but wasn't sure what she should do about it, if anything. *Best to let things work themselves out. I'm going to try and enjoy the male attention and quit worrying. Funny how quickly my life has changed.*

"Whatcha thinking about?"

"That I hardly recognize my life. It's as if I stepped into somebody else's shoes."

20

*I*t had been two weeks since a tearful Amelia had boarded her flight bound for Chicago, leaving her friend behind. Sophia had settled into a routine and was familiar with the lay of the kitchen. It didn't hurt that everyone was being so helpful. Gunner sauntered in and propped his hip against the counter, crossing his arms he stared at her.

"What?"

He grinned. "Nothing, you're just so darn adorable covered in flour. You've got some on your cheeks." She swiped her arm across her face leaving more flour than she'd removed.

"Here, let me." Leaning in closer than he needed to, he stroked his thumb across first one cheek then the other. Tilting her chin up he studied her face intently. "I missed a spot," he said, then brushed his finger across her bottom lip. Her breath hitched.

"Red, you keep looking at me like that and I won't

be responsible for what happens next." She licked her lips and he groaned.

"Oh, um . . . sorry." She turned away and placed the flour back in the plastic storage bin and snapped it shut.

Gunner shoved his hands in his pockets. "Let's go out this weekend. A proper date. Saturday night."

"D-date?" She said her voice small.

"Yes date. As in you and me . . . all alone."

"Are you sure? I mean what about me working for you and your dad and . . ." her voice trailed off.

"The way I see it, we're both adults, you're no longer a guest here so why not?"

She gave a half shrug and said, "Well . . . I can think of a few reasons."

"Name them, I'm all ears."

"For starters, you're far too attractive and sure of yourself."

"And that's a crime? Would you rather I be homely and awkward?"

"And . . . you have way too many admirers . . . it's intimidating."

"It shouldn't be. I'm only looking at you right now. There is nobody else."

She felt her face flush. "What about mixing work with our personal lives? And I'll only be here for a short time . . . and . . ."

"You're scared." He finished her sentence for her.

"Honestly, yes. I'm scared."

"Yet you're willing to hang out with a notorious player like my brother Elijah?"

"That's different."

"How?"

She gave him a dirty look. "Because it is."

"Great argument."

"It's hard to explain. I don't feel intimidated by Eli. I know where I stand with him. With you, I just feel more vulnerable."

He scratched his head. "Let me get this straight. You'll hang out with Eli because he's not intimidating and he's safe because you know he's not safe. You won't go out with me because I have too many admirers which somehow makes me untrustworthy?"

She fiddled with her earring. "I know that sounds silly. It's just . . . I'm attracted to you okay? I like you. Are you happy now?" she finally spit out.

He clutched his chest. "Did I hear right? Did the beautiful Sophia Russo just admit that she likes me?"

She wanted the floor to swallow her up and be done with it. "Okay."

"Okay what?"

"Date."

He gripped her chin and forced her to look at him. "You're saying yes, you'll go out with me Saturday?"

She bobbed her head and held up a finger. "On one condition."

"I'm listening," he said.

"That we take things slow."

"I'm good with that. We'll go at your pace, cross my heart." He reached out and tucked a strand of hair behind her ear.

"Am I interrupting something?" Sophia jumped when Eli's voice broke through their intimate moment.

Gunner nonchalantly turned to face his brother,

effectively blocking Sophia from Eli's view. She was grateful. It gave her a moment to compose herself.

"As a matter of fact, yes you are. You're like a burr in my shoe, big brother."

Elijah laughed. "That makes my day. Hey Soph remember that rodeo we talked about? There's one coming this way, about an hour drive from here . . . I'd like to take you. Becca said she'd cover for you."

"Um . . . I'd feel bad taking off of work."

"Don't worry about that. She's happy to do it and she's a pro. She's been helping Mama since she was a kid."

"W-e-l-l . . . I suppose . . . if you're sure she's okay with it."

"Yep. I'll fill you in on the details later. See ya around." Smirking, he winked at Sophia then turned to Gunner and said, "Little brother, there's some horses that need tending to. I'd have thought you were on vacation or something."

Gunner snorted. "Every day is a vacation for you."

"Ha! Adios," Eli said. Turning on his heel, he left the kitchen, whistling.

"Well, that was annoying."

Sophia's nose crinkled. "The timing was a bit unfortunate . . . you know we had talked about the rodeo a while back. Um . . . I . . ."

"Soph, no need to waste your time worrying about me. I'm a big boy. Just remember that Eli is like a little kid in a toy store when it comes to women. Don't take him seriously. Seems you've already figured that one out, but even I have to admit, he has a way of charming his way into a lady's heart. You'll enjoy the rodeo and there's no one better to show you than our own home-grown bronco rider. Just be careful."

Her mouth curved into a smile. "And I'm a big girl."

He flashed that potent grin. "And you like me."

"Gunner?"

"Yeah?"

"Don't get cocky."

He laughed and grabbed her hand, bringing her palm to his lips. "Never. I'd better get back to work. Remember, tomorrow's farmer's market. We'll take the truck right after breakfast."

"I'll have my list ready. I love farmer's markets. It's one of my favorite things to do."

"Added bonus, we get to be together."

"That too," she said.

"Later then."

After he left, Sophia leaned against the counter deep in thought. *I've really gone and done it now. Two dates with two different men who happen to be brothers. Geesh! To top it off . . . I told Gunner that I like him. Dang it!*

Becca interrupted her musings. "Hey, just checking in. You're killing it by the way."

"Thanks Becca."

"You look worried," Becca said.

"I do? No, I'm fine. Just organizing my thoughts."

"Does it have anything to do with my brother?"

Sophia bit back a laugh. "Which one? Am I that obvious?"

Becca smiled. "I reckon if it'd been a snake, it woulda bit me. I'm guessing since you're a smart girl, it'd be Gunner. Eli is not the settling down kind of guy. I love him, but I wouldn't wish him on any woman. If you want a good time though, he's unparalleled."

"I'll keep that in mind. I'd already kind of figured that one out. I just haven't figured out Gunner."

"Truthfully? He's probably had his fair share of flings, but he's only been in love once, far as I can tell, and that nearly broke him. His fiancée, who was also in his band, left him to hitch herself to a bigger star. He was gutted. He's been a little gun shy since then."

Sophia pondered that for a moment. "Love can be brutal."

"Yes, it can. I've had my heart broken a time or two myself."

"You're all so different, it's hard to believe you come from the same family."

Becca laughed; her face alight with amusement. "That's for sure. My mom had her hands full with us. She was beside herself when I followed in Eli's footsteps and joined the rodeo circuit. Two of us in a high-risk sport was two too many."

"You were in the rodeo?"

"Yes, briefly. I was in the pro-circuit in my early twenties. Barrel racing. I picked up a few trophies along the way."

"That is so cool Becca. Why'd you quit?"

"It's a lifestyle and I quickly grew tired of it. After me and my ex split, I left. He was a bull rider. Not to mention its hard on the bod. But I do miss the thrill of it . . . and being surrounded by cowboys every day."

"I hear that," Sophia said.

"I'll be going then. Let me know if you need anything. And Sophia, Gunner is a good guy. I'm not just saying that because he's my brother. He's a softie underneath that cowboy swag."

"Thanks Becca. I'm glad to be getting to know you. I'm going to miss you when I leave."

"I feel the same. Text me if you need anything. Ta ta."

Sophia's brow furrowed. She tried to imagine what that must have been like for Gunner to lose not only his lover but his bandmate. *Interesting . . . was he really over her?*

She grabbed a dish towel and scrubbed down the butcher block counter before mopping the floor, then headed back to the small cabin she'd been assigned in her new role on the staff. As always, the glorious view of the mountains, the horses dotting the landscape and the trees rustling in the breeze left her feeling peaceful . . . and grateful to be here.

21

*G*unner called through the wooden screen door. "Knock knock."

"Come on in. I'm almost ready."

He stepped inside and stood at the threshold feeling like he'd just downed a quart of expresso. His hair was still damp from grabbing a quick shower. He'd been running late after dealing with a colicky horse.

Sophia entered the room.

He whistled a low wolf call and said, "Wow, you look gorgeous. Every guy is going to wish they were me."

Her hair fell thick and shiny around her shoulders and down her back. She wore a yellow sleeveless crop top with white linen harem pants that hung low on her hips leaving a tantalizing view of her slim waist and flat belly. His eyes were caught by the navel piercing with a diamond studded ring. *Sexy.* He followed the trail down to her feet in flip-flops with painted pink nails

and back up to her face. Her shy smile sent a burst of
heat through him. She hesitated so he extended his
hand to her and she took it.

"Are you hungry?"

"Starving," she said.

"Good. This little diner serves the best trout and
bison burgers this side of the Rockies. They have daily
specials too. Their chicken fried steak is as good as
anyone's, and if you're really brave . . . you can order the
Rocky mountain oysters."

"No thank you! I refuse to eat bull testicles even if I
am a chef. I have to draw the line somewhere."

He interlaced their fingers and they walked
leisurely to his Silverado. Her wrist bangles made a
tinkling sound as their arms swung. The sun was warm
but the slight breeze tempered the heat. He opened her
door and waited as she climbed in, catching a whiff of
something floral.

Sliding behind the wheel he glanced over as she
buckled up. He frowned. She seemed uncomfortable or
something. *Maybe she's regretting her decision to go out
with me.*

He tilted his head squinting at her. "Everything
alright with you Red?"

"Yes." She played with her bracelets then expelled a
deep breath. "Actually, I'm nervous. It's been a long
time since I've been on a first date. I'm a little rusty," she
confessed. She rested her head against the seat and
turned to look at him. "What about you?"

"Been a while for me too. Plus, there is the fact that
I really like you and I want to impress you so much that
you forget all about my brother or any other guy for

that matter." That made her smile and seemed to dispel some of her nervousness. He was relieved. He put the truck into drive and pulled out. After he turned onto the main road, he reached across the seat and grabbed her hand, squeezing it. "I'm glad you're here with me Sophia."

"Me too. I've been looking forward to this all day."

"Why don't you skip that rodeo?"

"I promised Eli. I can't back out now. It wouldn't be right."

"So, you're okay to leave me back at the ranch, tormented with thoughts of my brother seducing you? That's the thing that's not right."

"I'm sure you'll survive. You seemed to be fine with it before. In fact, I seem to recall you giving me your blessing."

He scowled. "I changed my mind. I don't want you anywhere near my brother. I'm selfish like that." He really wasn't kidding. It was driving him crazy that she was going out with Elijah. He had half a mind to show up there. He could take Clayton for cover. *Quit worrying and use the time to make her forget all about big brother.*

He parked in a small corner parking lot a block away from the diner.

"It's right around the corner from here," Gunner said. The red neon 'open' sign greeted them and he cupped her waist as they entered, her bare skin cool against his palm. He guided her as they followed their waitress Gretchen, who'd worked there as long as Gunner could remember. She seated them at an intimate booth in the back. He watched Sophia slide across the vinyl seat then sat down across from her.

"Specials today: pan seared trout with rice pilaf or veal cutlets and your choice of baked potato or home fries. Veggie of the day is broccoli. Here's the regular menu." She handed them each a menu enclosed in plastic. "What'll you have to drink?"

Gunner said, "They do serve alcohol here."

"A glass of white wine sounds lovely. What are you having?"

He glanced at Gretchen. "I'll have a Coors draft."

Gretchen left to fill their drink orders. Sophia studied the menu, and Gunner fought to keep from touching her. She glanced up and met his eyes, her mouth curving in a smile.

"Soph, I can't seem to concentrate on the menu. They could probably serve me sawdust smothered with gravy and I wouldn't know the difference." She laughed softly.

"I know the feeling." She closed her menu and reached her open palms across the table. His hands covered hers and he caressed her wrists with his thumbs.

"You've been haunting my dreams." He took a deep breath. "I swear, you're like a drug, everything about you, gets me right here," he said, lifting her palm to his chest. "I want to know all about you. What's your favorite song, your favorite color, your first love, your first heartbreak . . . how you feel about me?"

Her breath seemed to catch in her throat as she looked at him. "Gunner, I like you a little too much for my peace of mind."

Expelling his held breath, he smiled. "Well, the way

I figure it, even if we wanted to run away it's a little late for that."

"One draft for you Mr. Cane, and a glass of white wine for your lady friend."

"Thanks Gretchen. I think we're ready to order. Soph what'll you have?"

"The trout special, thanks. Italian dressing please."

"I'll have the filet, medium rare, baked potato, ranch dressing." She took their menus and then they were alone again.

"My first love was my dad. I was your typical daddy's girl. We lived in an apartment above the bakery and he'd sneak me downstairs late at night and let me help him. As early as I can remember, I knew that's what I wanted to do when I grew up. My dad is a real clown and he always made me laugh." Sophia smiled, her eyes unfocused as if she was going back in time, "We'd have flour fights, and he never worried about spilled milk or messes, baking was fun. I had my very own apron and stool to stand on. He'd play music and pick me up and dance around the kitchen. I loved him so, he was like a big kid and he was my hero . . . still is."

Gunner said, "Almost opposite of my dad."

She sipped her wine. "I know how lucky I am. My mom is great too. She was definitely the disciplinarian between the two of them, but honestly, I was a pretty good kid. I didn't really rebel that much; there wasn't any reason to."

"Then you went on to chef school?"

"Yeah. They scraped and saved every penny they could to help me realize my dream. After I graduated from high school, I worked in the bakery until I was twenty-one, then they sent me to Paris to study at Le Cordon Bleu. I stayed with a host family in France for free. They became like a second family to me. We still keep in touch."

"That took some courage. I assume you speak French then?"

Sophia smiled. "*Oui.*" Their food arrived and she leaned over her plate, sniffing her entree. "Smells delicious." She loaded her fork with the tender meat of the trout and took her first bite. Rolling her eyes heavenward she said, "Mmm, oh my, so good. Want a taste?" she said, offering him a bite. Gunner opened his mouth and she fed him.

"Oh yeah, that's what I'm talking about," he said. "Here, taste mine."

Sophia opened wide and sampled his filet. "Yummy, so tender." She swallowed then took another sip of wine. Continuing where they'd left off, she said, "What about you? When did you leave the nest?"

"I took off for Nashville when I was twenty-one. Broke my ma's heart and infuriated my dad, but it was something I had to do. I felt like I was suffocating here. My dad kept a tight rein on the family business and on us kids. Eli had already left for the professional rodeo circuit; I followed shortly after."

"Talk about courage. At least I had the support and blessings of my parents. You had to strike out on your own. That must have been scary."

"I was too young and dumb to be afraid. That came later." He took another bite, chewing thoughtfully.

Sophia said, "I'm a bit embarrassed to say that I'd never heard of you before I got here. Being a city girl and all, I haven't been much exposed to country music. I'm sorry."

"Don't be. Hardly your fault. Truth is, I was well known in Nashville and amongst the country music singer songwriters, but I hadn't hit it really big yet. They kept telling me I was just on the edge of super-stardom," he said, dryly.

"I think they were right. Everyone here but me seemed to know about you."

"We did go on tour with Miranda Lambert as her opening act. You've heard of her haven't ya? Talk about adrenalin rush. That was the highlight of my career."

"Gunner, don't say it like that's all in the past! There will be more highlights. I heard you sing; you've got a real gift."

"I messed it all up. Got caught up in the lifestyle and lost my way. I don't deserve it."

Sophia reached across the table and clasped his forearm. "That's a lie you're telling yourself to hide behind. You got hurt and now you're afraid to risk it."

He squinted at her, his eyes flickering with some hidden emotion. "Oh yeah? And what makes you say that?"

"Call it women's intuition . . . um . . . some articles I read . . . I know it's a dog-eat-dog world out there. It's the same in the culinary world. Believe me, I've been burnt myself."

"Aren't you doing the very thing you're accusing me of, running away from what you love?" He asked.

Her lips turned up. "Maybe. Hey, I didn't claim to have my own life together. Practice what I preach, not what I do." He laughed out loud, a warm husky sound that filled the booth. The waitress appeared to clear their table, and after they declined dessert, she left the bill.

"Let's blow this joint." After plunking down some cash, he grabbed Sophia's hand and pulled her out of the booth.

"Thanks Gunner. It was fabulous."

"You're welcome. Great food and even better company."

Gunner called out to Gretchen as they left. "Thanks, Gretch, and make sure you tell that lunkhead of a husband he outdid himself again."

She chuckled. "Thanks Gunner. Will do. Don't be a stranger."

They stepped out into the balmy night air. Reaching towards the sky, Sophia spread her arms wide and twirled around. "Look at the stars! I swear I've never seen anything like it. They're so close seems like I can touch them."

"Wyoming's known for some great star gazing."

When they reached his truck, Gunner turned Sophia to face him and placed his hands on either side of her shoulders, backing her against the door of his Silverado. Her eyes widened as he dipped his head down to softly kiss her. He felt her body stiffen then yield and she parted her lips. That was all the invitation he needed. He kissed her slowly and thoroughly until she was breathing hard and clinging to him.

Her body fit next to his perfectly. He was caught in her spell, her lips...so soft, her skin silky beneath his rough hands, the taste of wine as he dipped his tongue inside her mouth . . . he wanted more, needed more. . .

to explore every inch of her body. Her hands wrapped around his neck and she held him tight. His fingers skimmed her waist, touching her smooth bare skin, then coasted around to her back so he could tug her closer to him.

When she moaned, he lifted his mouth, resting his forehead against hers. "Sophia, I want you so bad . . . probably more than I've ever wanted anything." Her floral scent drove him half crazy, both feminine and sexy as hell. She was intoxicating. He wanted to give her everything she'd ever dreamed of. His voice came out husky and rough as he said, "You could ask me for about anything right now and I'd find a way to make it happen."

She tipped her head to look up at him, softly brushing a lock of his hair back. "Gunner Cane, you've somehow managed to slip past my defenses. I don't know whether to curse you or kiss you again."

"Sounds like a no brainer to me." She pulled him down for another kiss. He thought he might lose his mind when she flicked her tongue inside his mouth. Something inside him let loose. Heat and desire were overriding his senses and he only pulled away when he heard people approaching.

"Sophia, I'm not thinking straight. Let's get out of here," he said, breathing hard.

"Good idea," she said, her voice shaky. "I feel like a schoolgirl caught behind the bleachers."

Her dark eyes glittered like jewels in the light cast from the streetlamp. He framed her face with his hands and studied her kiss swollen lips, fighting the urge to kiss her again. "If you don't quit looking at me like that, we're going to get arrested."

She responded by brushing her fingertips over his lips. "Let's go back to my place and talk about it."

He opened the truck door and she climbed in. After they were on the road she reached over and laid her palm on his upper thigh. It was going to be a long-ass ride back to the ranch.

22

*S*ophia was fighting an inner battle . . . she was hardly a high school virgin but she'd never behaved recklessly when it came to sex. With both of her lovers, she'd taken her time and held back until she was sure it was serious. Now her body was telling her *to hell with that. I want him, what's the big deal —I'm thirty years old. Go for it.* The problem with that logic was it didn't take into account her heart.

She'd never felt this way about anyone in her life. She was practically unhinged with want . . . yet there was more to it than that. She was catching glimpses of what a future with Gunner might look like. *Yikes! Just thinking about his lips is making my stomach flip-flop. What is happening to me? I have a half hour to cool down and get it together.* Only problem with that was she didn't want to get it together. *Can I have sex with him and let go of any expectations? If not, don't do it. It's that simple. Oh God I wish Amelia was still here!*

Gunner picked up her hand resting on his thigh and placed it further down his leg. He cleared his throat and said, "Um . . . you know you're killing me, don't you?" She glanced up at him and his eyes scorched her face.

She licked her lips and felt bad when he squeezed his eyes shut as if in pain. "I'm sorry, I . . . it's not intentional. I don't know what's going on with me, I'm in uncharted territory with you."

"It's chemistry, babe. Pure and simple."

"Not so simple for me," she said.

He pressed the car stereo knob, and Thomas Rhett filled the airwaves, dissipating some of the sexual tension. "Good song. Appropriate, don't ya think?" He grinned.

She had to laugh as she listened to the words to the song *Make Me Wanna*. "Ha—pull the truck to the side of the road! Let's! This is definitely our song. Will you sing it for me some time?"

"For you, I'd do just about anything."

"Winning!" Her laughter filled the truck cab and she realized she hadn't been this lighthearted in a very long time. He began to sing along and as she listened, she thought it was probably the most swoon-worthy moment of her life. She knew in that instant that her decision was already made. She'd have him tonight.

He parked and killed the engine. His eyes were smoldering, his voice strained when he said, "I'll walk you to your cabin."

"Yes," she replied softly.

They held hands and when they stepped onto the

porch, she faced him and slipped her arms around his waist. "Come in."

"Sophia, I . . . I don't want there to be any regrets."

"There won't be."

"Are you sure about that?"

"Yes."

She released him and opened the door. He hauled her into his arms the second the door closed behind them and commandingly kissed her, allowing no time for second guessing. Not that she would have anyway. Responding to his persuasion she greedily kissed him back. His hands were everywhere. She tugged at his tee shirt, practically ripping it over his head, staring unabashedly when she saw his bare torso. He was exquisite. Bronzed, muscular, perfection. They both kicked off their shoes then she unzipped his jeans, feverishly sliding them down over his muscular thighs. He stepped out of them, kicking them to the side. He grabbed her shirt, yanking it over her head unceremoniously. Their movements were fierce and wild, both overcome by their passion.

They stumbled to her bedroom, half naked by the time they fell onto the bed, both panting as his mouth came down over hers. He unclasped her bra and sucked in his breath when her breasts spilled out. "Beautiful," he whispered. Tossing the lacy bra aside, he captured her swollen pink nipple into his mouth and suckled until she cried out. The tug of his warm wet mouth made something deep inside her break free. She trembled beneath him. Raking her fingers through his hair she held him to her, crying out his name when he reached inside her panties to touch her hot center of desire.

He lifted his head and met her gaze, his eyes hooded and glazed. He stood to pull off his underwear and her breath caught at his beauty. He kneeled on the bed and slid her panties down, his rough hands against her skin sexy and all male. He licked and kissed his way back up starting with her toes, traveling slowly over her thighs, her flat belly, nuzzling between her breasts, nibbling her neck . . . finally reaching her lips, he open mouth kissed her into delirium.

She felt no inhibition lying naked beneath him; she was red hot with desire. There was no thinking, only sensation. His musky smell, his hard body against her flesh, his ragged breath, his erection pressing between her thighs, a loud moan escaped her. When his tongue plunged deeper, she thought she might shatter. She wrapped her thighs around him, squeezing tight.

"Please," she panted.

"Please what?" he growled against her mouth.

"Please, I want . . . to . . . feel you inside of me," she pleaded.

He ripped open the condom packet he'd retrieved earlier from his jean pocket. Slipping it on, he pressed against her moist center and pushed hard into her as she arched beneath him. When he had completely filled her, he paused and she cried out in frustration. "Gunner, now!"

He began to thrust, slowly and torturously at first, and he moaned her name as she tightened around him from inside. Arms on either side of her holding his weight, muscles bulging, he began to ride her in earnest. Her hands grasped his shoulders as he plunged in and out, his staccato rhythm building to a peak. They both climaxed at the same time. His ragged breath matched her own as she floated, suspended in sensation. Her body convulsed and pulsated against his hardness as she felt him shudder.

When he was spent, he collapsed on top of her and buried his face underneath her wild mane, nuzzling against her neck. It was erotic to feel his hot breath against her bare skin, his chest slick with sweat pressed against her breasts, so sensual . . . she felt sexy and feminine. His weight pressing her into the mattress was at once comforting and arousing. She'd never felt so desirable, and utterly, completely satiated.

When she shifted under him, he said lazily against her neck, "Don't move. I want to stay like this." Those words made her melt inside. It was the sexiest thing she'd ever heard. After some time, he rolled onto his back taking her with him so she was now nestled snug against his chest their legs tangled together.

She slung her arm around him and buried her nose in his neck. Her voice husky she said, "Gunner?"

"Hm?"

"Will you stay here tonight . . . sleep here with me?"

He nibbled her ear. "You'd have to call in the sheriff to pry me out of here."

She smiled. "That's good." Her eyes felt heavy, her body languid. She was drifting off. Gunner's even breath told her he was already asleep.

. . .

*A*t the break of dawn, Sophia first became aware of arms wrapped around her and a warm hard body pressed against the length of her back. She sleepily nestled into the comforting embrace. Her eyes popped open when she suddenly remembered where she was and whose body was pressed against hers. *Gunner. Last night . . . Oh my God! I'm a goner . . .*

His palm stroked down her flat belly. "Mornin' Red," he said quietly. She felt his arousal pressing against her bottom.

Flashes of their lustful abandon from the night before made her belly do cartwheels. "Morning."

He pushed her hair aside and kissed the nape of her neck, sending shivers down her spine. "I was afraid it was a dream," he murmured against her skin, his lips doing numbers on her nervous system. Flipping over to face him, she met his gaze, studying his face . . . so handsome, his sexy morning stubble making him even hotter. She ran her finger between his brows and down his nose before tracing the outline of his lips. His eyes were warm pools of brown, still soft with sleep. The intimacy of the moment made her heart swell.

His eyes burned with desire and something more. "Soph . . . thank you for last night. I . . . um . . . as cliché as it may sound, I've never felt so connected with some-one . . . ever."

"It was like that for me too. Gunner," she hesitated, voice wavering she said, "I . . . I . . . really like you." Embarrassed by her admission, she buried her face against his chest.

"Tell me again," he said. Face still hidden, she

shook her head no. He kissed the top of her head and held her tightly against him. His voice low and husky he said, "Sophia, I really like you too." She stilled.

Her voice barely a whisper she said, "You do?"

He tilted her chin up forcing her to meet his gaze. Stroking her hair back, he kissed the tip of her nose. "I do. I'm completely smitten."

A wave of longing swept through her. She brushed his lips in a tentative kiss, then his open mouth came down on hers and she was lost again . . . he leisurely kissed her; unlike their frenzied lovemaking from the night before, this was slow raw seduction. He trailed his knuckles down her bare arm . . . her hip . . . outer thigh and back up again. His fingers skimmed her buttocks, leaving her a quivering mass of sensation.

He reached between her thighs and touched her while kissing her senseless. The heat slowly built until the tension became almost unbearable . . . *more* . . . "Gunner, ah . . . you're so good." She rocked her pelvis against his hand, urging him to move faster.

She felt his hardness pressing against her thigh then reached for him, smiling as he groaned. *Good, I'm not the only one.* Pushing him onto his back, she positioned herself on top, peppering kisses across his chest and down his muscular abs. She deliberately swished her hair against his skin, teasing him. When she reached the dusting of hair leading to his manhood, she snuggled her nose against him, aroused by his musky scent.

She grabbed the condom he'd placed on the bedside table the night before and tore the foil packet open with her teeth as he looked on, his eyes burning.

Her heart squeezed. With trembling hands, she rolled it on then hovered over him before mounting slowly. Sinking down his length, he filled her as she took him inside.

He cupped her breasts rolling his thumbs across her nipples. She arched back, rocking her pelvis, lifting up then sinking back down slowly, as he growled, "My God, you feel so good!" Impatiently he grasped her hips and thrust up to meet her, urging her to quicken the pace. Leaning over him, she placed her hands on either side of his head, breasts temptingly close to his face, her long hair brushing against him . . . her thighs fully engaged, she began to ride him without restraint.

Panting, she was ready to peak, her body coiled like a tight spring. He began to shudder beneath her, sending her over the edge. Wave after wave of sensation overtook her. Gunner pulled her against his chest, holding her tightly as they climaxed together. His labored breath matched her own.

"Holy hell, what was that?" Gunner said several minutes later. "Felt like a tsunami."

Sophia couldn't move. She rubbed her cheek against his chest and sighed contentedly. "Yeah."

He feathered his fingertips up and down her spine. "Yeah? Is that all you have to say?"

"Uh-huh."

"How about something like this." He pitched his voice up to mimic hers. "Oh Gunner, you are the best lover I've ever had. So manly, so sexy, I'm utterly captivated."

She giggled softly. "Uh-huh, something like that."

"You've ruined me. I hope you're happy."

She finally lifted her head and met his twinkling eyes. "Very."

"Kiss me," he commanded. She could look at him forever, she loved his warm smile and unruly mop of hair. She loved the way their bodies fit together and the way he made her feel . . . feminine, sexy, and beautiful. She gave him a quick peck on his lips.

"You call that a kiss? I want a real one."

She dipped down again and hovered over his lips, her nipples grazing his chest. Her body was still quivering from the aftershocks of the earthquake she'd just experienced. She covered his mouth and kissed him hard and heavy, dipping her tongue, kissing him until they were both breathless again. He suddenly rolled her over so she was on the bottom and he took control. Burying his fingers in her hair, he kissed her until she was nothing but a puddle.

Her alarm clock startled them both and she giggled. He glanced at his watch and groaned. "I wish we could stay in bed all day but unfortunately that's not going to happen. It's six-thirty."

"I've got to get showered and get to work," Sophia said.

Gunner rolled off her and stretched lazily. "You get up first. I want to watch that sweet ass walking away."

She stood and tugged at his hand trying to pull him up. "I don't want you to watch. I feel shy."

He flashed a smile. "Now you feel shy? Isn't it a little late for that darlin'?"

She turned and ran into the bathroom loving the sound of his warm laughter following her.

23

*S*ophia was humming off key, her arms elbow deep in dough when Gunner snuck up behind her, pulling her against his chest. "That tickles," she said, giggling as he nibbled her ear.

"Whatcha' doing? I thought you'd be finished up by now."

"I promised Chef James that I'd bake some French bread for him for tonight's menu."

"Oh. That's nice of you. Did you miss me?"

"Yes, but Gunner, be good. I'm working. Anyone could walk in."

"So? Who cares?"

"Me."

"I can't get you out of my head," he whispered, "Babe, I'm half-crazy thinking about last night."

She allowed herself to melt against him for a moment. It felt so right. Leaning her head against his shoulder she sighed. "It was pretty good."

"Pretty good? I'm insulted. Try mind blowing."

"Yes, all of that . . . now let me go. I'm covered in flour and dough and you're taking advantage."

"Okay, but only if you promise to give me all of your attention tonight."

"Deal."

He released her and stepped away. Gathering up some of the dirty dishes, he rinsed them off before placing them in the dishwasher.

"Thanks," Sophia said.

"I'm besotted and pretty much willing to do anything you ask. Best that you take advantage while you can."

"Why, is the meter running?"

"Not really. You're good . . . no expiration date."

She laughed. "What a relief."

They both turned when they heard someone clear their throat. "Sorry to interrupt," Becca said.

"You're not interrupting," Sophia answered quickly. She felt her cheeks heating.

Becca looked miserable as she gestured with her thumb towards the door. "Um . . . Gunner . . . there is someone here to see you," her voice trailed off. "I'm sorry." She lowered her head, wringing her hands.

"Sis, cut to the chase. What's the problem? You look like someone just died."

"It's . . ."

A sultry voice cut through the air, "Gunner, long time no see." A woman stepped around Becca and entered the kitchen. Sophia saw a stricken look flash across Gunner's face and she knew immediately that this was his ex-fiancée.

She was stunning and had the cool factor down in spades. Her nose was pierced and a small diamond stud sparkled in the sunlight. Her bohemian style long dress was split up the middle revealing tanned thighs and cowboy boots. Her ample cleavage was on display with the daringly cut vee of the dress design. A purple floppy cowboy hat sat prettily atop her long blond hair, which hung loose and tousled.

Gunner recovered and managed to mask his emotions behind a tight smile. "Hello, Natalie. Why are you here?"

"Is that anyway to greet an old friend?"

His lips twisted. "Is that what you'd call yourself?"

Natalie, suddenly noticing Sophia standing there, raked her eyes up and down Sophia's body. Sophia felt her hackles rise. *Who does she think she is, Lady Gaga? I hate her already.*

"Hi, I'm Natalie. You must be the cook."

"Yes, one of them. I'm Sophia." She was trying really hard not to compare herself to the perfectly coiffed woman smiling at her so condescendingly. Now uncomfortably aware that her apron was covered with flour and undoubtedly her hair a disheveled mess. Any lip gloss she'd had on was long gone by now.

Natalie turned away dismissively and walked over to Gunner, slipping her arm through his. "I've missed you. You still look good enough to eat."

He pulled away from her and said, "I'll repeat myself, why are you here?"

"Can we go somewhere private to talk?"

"I don't have anything to say to you."

"Gunner, I'm here on business and there's no need

to be so rude." She pouted, looking up at him through her lashes.

He jammed his hands in his front pockets and looked at Sophia, brow furrowed. "Soph, I'll catch up with you later. Okay?"

She nodded, not meeting his eyes. "Of course."

Becca said, "I'll get Little Joe to take over your group this afternoon."

He nodded and strode briskly to the door. Sophia watched him disappear around the corner.

Natalie looked coyly at Sophia and smiled. "Nice to meet you. I admire anyone working in the service industry. It's such hard work. Society's little worker bees."

"Buzz buzz." Sophia said, plastering a fake smile on her face.

Becca glared at her retreating backside. "What a bitch! And the nerve of that woman showing up here after what she did to Gunner. I feel so bad for him."

Eli appeared, scowling, sweaty and looking like he'd been rolling around in dirt, his dusty cowboy hat pushed back on his forehead. "What the hell is Medusa doing here?"

"Who knows? She says it's business," Becca said, worriedly.

"Yeah, sure it is. She knows how badly she messed up. I hope Gunner doesn't fall for it. He was supposed to help me with branding a few dozen cattle this afternoon, kind of a show and tell for the guests. I guess I'll have to catch up with Little Joe at the barn and enlist his help . . . just in case. I hope she's long gone by then."

"Me too."

Sophia felt like she was going to be sick. *Was it possible that he still had feelings for her? Would they be so worried about him if he didn't?* Becca pulled out her cell and began texting, presumedly Little Joe.

Baking had always been like meditating for Sophia —focusing on the task, creating something with her hands—it had helped her through many turbulent times. *So that's what I'll do right now.* She turned her attention back to kneading the dough like it was a lifeline. Finally satisfied that she had the perfect consistency, she shaped the dough onto the floured butcher block surface then placed them on a large baking sheet. She set them by the sunny window to rise again. Glancing at her watch, she calculated her time. They had to rise for thirty minutes then she'd return and throw them in the oven to bake.

Becca and Elijah were having a quiet discussion off in the corner and Sophia said, "I'll be leaving now. I'll finish up here after the dough has risen."

"Thanks for all your hard work Sophia," Becca said. Looking at Sophia, her brow furrowed with concern. "Sophia, are you okay? You look pale. Don't worry about Natalie . . . really. Gunner has moved on."

Sophia forced a smile. "I'm fine. You know us little worker bees."

Becca snorted. "Little worker bees, I'd like to stuff one of those loaves down her pretty little throat."

"Don't worry about it. I just consider the source."

"You're more forgiving than I am."

"I'm looking forward to our rodeo date," Eli said, winking.

"Oh . . . um . . . okay." She appreciated that Eli was

trying to make her feel better, but that was the last thing on her mind at the moment. She quietly left the kitchen and headed back to her cabin. She needed to clear her head. She couldn't help it; she was beyond anxious to know what business the famous Natalie wanted to discuss with Gunner. *It's probably an excuse to see him again.* She reached up and massaged her neck. She'd know soon enough, but she still felt sick to her stomach. *Why did she have to show up now? The timing couldn't be any worse after the night they'd spent together.* She threw herself onto the bed and buried her face in her arms and sobbed.

24

*G*unner waited until he was outside the lodge before he stopped and faced Natalie. He glared angrily, "You aren't welcome here."

"I know that, but after you hear what I have to say you may feel differently. For me, it's worth a dose of your scorn."

"Follow me." He pivoted on his heel and briskly walked away.

He entered the office building next to the barn and turned on the lights. "Have a seat."

He sat and glared at Natalie as she perched on the edge of a chair across the desk from him. She was still as beautiful as when they'd first met, but he felt nothing. There wasn't even a spark of interest. It was as if he were looking at a stranger. She wasn't the least bit nervous or remorseful. Her hubris had always bordered on narcissism. He'd been so enamored with her that he hadn't caught on to that until much too late. He'd hoped to never see her again and now here she was . . . in Wyoming.

She smiled provocatively. "You are as handsome as ever. Gunner . . . I . . ."

He held up his hand. "Stop right there. Let's get something straight, I'm willing to hear you out since you came all this way, but know this, my feelings for you are dead. If this is about business then spit it out. I'll give you a half hour. If it's personal this meeting just ended."

She raised a perfectly arched brow. "My, my but you've changed. Did I do this to you?"

He crossed his arms and tipped back his chair. "The clock's ticking."

She pouted. "Fine then, have it your way. I was hoping you could at least be civil."

"This is as civil as it's going to get."

She huffed out a breath and said, "I was approached by Miranda Lambert's manager. They want us to get our band back together and be her opening act next spring. She'll be releasing her next CD and she wants us to join her on a promo tour."

"No."

"No? Just like that? All the band members are in. We need you. Do you really feel so cavalier about your friends that you can selfishly ruin this opportunity for them?"

"You certainly didn't give a damn before when you left us to further your own career."

She waved her hand dismissively. "That was in the past. This is now."

"So, I take it you approached the band before talking with me?"

"Yes. I figured you'd be the only hold up."

"Things didn't go the way you'd hoped with your superstar and now you come back to us?"

"Yes. Spin it however you want but we have another shot. Why not take it?"

"I have my reasons."

"Oh right, your reasons . . . just what exactly are your reasons? It never made any sense to me . . . you leaving when your career was taking off." She scoffed, "I never believed for a second that it was because you'd done your time. Tell me the truth. What was the real reason you left?"

"None of your business. Is that all then?"

"Gunner, listen to me and listen good. You haven't been gone so long that people have forgotten you. Your fans will be so happy to have you back that your resurrection, if you will, will only catapult you to the top. Phillip Krauss personally asked me to come and speak with you. He believes in you. So do I."

"Give me a break Natalie. Do you think I give two shits about whether you believe in me or not?"

Her eyes flickered for a moment before she veiled them. *If that hurt, too bad. She deserved it.*

He had a momentary prick of conscience then brushed it aside.

"You don't have to answer now. Take a few days to think about it. Phillip will be following up. You'd be a fool to let this opportunity go. There's no question you were born to be a star. No one out there sounds like you. Your natural talent is a gift. Don't make the mistake of squandering it."

"We're done here," Gunner said as he stood.

"At least let Phillip fly you out to Nashville to hear his offer. He'd like us to put together our own CD before the tour so we can promote ourselves as well. You know as well as I do that opportunity only knocks so many times. Are you really ready to throw away your dreams?"

Gunner's jaw tightened. "I've finally accepted this is where I'm supposed to be. I don't need anything more. Have a safe trip back. And Natalie? Don't ever contact me again."

Natalie stood, slinging her purse strap over her shoulder, she said, "You've changed and it's not a good look. Don't mess this up for everyone. Think long and hard before you turn it down. It's not just about you."

He snorted. "That's priceless coming from you. Get out."

"I'll leave but I haven't given up. Phillip will be in touch. Think about Randy and Jimmy . . . and Dirk. Randy has a wife and two kids . . . Jimmy's barely scraping by on his studio work. Dirk's doing okay but he could use the break. Maybe you're so privileged that you've forgotten what it's like to be a struggling musician, but they need this." After delivering her final blow she walked out the door.

Gunner sat there as memories swept over him. He thought about when he'd first arrived in Nashville full of hopes and dreams. His first open mic . . . his first paid gig . . . the night he'd met Randy at a bar and they'd gotten drunk together and The Trailers was born. How they'd hustled to get the rest of the band together . . . how he'd felt the night Natalie blew him away with her audition. He buried his face in his hands. *Is it enough? Is it enough to be here working on the ranch? Has my dream really been laid to rest or am I fooling myself? Hell if I know.*

"Knock, knock," Beau said sticking his head through the open door. "Am I interrupting anything? Who the hell was the babe that just left?"

Gunner blew out his breath. "What do ya need?"

"Dolly came up lame. Looks like she has a hoof abscess. Do you want me to call the farrier?"

"Yeah, that'd be good."

"Are you alright? You look kind of pale."

"Yeah, I'll survive. I just had a battle with a rattler and I'm not sure who won."

"Ah . . . the blonde who just left. . . your ex I take it?"

"Yeah. Ex fiancée and ex band mate."

"She's gone. She hopped in her car and took off."

"Good. I'll be along shortly to check on Dolly."

"Okay chief. If there is anything I can do . . ."

"Thanks Beau, call the farrier. That's it."

Beau tipped his cowboy hat and left Gunner alone again with his thoughts. The morning glow of waking up next to Sophia felt like weeks ago. His shoulders slumped as he turned out the lights and headed towards the barn. Despite his confident declarations to Natalie, he was filled with uncertainty. What about his friends? His bandmates had always been there for him. Could he turn his back on them now? Had the mistakes from his past really been buried? Did he even deserve this second chance?

He knew he should check in on Sophia but he was

way too raw. He needed space and time . . . and to keep busy. The best way he knew how to make any decision was to set it aside. Stewing and turning it over and over in his mind was like being on a hamster wheel, didn't do a lick of good. He'd check on Dolly then ride out and inspect the fence lines . . . blow off memories crowding his brain and clouding his thinking. The answers would come . . . they always did.

25

Sophia entered the lodge then headed straight for the lounge. She waved to Hank who was washing bar glasses and plopped on a stool. He dried his hands and came over to take her order.

"The usual?"

"Yes please."

As he opened the bottle of wine, he glanced up at her, "How's our journalist friend?"

"I haven't heard from her for a few days so she must be up to something."

"I hated to see her go. She's a lot of fun."

"A wild one that's for sure. She really liked you too. She's going to try to come back for a short visit before my time is up here. I'm sure she wouldn't mind hearing from you. Hint hint." Sophia smiled.

"I've got her number. I'll give her a call soon."

Sophia snuck another glance at the door and tried to convince herself it didn't matter that she hadn't heard from Gunner since he'd left with Natalie. *It must have been a shock to see her again. He didn't look happy about it that was for sure . . . still . . . she's so beautiful.*

"So, did you get to meet the famous Natalie Storm?" Hank asked casually, as he wiped down the bar countertop.

Sophia's eyes widened. "You dare to bring up the elephant in the room? So brave."

"She's a real piece of work that one is."

"Is she still here?"

"Rumor has it she took off pretty quick."

Sophia looked down. "Oh."

"It had to be like a kick in the teeth for my old friend."

Sophia frowned. "That bad huh?"

"Yeah, but I wouldn't worry about it too much."

"Worry about what?" Gunner said, as he hopped on the stool next to Sophia.

"Gunner!" Sophia said.

"Sorry I dropped off the face of the earth for a bit. I had some things to work through." He eyed her intently. "You okay?"

She turned her face away. "I'm fine. I understand."

"Beer?" Hank asked.

"Make it a shot of tequila."

Hank arched his brows and reached for a shot glass. After pouring a hefty portion he grabbed several lime wedges and sat the saltshaker next to the glass.

Gunner sprinkled some salt on the back of his hand then licked it. Watching him stirred up a flash from the previous night...his tongue against her skin. . . He grimaced as he threw back the shot, then quickly sucked on the lime wedge.

"That makes me pucker just watching you," Sophia said, determinedly tamping down her desire. She touched his arm. "How about you? Are you alright?"

He shook his head. "Not really."

"Do you want to talk about it?"

"Not much to say. Natalie was here to deliver a message. A big record label wants me and my old band to sign on and do a tour with Miranda Lambert. Apparently, we made an impression on her when we opened for her before. I said no."

Sophia gasped. "But Gunner . . . why? This is your dream. You can't just say no."

"Sure, I can. Phillip, the head of the label, has been calling wanting me to at least meet and hear him out. I guess he got frustrated and decided to have Natalie yank my chain. I'm not too happy about that tactic."

"What was so terrible that you had to walk away?" She caught a look exchanged between Hank and Gunner. *Hm.* Hank went to serve a couple waiting at the end of the bar.

"Soph, my story is nothing original. The lifestyle was brutal with little to show for it. Being adored by the fans might sound like a dream, but in fact it made me half crazy. Hard to tell who liked me for real or just wanted something from me."

"That must be hard."

"When the people you trust are setting you up then waiting for you to fall, it is hard to handle. Late nights I'd be so wired from the show that I'd drink to get some sleep then get up and do it all over again. The shows themselves were what I lived for, and the jam sessions. Making music. It's what I love . . ." His eyes became distant. "But after a while, it seemed that the music became secondary to the lifestyle."

Sophia pondered that for a moment before replying. "After having a break . . . maybe you've gained a clearer perspective, don't you think you could figure out how to change it?" Sophia said softly. It broke her heart to see the pain in his eyes and made her forget about her earlier doubts.

"Maybe. Problem is . . . before I left Nashville, I got in some trouble, not of my making, but it'd be hard to prove otherwise."

Hank walked back after serving the guests and jumped back in on the conversation. "Here's my two cents worth. Go and hear what he has to say, then decide. It will give you a taste of Nashville again. Get a feel for the label and go from there."

Gunner pinched the bridge of his nose. "I'm afraid if I open that door again, I'm setting myself up for more misery. I've re-adjusted to the ranch life. This is my home, my roots."

"And it'll always be here," Hank said.

Sophia squeezed his arm. "He's right, you know."

"Why don't you sleep on it. You'll get your answer," Hank said.

"I thought I had my answer, but obviously not, because my thoughts are like a dog chasing its tail."

"Been there my friend. Now if you're as smart as I think ya are, you'll let this beautiful redhead take your mind off your troubles."

Sophia leaned in real close to Gunner's face and

stared at him. "I'm going to be real disappointed if I can't manage to do that."

His smile didn't quite reach his eyes, but he reached for her hand and held it. "I'll be alright. You don't have to worry about me."

"I know you will." She squeezed his hand and he squeezed back. She leaned close, her lips brushing his ear and whispered, "Want to spend the night again?"

"Yes," he said, without hesitation.

Voice husky she said, "Let's get out of here then." Sophia slid off her stool and pulled him along. He threw a bill onto the bar and waved goodbye to Hank who stuck his thumb up.

"Have fun," Hank called to their retreating backs. Without turning Gunner waved his hand in the air as his other arm wrapped around Sophia's waist.

26

*G*unner was only half listening as the flight attendant instructed all passengers to return their seats to an upright position and stow the trays in preparation for landing. After a few days of soul searching, he was moments away from landing at the Nashville International Airport. His emotions were all over the place. One minute he was dreading it and the next he felt excited.

He didn't need to stop at the baggage claim because all he'd brought was a carryon. He'd only be here for a couple of days. Plenty of time to meet with Phillip Krauss and his former bandmates. He scanned the faces in the terminal and spotted Randy right away. Randy looked so glad to see him that Gunner choked up for a second.

"Dude! Man is it ever good to see you!" Randy said grabbing him in a big bear hug.

"You too. I've missed ya."

"This is exciting bro."

"Don't get your hopes up too high. I'm here to see what they have to say."

"You ever had any more trouble with those photos?"

Gunner slung his bag over his shoulder. "Nada. Which is weird."

"I've never seen hide nor hair of that Harper chick again after that night."

"Makes sense since the band split up shortly after."

"True," Randy said. "It's still strange how it all went down."

"Yeah. I'm in a better place about it all now. Being back with my family helped me get my head on straight."

"Good to step back once in a while. Get some perspective," Randy said.

"You sure Cindy doesn't mind me crashing at your place?"

"She wouldn't have it any other way. Plus, Pete is excited that 'Uncle Gunner' is coming. It's been too long."

"Yes, it has."

They exited the terminal and headed for the parking lot.

"Gunner!" Cindy rushed to greet him with their toddler JJ perched on her hip. "Say hi to Uncle Gunner," she said. Instead, JJ shyly burrowed his face into his mother's neck.

"Where's Pete?" Gunner asked, referring to their seven-year-old.

"He's in the playroom with his cousin. Pete!" she yelled. "Uncle Gunner is here."

He heard laughter and then Pete ran out and barreled right into him. Laughing, Gunner scooped him up and hugged him tightly. "Hey buddy. Let me take a look at you. What happened to your two front teeth?"

"Lost 'em. I got ten bucks for each . . . from the tooth fairy."

"Wow. That's quite the haul. Who's your friend?"

"Conner. He's my cousin."

"Howdy Conner. Did he share any of his profits from the tooth fairy with you?"

"Nope." Conner stared up at Gunner wide-eyed.

Cindy laughed. "Can you tell he's a fan? Pete talks about you all the time . . . and plays The Trailers until I'm ready to scream."

Gunner chuckled. "Good taste."

"Pete why don't you and Conner show Gunner to his room. Gunner, get settled in. I've got chili cooking. Please make yourself at home. I've got towels set out on your bed."

"Thanks, Cin. Please don't go to any extra trouble for me."

Pete grabbed Gunner's hand and happily pulled him down the hall to his room. "Uncle Gunner, are you moving back? I heard Mom and Dad talking about the band getting back together."

"We'll see. Not really sure."

"Aw, come on . . . please . . . say yes. We need you. My dad needs you."

Gunner felt like he'd been sucker punched. It was one thing to think about it from the back of a horse on the other side of the country, but being back here with his friends, he felt responsible. The decision now weighed about a thousand pounds. As Natalie had pointed out, it wasn't just about him. Whether he said yes or no would affect his bandmates and their families. *I have to stay clear-headed and not collapse into emotion. It has to work for me as well. It might not be all about me but I count too.*

He threw his bag onto a chair and the boys jumped onto the bed and turned it into a trampoline, which quickly disintegrated into a wrestling match. Randy stuck his head in the door and ordered the boys out of the room. "Give Gunner a break. Go play in your room."

"Okay, Dad. Let's go, Conner."

Randy watched them go with an indulgent expression. "Never thought I could love anything so much."

"Who'd have thought, huh?" Gunner said, "You're a great dad. It suits ya."

Randy shook his head. "Talk about perspective . . . my priorities did a complete one-eighty after becoming a dad . . . and a husband. Cindy is the best."

"Yeah, you're a pretty lucky dude."

"I hope you can find someone special Gunner. You got dealt a bad hand with Natalie, but there's lots of good women out there."

"I'm actually kind of seeing someone. She came as a

guest and stayed to help out after mom got hurt. Her name is Sophia. She's pretty special."

Randy's blue eyes lit up and he slapped Gunner on the back. "That's great news. I want to hear all about it."

"Yeah, well we'll see. It's new and she's from Chicago."

"People move all the time, and also maintain long distance relationships. It's not like the old wild west, where if you left home for the frontier you never saw your family again. I'll let you settle in. Come on out when you're ready."

"Thanks. I'm going to give Sophia a call and let her know I've made it. See ya in a bit."

"Lock your door behind me or there'll be no guarantee of privacy."

"I don't mind. Remember, I had three siblings. We had no boundaries whatsoever."

Randy grinned. "It's so good to see ya."

Gunner nodded. "It is."

After Randy left the room, Gunner pulled up Sophie's number. She picked up right away.

"You made it," her soft velvety voice felt like a caress.

"I'm here. Only problem is, you're not."

"I know. I feel the same over here."

"You'd love Randy and Cindy. They're good people. I hope you get to meet them sometime. They've got two kids. Pete is seven. He's grown like a weed since I saw him last. JJ is two. I'll admit to being a little envious."

"It must feel weird to be back there."

"A little. Good to see my friends though. How was your day?"

"Other than Lenny knocking me over, uneventful."

Gunner laughed. "I swear that dog is in love with you. But then again, who isn't?" She didn't respond, not even a chuckle.

"Red, you still there?"

"I'm here," she said quietly. "I'll let you get back to your friends. Be careful and don't pressure yourself to come up with the answers right away. Tell them you'll think about it."

"I'll do that. I miss you."

"Me too."

"I'll call you tomorrow. We'll probably meet out at our old watering hole later tonight then tomorrow is the big meeting with the record label."

"Good luck." As if reading his mind, she said, "Don't take it all on your shoulders. You're not responsible for everyone. Be true to yourself."

"Thanks, Red. I'll keep that in mind. Be good. Don't let that brother of mine move in on you while I'm gone."

He could hear the smile in her voice when she responded. "Not a chance."

"Good. You'll be the last thing I think about before I drift off to sleep and the first thing on my mind when I wake up in the mornin'."

"There you go again . . . melting my heart. Bye, Gunner."

"Bye, Soph."

Gunner disconnected. Feeling restless, he went into the en suite and splashed his face with cold water before heading back out to visit with his friends. He was shocked at the longing he'd felt while talking to

Sophia. He realized it the minute he heard her voice . . . that spark of hope that maybe he could have it all. . . He wanted what Randy and Cindy had. His happily ever after. The rest was just extra. It didn't mean anything if there was no one to share it with.

27

*S*ophia glanced at her caller ID and saw that it was Amelia. "Hey, you've been MIA. Didn't you get my message yesterday? I was beginning to get worried."

"No need. Guess where I'm at?" Amelia said.

"I give, where?"

"Nashville. I'm on a stakeout, sitting in front of the Ringside Café."

"You're where?"

"Nashville Tennessee. My amazing investigative skills have led me here. I'm sitting in front of the in-place for musicians. Tonight, is open mic and I'm hoping to run into Gunner's old manager Greg Harlow. Did some snooping and found out he's broke . . . close to bankruptcy. Apparently, Gunner must've been his main cash cow."

"So? What would that have to do with Gunner quitting?"

"You never know when you might pick the right thread and things begin to unravel. That one thing that leads to another. Maybe Gunner left Greg for a reason. They'd been together for ten years. He was Gunner's first and last manager. I'm sure Greg wasn't too happy about Gunner quitting. Plus . . . are you ready for this? Gunner dated Greg's sister Amber briefly, then dumped her."

"Oh."

"Anyway, this bar is the place where you go when you're scouting for new talent. Sometimes you can get lucky and some star will pop in and do a set. I thought it was a perfect place to casually snoop around."

Amelia's voice dropped to a whisper. "On my God. Gunner has a doppelgänger. I swear if I didn't know better, I'd say that's him just about to cross the street right in front of me."

"It's probably him. He's in Nashville right now."

"What?" she sputtered. "Yikes! Why didn't you tell me? Hold on a sec, I've got to duck down."

Sophia could hear rustling and smiled. "Gunner is there for a couple of days to meet with a new record label. They're doing their best to entice him."

"Wow. What kind of fate is this?"

"Not fate, just a coincidence. Now what are you going to say when Gunner sees you?"

"I'll tell him the truth. That I'm on the job. I just won't say it's about him. My cover story is that I'm following the latest talents and doing a story for Country Music magazine. And it's partly true. I shopped a piece about the Austin-versus-Nashville music scene to them and they're interested. So, this is all research anyway, even if I don't unearth the *big* story. Plus, I can write it off as a business expense."

"That makes me feel a little better. I hate keeping secrets. Things are getting more serious between us. If you do find out anything, you have to talk to Gunner about it before doing anything with it. Promise?"

"I write under my pseudonym. He'll never know it's me unless you tell him."

"That's not the point. I will know."

"Look, if nothing turns up in the next day or two, I plan on dropping it anyhow. Don't worry. I wouldn't do anything to harm Gunner. You know I think he's a great guy. But this could be a major breaking story and, yes, I promise I won't run it unless he gives me the okay."

"If he wanted everyone to know he'd have issued a statement by now," Sophia pressed.

"Gotta go. I'm going to go on in and see what I can find out. Bye."

Before Sophia could respond, Amelia hung up. Sophia stared at the phone then laughed. Amelia was a thrill seeker and that would never change. It was one of the things she loved the most about her friend and the thing that drove her the craziest. But it did make her a great freelance journalist. She had no fear. Sophia crossed her fingers that this time Amelia would fail. Let her do the subdued article comparing the two music cities and leave Gunner's past where it belonged. She trusted that her friend would act with integrity and would consider her feelings, so for now she'd have to let it go.

28

*G*unner was not happy to see Natalie waving them over upon their arrival. He glared at Randy. "Not cool."

"I didn't know she'd be here; I swear. Obviously, she knew you were coming to town for our meeting, but she made a lucky guess about tonight."

"I'm not sitting with her."

"Look, Jimmy, Sam and Dirk are already sitting at her table. Suck it up. If things work out, you're going to have to make peace with her eventually." Gunner was pissed, but he followed Randy over and sat in the seat furthest away from Natalie.

The bar was crowded and noisy. There were two musicians on stage tuning up their guitars and doing a sound check. Everyone greeted him enthusiastically. It felt like time had stood still and he'd never left. These guys were like brothers to him. When you were on the road, touring for weeks on end, you either ended up hating each other or you got real close. They'd been fortunate.

Natalie took charge and waved the server over. After pushing through the bodies to get to them, the waitress took their drink orders and disappeared back in the crowd.

"I'd hate to be a server here," Randy said.

Jimmy said, "We put your name on the play list Gunner. We thought just you and Natalie on her fiddle."

"I didn't bring my guitar."

Dirk said, "I brought mine."

"No."

"Come on Gunner, dip your toe in the water. It's been a long time between performances," Jimmy said. Their beers arrived along with the shots of bourbon Natalie had ordered for each of them.

Jimmy held up his shot and gave a toast. "Here's to the nights we'll never remember with friends we'll never forget."

Gunner's eyes met Randy's warily, who gave a half shrug before tossing back his shot. *Must be a coincidence. Randy is the only one in the band that knows about that night. Don't be paranoid.*

The guys on stage were good, not great. After finishing their set, the owner of the bar announced Gunner and Natalie were up to play next. Gunner was startled to be called so soon. "Dirk it's your guitar, you go up."

"I don't have the chops that you do. I'm only good for backup. Go on. It'll be a good re-entry."

Reluctantly Gunner followed Natalie up on stage.

Dirk went along to grab his guitar from the backstage dressing room and handed it to Gunner. Natalie did her sound check with the fiddle then Gunner checked his guitar. Surprisingly, he wasn't nervous; instead, his entire body was humming with energy. Charged and ready to fire.

They were introduced. "You all might remember these two, it's been a minute, but we're lucky as all git out to have Gunner Cane and Natalie Storm back on stage together for the first time in way too long. Put your hands together and show them some love."

There were cat calls and cheers from the crowd as Gunner played a few chords and greeted the audience. "Hey y'all, great to be out tonight. We're going to play an old favorite, 'Wagon Wheel' by The Old Crow Medicine Show. We've got the beautiful and talented Natalie Storm on fiddle and harmony. I'm Gunner Cane."

Gunner led with the guitar and after several bars, Natalie put her bow to the strings and began playing along. When she played the fiddle, her whole body played the fiddle. Her foot tapped along as she dipped and bowed over her instrument. Gunner glanced at Natalie. She had such a stage presence . . . mesmerizing. He remembered when she used to take his breath away. Everyone was on their feet with this boot stomping crowd pleaser, and singing along. It was like they'd never taken a break. Even if their relationship had gone up in flames, they'd always made great music together.

Gunner looked out at the crowd and did a double take. *Is that Amelia? If it isn't, she's got a twin.* Their eyes met and he nodded to her. She glared back then snapped a picture of him with her phone. *Shit!* Amelia was standing right next to his old manager, Greg Harlow, who unlike the rest of the crowd, stood stiffly with his arms crossed and a pinched look on his face. Gunner didn't miss a beat.

When they finished the song Gunner said, "That's all we got for ya tonight. Leslie Fischer is up next. Thanks everyone, until the next time." He tipped his cowboy hat and left the stage.

*G*unner headed straight for Amelia. "Small world. What are you doing in Nashville?" he said.

"I'm working on a story for Country Music Magazine. What about you? Besides being back on stage with your ex. Does Sophia know about this?"

"No, because I didn't know myself until about a half hour ago."

"Didn't look like you were hand cuffed or anything like that."

"It's strictly business. I'm here to meet with a record label."

She squinted at him. "So, I've been told. Was this open mic performance part of the audition then?" She said this with a saccharin sweet tone, dripping with sarcasm.

"Look Amelia, I get that you're protective of Soph, but I've got nothing to hide here. I have no feelings for Natalie. None."

"My friend had her heart ripped out and stomped on by the last Romeo and I won't watch someone do it to her again."

"I have no intention of hurting Sophia. I really like her."

Amelia stared at him intently. "You'd better be telling me the truth."

Gunner reached for her arm and gripped it. "Look, I don't have a crystal ball . . . we're getting to know each other, but I promise you I only have eyes for Sophia. Period."

He could see Amelia relax and her obstinate expression gave way to some warmth. Amelia glanced over at Gunner's table and his eyes followed. *Looks like Natalie has a date. Good.* She was sitting on the lap of a young, good-looking guy and his hands were possessively around her body.

"See. She's got a boyfriend. Now do you believe me?" Gunner asked.

Her eyes sparkled mischievously. "We'll see. You'd better be on your best behavior."

Gunner slung his arm over Amelia's shoulder and hugged her. "I'm glad Soph has a friend like you."

"I'm the lucky one. I like you Gunner. Don't you dare disappoint me."

He grinned and saluted her. "Yes ma'am. Got it."

She hugged him back, then said, "I've got to do some sleuthing."

"I'll be taking off soon. Good luck on your article."

"Thanks. You sounded amazing by the way. I hope you get back to it. That's where you belong."

Amelia's praise touched something deep in Gunner and he swallowed. "I didn't realize how much I missed it until tonight. Thanks for that, Amelia. I appreciate your support more than you know. I feel like in this sea of sharks, it's good to have you here."

She punched his arm. "Don't go all soft on me."

"Never." He returned to his table where another beer and shot awaited.

Natalie introduced her date as her boyfriend, and he seemed like a nice enough guy. Gunner was relieved. She hadn't made any untoward advances but he'd been wary of her intentions. She appeared to be into this guy and that was a game changer for him. It opened the door for him to seriously consider reuniting with the band. *Maybe I can return to my first love.*

Since they had the meeting the following day, they all left before midnight. As Gunner drifted off to sleep, he felt lighter than he'd felt in a long time. He was filled with anticipation for the future . . . which he hoped included not only music but the beautiful redhead waiting for him in Wyoming.

29

*G*unner was returning today and Sophia could hardly wait. She didn't want to think about how badly she'd missed him. Her date with Eli to the rodeo had been fun and lighthearted but it was apparent that he understood where her interests lay and he was far from ready to settle down with one woman. That didn't mean that he wouldn't use the situation to rib his brother; he'd even said as much.

Becca sliced the tomatoes for lunch prep this morning because someone had called in sick.

"Is Amelia still coming for a visit?" Becca asked.

Sophia tossed some lettuce into a colander then rinsed it under the water faucet. "As far as I know she's going to try, unless something with work comes up."

"Two more days and we'll have some time off." The ranch shut down from hosting guests for a week several times per season to give the horses and staff a break and to catch up on everything that got pushed aside during peak tourist season.

"I know. I'm ready."

Becca's lips turned up. "And . . . Gunner will be home."

Sophia sighed. "That too."

"I think you guys are perfect together. You have my stamp of approval. Mom's too."

Sophia felt her cheeks grow warm. "Oh . . . um . . . what did your mom say?"

"She loves you! She said you're as nice as you are pretty and that Gunner is lucky that he caught your attention."

"She did not!"

She held up her palm. "I swear."

"That is so sweet."

"You showed your true colors when you volunteered to help without even thinking about it. That is a sure sign of a good and generous heart."

"It was nothing. Really, anyone would have done the same."

"Not true. And Soph, you fit right in here. I feel like I've known you my whole life." Becca pulled out the rolls from the oven and placed them on a rack to cool. "If you want to go get cleaned up . . . I don't think we need you in the kitchen anymore. Right Char?" The assistant nodded her head in agreement.

"If you're sure, I'll take you up on that."

"Go."

Sophia already had her apron untied. "Bye then, and thanks."

"See you later," Becca and Char called out, but Sophia didn't hear them because she was already out the door.

*S*ophia tried on and discarded several outfits before deciding on a one-piece white linen jumpsuit. It checked the right boxes for celebrating with Gunner . . . sexy, dressy yet casual, and the sleeveless top accented her slim tanned arms against the light-colored fabric. It belted at the waist and the wide legged pants were loose fitting. The overall affect flattered her slim hips and long legs. She smiled at her reflection, pleased with how well the outfit complimented her physique.

As a final touch, she added a pair of dangly silver earrings and bangled bracelets then slipped on a pair of thin-strapped pink sandals. *Hm, hair up or down?* She rooted through her bag and found her wide white headband. With her hair pulled back from her face, her eyes looked larger and it somehow made her features more delicate. *Not bad. I guess a little mascara and pink lip gloss will do it. Now all I have to do is wait.*

*S*ophia sat on the front porch and tried concentrating on her book, but after reading the same line a half dozen times, she gave up. *Besides he'll be here any minute.* As if she'd willed it, she heard truck tires on the gravel lane and stood up. *Gunner. He's here.* She watched the truck stop right in front of her cabin and he stepped out. He glanced over at her with an inscrutable expression.

She waved excitedly. "Gunner!" He gave a half-hearted wave back and went around to the truck bed to grab his bag. She rushed out to greet him. When she reached his side, he turned toward her and she threw her arms around his neck. Standing on her tip-toes she gave him a quick peck on the lips.

"Congratulations! I'm so excited for you." Her smile died on her lips when she saw how dull and listless his eyes were. "Gunner, what's wrong?"

"Nothing. I changed my mind is all."

"What? What do you mean? Last night you were so excited . . . you said you were going to take this chance. Gunner, why?"

"I realized it's not for me. I'm content here at the ranch."

"But . . ." She shook her head, confused by his sudden change of heart.

"I don't want to talk about it right now. Soph, I need you to support my decision and not question it. Can you do that for me? Please?"

"But Gunner . . . I . . . I'm worried. This is the opportunity of a lifetime. It's your time. I feel it here." She grabbed his hand and placed it over her heart.

"Look Sophia, this is hard enough without your disappointment on top of it. I asked you to let it go. Why are you pushing me?"

She jerked away like she'd been slapped. Her eyes stung with tears. "I'm sorry you feel that way. I was trying to offer my support. I didn't realize that would be a burden to you." She turned and ran back to her cabin, the screen door slammed shut behind her.

She stood frozen, stunned. What could have happened between her conversation last evening when he was euphoric after his meeting with Phillip Krauss and now. She felt like she'd suffered a whiplash. It didn't make any sense. She covered her face with her palms. *Ah, but he just told me where I fit in his life. Basically, he told me MYOB. Plain and simple he told me to butt out. Fine. No problem. Have a nice life, Gunner Cane.* She ignored the knock on her door.

"Sophia, can I come in? I'm sorry . . . please forgive me." He was met with silence. "Soph please let me explain. I didn't mean to lash out at you." She heard the screen door open and his boots on the wooden floor. She kept her back to him.

He wrapped his arms around her from behind and pulled her against him, hugging her tightly. "I'm an insensitive ass. I'm sorry." His voice sounded ragged and Sophia thawed a little.

"I know I did a complete turnaround and you have every right to ask about it. I'm really sorry for shutting you out."

She relaxed into him and felt his sigh of relief. She turned to face him and wrapped her arms around his waist. Her voice was muffled against his chest. "I'm sorry too. I overreacted. You asked me to support you and not to question your decision. I was so surprised that I didn't hear you."

She felt his nose burrow into her hair. "Aw Soph, this life isn't for the weak of heart, is it?'

"It's going to be alright no matter what. It was

always a win-win decision anyway. You have a great life here, Gunner. Don't you forget that."

His voice sounded choked up when he responded. "Yeah, I'm one lucky bastard." Sophia patted his back and made soothing sounds as she comforted him. Something bad had happened . . . she knew it . . . but for now, Gunner needed space, not prying.

30

"*P*our me another shot," Gunner said, his speech slurred.

Hank exchanged a worried look with Sophia. "Don't you think you've had enough my friend?"

"Jush keep pouring till I tell ya to shtop. I'm gonna go take a piss." He stood unsteadily and weaved his way to the restroom.

"He's cut off. I should have done it before the last round."

"Don't blame yourself, Hank. It's hard to say no when he's so insistent. He seemed like he was handling it until this last shot."

"I'll help you get him back to your cabin. I'm thinking we shouldn't take him home to Mom in his current state."

Sophia sighed. "I agree." A guest called out to Hank and he went to serve them.

Sophia took a sip of wine, her brow creased with

worry. Gunner's cell phone pinged from where he'd left it on the bar. She leaned over it trying to see who the message was from. *None of your business, Sophia Russo.* She sternly chided herself even as she reached toward the phone and swiped the screen. There was no name associated with the text and despite her inner self screaming to stop, she opened the message. Gasping she quickly covered her mouth.

Oh my God! Why is there a picture of Gunner naked in bed with some young girl? Did this happen last night? Is that why he is so weird? Soph, think . . . get a grip . . . She studied it more thoroughly. *First off, he's passed out. So is the girl. This is no selfie. Second, his hair is longer in this photograph so it's not from last night. Okay . . . that's good.* She scanned the other incoming messages and saw several more compromising photos with the same girl in the same setting and a message saying, "Welcome back to Nashville, in case you forgot." She saw Hank finishing up with his customers and pushed the phone away.

"I'll go check on Gunner, make sure he's not passed out in the men's room," Hank said.

"Good idea. Oh wait, there he is." They both watched as Gunner made his way, unsteady on his feet.

Hank put up a 'be back in five minutes' sign then lifted the bar panel and stepped out from behind the counter to assist his friend. "Hey bud, let's get you out of here."

Sophia grabbed Gunner's phone and got on his other side, wrapping his arm across her shoulders. They both walked him to Sophia's cabin, depositing him on her bed. "Will you be able to take it from here?" Hank asked.

"Yes, go. I've got it."

"Okay." He looked down at Gunner and shook his head. "Keep me posted."

"I will. Thanks, Hank."

After he left, Sophia removed Gunner's boots and shirt then threw a light blanket over him. It was only nine o'clock but she decided she was ready for bed so she brushed her teeth and changed into her tee shirt and crawled in beside him.

She turned on her side and studied him while he slept. His thick dark lashes fanned his cheeks . . . such a beautiful man. Watching his chest rise and fall, his breath deep and steady, she traced the outline of his mouth. He looked so vulnerable in sleep. *Who is this man lying beside me?* Her mind raced, every explanation she came up with quickly discarded.

Uneasy, she pressed her palm against her tight belly, which felt like it held a ball of yarn the size of a baseball. *What do I really know about this man? Is he everything he seems to be or are their hidden parts even his family doesn't know about? Is this girl in the photo the reason he gave up on his career? Why did she say 'In case you forgot'?*

Sighing, she brushed his hair back from his brow then closed her eyes. There was nothing to do about anything tonight. She'd have to wait and see if Gunner planned on sharing this with her . . . If he didn't, she wasn't sure what she'd do about it. He groaned and mumbled something in his sleep then slung his arm around her, pulling her body against his. She snuggled her cheek against his bare chest, inhaling the male scent of him as she finally drifted off to sleep.

"*R*ise and shine," Sophia said as she sat on the edge of the bed holding a steaming mug of coffee in one hand and a bottle of aspirin in the other. Gunner groaned and opened one eye squinting at her.

"Aspirin," he croaked.

She held up the bottle shaking it. "Right here."

He pushed himself up onto his elbow and reached for the coffee. His naked torso was nearly her undoing. *Oh my.* She swallowed, as her gaze roved over his broad muscular shoulders and toned chest. His bicep flexed as he raised the cup to his lips. She felt like jumping on top of him . . . to hell with everything else. *Why does life have to be so complicated?*

Thankful that there were no guests to feed, she wished they could roll around in bed all day. "I'll make you some scrambled eggs, if your stomach is up for it."

"Let's see how the coffee stays down."

Sophia opened the aspirin bottle and he held out his palm so she could shake a couple into his hand. He tossed them into his mouth and took a big gulp of coffee to wash them down.

Sophia could look at Gunner all day and then some. Even hungover he was the sexiest man she'd ever laid eyes on. Everything in her responded to him. Despite the text messages from the night before, her body had a mind of its own. Her skin tingled and she met his smoldering gaze, drowning in the warmth of it.

"Soph," he said, placing the mug on the bedside table. He caressed her cheek then reached for her, pulling her down next to him, he buried his nose in her hair. "When you look at me like that, I go a little crazy," he said gruffly.

A wave of desire coursed through her, overriding that nagging voice in the back of her mind. Her palms flattened against his chest, and she kissed him just below his ear then trailed kisses up his neck, along his jaw . . . until she reached his mouth and softly touched her lips against his. He opened his mouth; his palm cradled the back of her head pulling her hard against him as a moan escaped. Deepening the kiss, his tongue explored with increasing passion. She felt his breath quicken beneath her palms still splayed over his chest.

He flipped her onto her back, reached down and stroked her through her panties. She gasped, breathless as his lips found a sensitive spot just below her collar bone. He pulled her tee shirt off and she buried her fingers in his hair. She cried out when he latched onto her nipple. He sucked it into his mouth sending waves of heat and sensation racing through her.

Rising up, his smoldering eyes pierced hers as he unzipped his jeans and tugged them off. Before tossing them aside, he searched his pockets until he found the foil packet he was looking for. Her impatience took her by surprise. She needed to feel him inside of her. Wiggling out of her panties she opened her thighs as he slipped on the condom. His eyes never left hers as he plunged inside her moist warmth, filling her completely. He paused, then took her with a fierce possession as she wrapped her thighs around him, her hands clasped around his neck. They came fast and explosively.

"I never knew it could be like this," she whispered softly against his neck, after her breathing had returned to normal.

He touched her face; her riotous fiery hair fanned the pillow, tumbling in loose waves around her breasts. His intense gaze sent a burst of emotion through her. Then he gave her a soft sweet kiss and she knew she'd never be the same. His phone pinged, signaling that he'd received a text message, and the memories from the previous evening came flooding back to her, the text effectively bursting their bubble. *Well shit.*

31

*G*unner felt Sophia stiffen when his cell phone pinged. Remembering the photographs, he was suddenly filled with dread.

"Aren't you going to get that?" Sophia asked.

"It can wait."

"Whatever." Sophia reached for her tee shirt. She pulled it over her head as his eyes devoured her. Her breasts were perfect, round and firm, the nipples pink and swollen, her skin creamy and soft. He wanted to kiss every inch of her. She got out of bed then bent over, slipping her panties on. Her hair hid her face so that he couldn't read her expression.

"Whatever? What's up with that?" he asked, reaching over to stroke her thigh.

"Nothing."

"Sounds like something."

"I'll go make breakfast," she said and left him there scratching his head.

. . .

*H*e watched her as she stirred the egg mixture in the skillet, and waited for the toast to pop up. She wouldn't meet his eyes. "Hey Soph."

"Hm?"

"Did I do something wrong?"

"I don't know, did you?"

"Not that I'm aware of."

She turned off the burner and scooped the eggs onto two plates as he buttered the toast. She raised her brows. "Orange juice?"

"No thanks. I don't think my stomach is up for it. I'll pour you a glass though."

"No thanks."

They sat at the island counter, facing each other. Sophia kept her eyes downcast, focusing on her plate. "That must be some fascinating scramble," he said softly.

She looked at him through her lashes. "Did you check your text messages yet?"

"No, why?"

"Just wondering. Maybe you need to be alone for that."

"Sophia, what the hell is wrong with you?"

She crossed her arms, her expression mutinous. Gunner pinched the bridge of his nose. *Guess she didn't like that approach.*

"I'm suddenly annoyed about last night. You got so drunk we didn't have a chance to talk about your meeting with the record label . . . why you changed your mind."

"I'm not up for a deep discussion right now Soph. I'll fill you in later."

Her lips tightened. He thought if he were watching a cartoon, he'd probably see steam coming out of her ears. "Fine."

"Doesn't sound 'fine'."

"Gunner, I guess you call the shots. You'll fill me in whenever you feel like it. It doesn't seem to matter that I've been excitedly cheering you on . . . waiting to hear about it." She impatiently brushed away tears.

Gunner stood up and walked around to stand behind her. He leaned over and wrapped his arms around her waist. "Are you crying?"

She sniffled. "No."

Nuzzling her neck, he said, "I promise to fill you in later. Suffice to say, I'm not going to accept their offer. I'm done."

"But . . ."

"Soph, let it go for now . . . please." She pulled his hands away from her waist.

"You should finish your eggs before they get cold."

"They're probably frozen by now with the cold air you're throwing my way."

"Ha ha. I'm going to take a shower. You can let yourself out." She picked up her plate of untouched food and pitched it, then rinsed off the platter and went to take her shower.

. . .

*G*unner went from Sophia's straight to the office and closed the door behind him. Pulling out his phone he checked the most recent text. It was from Hank checking to see how he felt. He pressed the phone icon and called his friend.

"Hank, sorry about last night."

"You're fine. I was worried because it's not like you to get wasted like that."

"Hank, I was all set to go for the deal . . . but before I left Nashville, I got another text like before."

"You're shitting me, right?"

"No. I wish I were. The message along with it was 'Welcome to Nashville. Just in case you forgot.' Nice huh?"

"Maybe it's from her . . . the fangirl in the pictures."

"Her name is Harper. Jeez I don't know; it doesn't seem to fit. Why would she send them and not follow up or ask for anything? I've never heard from her again after that night unless she sent these photos."

"Seems like someone doesn't want you back in Nashville."

"That's what I'm thinking. Bottom line is this, if someone decides to leak the photos I'm done. Why put the time and effort into the music, only to have my reputation destroyed later? Seems like if I lay low, it all goes away."

"You don't know that for sure."

"It looks bad no matter what. Who is going to believe that I was the victim? Nobody."

"You could get it out there first."

"How? It'd be a trial by public opinion. Everyone

loves you when you're on top and loves it even more when you fall. Those photos are damning, they tell a story and no matter what I say to the contrary, I'll be smeared."

"You've got to find a way to get to the bottom of this. You've got one life to live, don't give up on your dreams."

"I've got my mind made up. Can you imagine what this would do to my mom? Nope, not going there."

"Have you told Sophia about it?"

"No. I'm too embarrassed."

"She's crazy about you dude. I'm not saying it will happen, but if this does get out, it'd be better coming from you than a tabloid."

"I know you're right but I'll have to think about it. I can't just blurt it out. It has to be the right time."

"Maybe you should talk to a lawyer or someone in law enforcement . . . see what your options are."

"Maybe. Today I'm doing good just to recover from poisoning myself; I'll see what tomorrow brings."

"Your call. I'm here for ya."

"Thanks, Hank." Gunner hung up and stared at the wall. He needed a break from thinking. Maybe a trail ride would clear his head. He'd deal with Sophia later.

32

*G*unner slipped a bareback pad onto Amitola and jumped on. She was sound now. The farrier had given him the okay to ride her. He'd start out easy, keep it at a walk for today. She pranced in place as he mounted, seemingly glad to have him on her back again. He'd felt a deep connection to this filly since day one and he'd swear she knew he'd rescued her from the slaughterhouse. They were a team. She was skittish with anyone else on her back but him. She trusted him and he knew she'd walk through fire if she had to, just to keep him safe.

There was something about riding without a saddle that satisfied him. He liked feeling the warmth of her body and the muscles beneath his seat. With no barriers between them, they could detect even the subtlest of movements. His thighs rested against her barrel, hypnotically swaying back and forth as she walked down the trail. Her ears were moving forward and back, signaling to him that she was alert and paying attention to him and her surroundings at the same time.

"Ah girl, it's good to be out here with ya." She blew out her nose, snorting contentedly. He patted her neck. It was a clear sunny day and the sky was a brilliant blue, not a cloud to be seen. He let Amitola have her head. She knew where to go . . . their favorite spot by the river. The mountains comforted him. Made his troubles seem less. *I had my shot. I can be content with this life. I've made my peace with it.*

When they reached the river's edge, he encouraged Amitola forward and she tentatively stepped into the water. He laughed as she pawed playfully, splashing him with her antics. The cool water was refreshing on this hot summer day. His pant legs were soaked by the time they headed back. He let his thoughts wander as he rode along. They naturally drifted back to Sophia. *How much to tell . . . what to say . . . or should I drop it? Why dredge up the past when I've made up my mind? She'd never understand. Hell, it looks bad even to me. I wouldn't believe it either. It was before I ever met her anyway. Time to bury the past and quit while I'm ahead.*

Beau was waiting for them when they reached the barn. "How'd she do?"

"No hint of lameness. I only walked her today. Next time I'll try a trot." He jumped down and Beau reached for the reins. "That's okay Beau, I'll take care of her."

"Sophia was looking for you."

"Oh?"

"I told her you were out on Amitola."

"Hm."

"She seemed anxious to find you."

"Okay, thanks."

"Boss, I know it's none of my business but Eli said you may be going back to Nashville. Is that true?"

"I was considering it, but how could I leave all of this?"

"It'll be here. Not that I wouldn't miss ya, but you could live here between touring and recording. Best of both worlds."

Gunner smiled. "Trying to get rid of me?"

"Course not, but I reckon it'd be a waste for you to give up on your music."

"Now what would be the bigger waste, hm? Look around you." He swept his arm toward the mountain range. "I'm living in a little corner of heaven already."

Beau looked down at the ground and shuffled his feet. "I reckon."

Gunner lightly punched his arm. "Why are you looking so down about it? I'm content."

"If you say so."

"Don't you have something better to do than give an old cowboy advice?" Gunner said as he tied Amitola to the fence post. He grabbed a hoof pick from the bucket of grooming tools and bent over her leg, tapping her to lift.

"I got the hint. See ya around."

Gunner took his time, carefully brushing her from head to tail. When he was done grooming, he gave her a couple of carrots and turned her out with the rest of the herd. She went galloping out to meet them. As usual just being in the presence of a horse for the afternoon soothed his soul.

He took his cowboy hat off, raking his hair from his brow, before placing it back on his head. He returned everything to the tack room and made his way back to the main house for a shower. He knew he was avoiding the inevitable, but he needed a little more time before facing Sophia.

33

*S*ophia stretched out under an umbrella on a chaise lounge by the pool and closed her eyes. It was hot out and it was nice to have it all to herself. No guests . . . just her and her monkey brain. *Why can't I turn off my brain? It's really none of my business anyway. On the one hand, Gunner doesn't have any idea that I saw the photographs so I can pretend I didn't. But if this is the reason he's giving up, it must be significant. But if I can't trust him, what's the point?*

Alarm bells went off in her brain. This brought up her past big time. When she'd caught her fiancé in bed with another woman, she'd been rocked to her core. The worst of it was that it'd made her doubt herself and her own judgement. How could it have been going on right under her nose and she hadn't had a clue? It had undermined her trust and belief in herself. That had been the cruelest fate of all. She had thought she'd finally put that to rest but this was making her feel crazy. *I can't do this again.*

Finally, between the sun and the calming sounds of nature, she began to unwind. Rolling onto her stomach she rested her cheek against her forearms and dozed.

Still half asleep, she swatted at something tickling the back of her thigh. Rousing, she realized that it wasn't an insect, it was fingers stroking up and down her leg. Her eyes shot open. "Gunner!"

Gunner was perched next to her on the edge of the lounge chair. "Hey darlin'. Heard you were looking for me."

"You're late. That was about six hours ago."

"I'm sorry."

Sophia turned onto her back and sat up. Gunner stared at her; his eyes hungry as he scanned her bikini clad body. She suddenly felt naked and crossed her arms over her chest, glaring. "I'm discovering that you're pretty good at running."

"How's that?"

"I seem to recall you apologizing just the other day for disappearing."

"Soph, I'm sorry. I have a lot on my mind."

"I guess I'm not important enough to share it with then."

"It's not that. I don't want to burden you."

"So altruistic of you. You're a hell of a guy."

He blew out his breath. "You're mad."

"Who me?"

"Soph, what can I say?"

"Look, I didn't say anything when you followed your ex back to Nashville, I trusted you. Now you get back and want to go off to your cave and lick your wounds all by yourself . . . fine. But, don't expect me to wait around for you. Call me old fashioned, but in order for relationships to progress . . . well . . . I think it requires trust and intimacy. If you're keeping everything bottled up, then I can safely assume you don't care about me as much as I do about you."

"I told you . . . I decided that Nashville . . . the scene . . . it doesn't fit for me anymore."

"Oh really? I'm not stupid. I talked to you right after your meeting and you were very excited about returning. What happened between then and when you got back? Girl troubles perhaps?"

Sophia watched pain dance across Gunner's face. He shrugged, then shuttered his expression. "I slept on it. That's it. End of story. No drama."

"And that's it? No big a-ha moment?"

Propping his hands on his thighs, he bowed his head. "Sophia, it's a dog-eat-dog world . . . I just got a dose of it and remembered why I left it all before."

Sophia's heart sank. She couldn't force him to confide and she wasn't comfortable outing him. If he didn't want to tell her, maybe he did have something to hide.

"Gunner, I think its best if we back off of things right now. I only have a couple of weeks left here and maybe this is where we leave it."

"What? Surely you don't mean that. You're mad, I get that. Let's take a deep breath . . . give yourself time to think about it."

"I have thought about it. I can't invest in someone who runs away every time he feels pain or holds back on me. It pushes all of my buttons. I have my own baggage. I can't trust someone who runs or hides. I'm not saying that couples aren't entitled to privacy, but it feels like you're keeping something important from me. That's okay. It's just not right for me."

Gunner tried to pull her to him but she stiffened. Her chest ached and she wanted to collapse into his arms and cry her eyes out, but instead she pushed him away. "I'm sorry Gunner. I care about you, maybe too much. I need a break right now."

"Now who's running?"

Her tears turned to fury as he threw her own words back in her face. Teeth clenched she said, "Let's make a deal. When you decide you're ready to tell me what really happened in Nashville, I'll be all ears. Until then, you're damn straight I'm running. As fast as I can. How's that?"

Gunner stood, glaring down at her. "If that's the way you want it, not much else to say now is there?"

"Nope."

She watched as Gunner stomped off. Fuming, she grumbled to herself. *So what if he's hurt and mad. So am I. He can go crawl in a gopher hole for all I care.* She got up and dove into the pool to cool off. She did laps until her arms were shaking then crawled out and headed back to her cabin. She'd make herself as scarce as possible. *Two can play that game.*

34

*S*ophia reached into her back pocket for the carrot and broke it in to several pieces. A couple of the horses had come running when she called to them from her perch on the split rail fence. One of them was the beautiful Amitola. Three days had passed since her fight with Gunner. They'd been successful in avoiding each other. Since the ranch was on a break, the guys were out all day tending to fence lines and cattle, doing regular maintenance to the barn, as well as baling and stacking hay.

She was feeling a little restless, and decided to ask Beau if she could ride one of the horses around in the ring. She found him standing in the back of a truck bed, sweaty and covered in hay, tossing bales down to Elijah to stack.

Elijah stopped immediately and gave an apprecia-tive wolf whistle. Putting a hand over his heart he said, "Legs to die for. Be still my heart."

She smiled. "Can I borrow a horse?"

Beau jumped down from the truck bed and brushed off his shirt. "You're not thinking of going off by yourself are ya?"

"No, I thought maybe I could ride in the ring."

"Sure. Who do ya want to ride?"

"Silly question. Pirate of course. I'm nothing if not loyal."

"Do you want me to grab him for ya?"

She shook her head. "No, I'll do it."

"Just grab his halter and go fetch him."

"Thanks guys. Don't work too hard." She had been wanting to try riding bareback so now was her chance. She found Pirate and slipped on his halter. He followed her willingly to the ring and she tied him to the fence and groomed him. *I'm not even going to use a bare back pad.* He waited while she bridled him, then stood patiently by the fence rail so she could climb onto his back.

His coat was soft against her bare legs. She tapped her red cowboy boots lightly against his sides, urging him forward. Remembering what Gunner had taught her, she relaxed her seat and concentrated on feeling his motion so she could move with him. She closed her eyes for a moment to settle into her body. Pirate blew out a big breath and she felt him relax under her. "Good boy." She leaned forward and patted his neck.

Bareback riding was so different from sitting on top of a saddle. A little harder to balance without the stirrups but she caught on quickly. The more she relaxed the easier it got.

I think I'm ready to try a trot. She squeezed her

thighs together and he picked up a trot. She lurched forward almost toppling off, but managed to regain her balance. Her ponytail bounced up and down, the gait jarring her with each stride. *Breathe Soph. Soften.* The second pass around the ring was much better. She was actually sitting the trot without bouncing. She found herself grinning from ear to ear. *This is great!*

She'd been so focused on her riding that she hadn't noticed Gunner appear. He was standing by the gate watching her. His eyes were intense and haunted. She allowed her gaze to wander down his body. The white tee shirt hugged his torso and the Levi's hung low on his hips. She unconsciously licked her lips when he pulled his tee shirt up to wipe the sweat off his face exposing his ripped abs. She brought Pirate to a walk and the next time around she stopped beside the fence where Gunner was waiting. Lenny and Clifford were by his side, tails wagging.

"You're a real natural," he said.

Her cheeks warmed from the compliment as little alarm bells went off. "Thanks. I remembered what you taught me. You're a good teacher."

His eyes pierced hers. "I've missed you."

"I wasn't that hard to find."

"You said you wanted space."

"True. I did say that." She hopped off Pirate and Gunner opened the gate so she could lead him out.

"Can we talk?"

"I don't know, can we?"

"Seriously Soph. Is this the way you're going to play it?"

"Gunner, I'm not playing, that's just it. I meant what

I said. Have I missed you? Yes. Does that change anything? No."

"Let's have dinner at your place tonight. I'll bring everything and cook for you. Then we'll talk."

She had missed him like crazy and found herself softening. His gaze wreaked havoc on her nervous system. He looked so forlorn that she found herself agreeing.

"Dinner. That's it, just dinner."

"Yes," he said, pumping his fist. "What time?"

"I'm free anytime."

"I'll clean up, then go in town to grab a few things and meet back at your place around six. Sound good?"

She bit her lip. "Okay."

He started to reach for her but her look stopped him. "I'll see you at six."

"Six." She agreed.

She watched until he and the dogs disappeared around the corner before untacking Pirate. She sighed. "Pirate, what did I just go and do? I'm hopeless."

Pirate pawed the ground, eagerly awaiting his treat. He munched on the apple slice as she walked him to the pasture for turn-out.

"Thanks for the ride." He pivoted sharply and nickered as he ran to greet his herd.

35

*G*unner perused the produce aisle for inspiration. He got lucky . . . they had radicchio. That was going to make his life a whole lot easier. Radicchio, red onions, some dry red wine, lots of fontina cheese and pasta—he'd learned to make one of his favorite dishes from an old Italian friend in Nashville. Luigi had owned a restaurant and he'd gotten to know him as a regular. He grabbed a Sara Lee cheesecake from the freezer section for dessert and was on his way.

His fingers drummed the steering wheel . . . unsure about tonight . . . how much to share, what to say, embarrassed by the photographs. *They make me look like the world's biggest player. The fact that Harper looks so damn young makes it that much worse. How can I expect Sophia to understand or believe that I'm innocent? Maybe its best I leave the part about the photographs out of the discussion.*

He pulled in front of Sophia's cabin, killed the engine, grabbed the bags and went to slay his dragons. "Hey, I'm here," he called through the screen door.

"Come on in."

He entered and saw Sophia lighting a candle over the fireplace mantel; she turned and looked at him, smiling as she blew out the match. *Good sign.* She had on a silky white sleeveless top tucked into a pair of black shorts and she was barefoot. Her hair was loose and she reached up to tuck it behind her ears. It framed her lovely face and fell in waves around her shoulders. His chest tightened. Memories of their lovemaking came flooding back and sent a ripple of desire through him.

"Make yourself at home Chef Gunner."

He cleared his throat. "Um . . . okay." He unpacked everything and pulled out the chopping board and knife and began peeling and slicing the onions. Arms crossed, she leaned her hip against the counter and watched him chop.

"You're pretty good with a knife."

He grinned. "I had my fair share of kitchen chores growing up."

"Anything I can do to help?"

"If you're ready for wine, maybe pour us a glass. Otherwise pull up a stool and relax."

She went to the fridge and pulled out a bottle of white wine. Filling their glasses, she brought his over, setting it within his reach, then plopped down on a stool and took a sip.

"I'm a bit out-classed . . . but I may as well die standing up. Never thought I'd live to see the day I'd be cooking for a Cordon Blue chef," he admitted. He grabbed a pot for the pasta and filled it with water then set it on the burner to heat.

"Don't be intimidated. Full disclosure . . . I love Taco Bell, so no worries."

"Ha—!"

"How was your day?" she asked.

"Busy. Lots to do before the next batch of guests arrive next week."

"Becca tells me your mom is almost ready to take over the kitchen again," Sophia sighed. "Maybe as soon as next week."

He glanced up from chopping and caught a moment of sadness cross her face. "It's been great having you here. You could stay on permanently you know. We could use another chef. Sorry, does that make me sound like an ingrate? I guess I'm a greedy bastard after all."

She chuckled, then said softly, "It's been real nice, Gunner."

He threw the ingredients in a pan and began sautéing. She came up behind him and put her arms around his waist, resting her head against his back. "I missed you, too."

He froze. He had to use restraint not to ditch the cooking and haul her into his arms. "Thanks for that."

"I just wanted you to know. It doesn't change anything, but I needed to say it."

"Got it."

She squeezed him then let go, leaving him feeling oddly bereft. She set the table and lit two tapered candles, adding to the romantic ambiance. "Music?"

"Sure."

"Any requests?" she asked.

"You pick."

She put on some soft jazz and it fit the mood perfectly. He drained the pasta then filled two bowls and added the radicchio mixture on top. Placing them on the table he said, "Hurry up and stir your pasta."

"Looks delicious."

He sat across from her and watched her take a bite and waited. Her eyes closed and she made approving *mmm* sounds as she chewed.

"Oh my God! This is fabulous!"

"Glad you like it. Dig in, there's more where that came from."

They ate in silence for a few minutes then Gunner decided to take the bull by the horns. "About Nashville . . . my decision . . ." Her fork stopped midway to her mouth and she paused.

He quietly continued. "The way it went down last year, I thought one way and found out it was another. It got to the point that I was looking over my shoulder constantly and didn't know who to trust. I'm not made that way. People I thought were my friends turned on me. My record label hung me out to dry, my manager and I fell out because of my own stupidity. Wasn't pretty."

"I guess the further you get to the top, the more competitive and jealous people get. I can relate, I experienced that as well in the culinary world. Actually, I got fired," Sophia shared.

He studied her face, fascinated by the array of

emotions flickering in her eyes. "Fired? I had no idea," he said.

"Not something I'm particularly proud of. Wasn't my fault but who cares. The end result was the same."

He wiped his lips with his napkin and continued. "I let my manager Greg talk me into dating his sister. It was on the heels of my breakup with Natalie and I was nowhere near ready to date. She'd been pestering him to fix us up. It was mistake that cost me and unfortunately her. After a month I broke it off and she had a break down."

"Oh no. I'm so sorry."

"Needless to say, Greg wanted to kill me, I was sick over it, and our sophomore release tanked in the charts. Dark days for sure. So, I quit."

"You walked away?"

"Yep. I'd had my fill. I gave it ten years of my life. I know everyone told me that I was on the cusp of the big break, but I couldn't take any more."

"What was the straw that broke the camel's back?" she asked.

He hesitated. *Do I tell her? This is the perfect opening.* "I . . . um . . . it wasn't one thing it was the culmination of everything."

"And now? You seemed gung-ho after meeting with the new record label. What changed your mind?"

Gunner pinched the bridge of his nose. He tried but couldn't get the words out. An image of the photos flashed through his mind and he felt a flush rush up his neck. It was like a mental block. He couldn't meet her eyes as he replied. "I guess after sleeping on it and being in Nashville for several days, the reasons I left came back to me and I realized nothing had changed."

"And that's the *only* reason why you changed your mind?"

He looked at her, warning bells going off as he caught something in her tone of voice. "Isn't that enough reason?"

"It is, but I'm asking you if there is more to the story."

"This is beginning to feel more like an interrogation than a discussion," he countered.

"I asked you a simple question. Why are you getting defensive?"

"Who's defensive?" He challenged. Even as he said it, he knew this discussion was going in the wrong direction. He set his fork down and took a deep breath. "Sophia, is there something specific you'd like me to say?"

"The truth."

"Everything I told you is the truth. What more do you want me to say?"

"Nothing. End of discussion. I'm sorry things didn't work out for you."

He tried to lighten the mood. "Hey, I'm over it. I'm still able to do something I love. How many people can say that?"

"I'm happy for you."

"Are you ready for dessert?" he asked.

Her voice was very chilly when she answered. "Sure. Then I think I'll call it a night."

"Only after I do the dishes."

"No," she said sharply. His eyes widened, then as if

she realized how she'd sounded she added, "Thanks for the offer but I'm exhausted. I'll let them go until tomorrow. Really."

"If you insist."

They ate their cheesecake in silence. As Sophia closed the door behind him after a subdued goodbye, he stood on the porch racking his brain to figure out how things went from bad to worse. He had half a mind to pound on the door and go back at it. It was almost as if she knew about the pictures. *Come on Gun . . . there's no way.*

As he got ready for bed he came to a decision. He was heading back to Nashville to get to the bottom of things. It was no longer about whether or not he returned to his music career, now it was much more personal. He didn't want anything to get between him and Sophia. This was a threat and his reputation and peace of mind were worth something. Since Eli was leaving next week to return to the rodeo circuit, it was now or never. *If I can get the courage up to tell Sophia about the photographs, I'll ask her to come along.*

36

*S*ophia paced back as she talked to herself. *Why is he hiding the photographs? I know it would be humiliating but still . . . how could they take their relationship to the next level if he couldn't trust her.* She punched in Amelia's number and she answered on the first ring.

"Help," Sophia said.

"What?" And the story poured out.

"Hm. Well I can't say I blame him for wanting to keep that from you," Amelia said.

Sophia sputtered. "Whose side are you on?"

"Yours . . . but . . . it was in his past and can you imagine how hard it would be to say . . . oh and by the way darlin', here are some pictures of me naked in bed with some young chickee. Why didn't you fess up and tell him you saw the text?"

"W-e-l-l . . . I feel bad about snooping."

"See, you're withholding information too."

"That's different."

"How?" Amelia said.

"Because, it just is."

"Hm. Glad you're not my lawyer."

"Since you're still in Nashville, can you look into it for me?"

"On it. If you promise to give Gunner a break. That text message was definitely a threat. It's easier to smear someone than it is to clear your name. Gunner knows this."

"What if there's more to Gunner than we know? Another side."

"I don't believe that and neither do you," Amelia said firmly.

"I didn't think that about Scott either and look what happened."

"I could kill Scott for what he put you through. Gunner is nothing like him. You know I always thought Scott was a pretentious asshole. I hate to break it to you, but I wasn't that shocked by his behavior."

"So, you've said."

"Don't forget, you were in the same position that Gunner is in at the restaurant and you didn't fight . . . that didn't mean you were guilty. Sometimes it's not worth fighting the establishment. How can you not see that?"

Sophia felt sick. Her face heated with shame as she realized she'd been quick to judge Gunner of things she'd been guilty of herself. She hadn't given him the benefit of the doubt.

"Listen, don't obsess over it tonight. I'll dig around. I'm on a mission now to get to the bottom of this. I've got a few leads going, I'll call you the minute I find out anything. Get some sleep."

"Thanks. But now I feel awful. I'm a terrible person. What am I going to do?"

"Talk it out. You'll know what to say. Tell him you saw the photos and see what he has to say."

"You're saying I should just admit I snooped through his phone?"

"Yes."

"Yikes. I hope I can get up the nerve."

"You can and you will. It's late. Get some sleep."

"Yes ma'am. I'll let you know how it goes."

"Night," Amelia said.

Sophia plugged her phone into the charger and went to brush her teeth and get ready for bed. Minutes later she crawled between the cotton sheets and stared at the ceiling wide awake. *How could I be so dense? I let my fear cloud my judgement. I hope he can forgive me.* After tossing and turning for most of the night she finally fell asleep as the roosters crowed.

Sophia jerked awake and looked at the bedside clock. *Eleven o'clock?* Her conversation with Amelia came flooding back and she jumped out of bed. *I have to find Gunner.* She put the coffee on and went to shower.

a half hour later she found him in the outdoor arena lunging Amitola. His shirt was off and his tanned skin glistened with perspiration, the muscles defined from exertion. His back was strong and sculpted, the broad shoulders tapering down to narrow hips. Remembering him naked in bed next to her, she felt weak kneed. *Mm . . . all muscle.* Her nervousness grew when he glanced up and brought Amitola to a walk . . . his expression inscrutable. Nodding his head, he acknowledged her then continued his cool down.

Sophia walked out to him. "How's she doing?"

"She's almost there. About ninety-five percent healed. Another week and she'll be as good as new."

"Gunner, we need to talk. Do you have some time after you finish up here?"

"Sure." He clicked his tongue then said whoa and Amitola stopped beside him. "Let me turn her out and we'll take a walk."

They walked along slowly, each lost in their own thoughts. Sophia was racking her brain to come up with the best way to bring up her transgression. It was embarrassing and not like her at all. She glanced up at Gunner noticing the wind ruffling his hair. He was squinting from the bright sunshine and she stopped herself from reaching up to touch his face. The laugh-lines fanning out around his eyes only enhanced his good looks and made her want to trace them with her fingertips. *He'll be just as handsome at eighty as he is now.*

"Let's find a place to sit and talk." Gunner said, taking her hand. He led her away from the barn to a shady spot beneath an old maple tree. He sat, pulling her down beside him. They leaned against the trunk, shoulders touching, legs stretched out, staring at the spectacular mountain view. It was so vast you could see for miles and miles. The varying brown hues of the scrub and dusty dirt cow trails contrasted with the myriad shades of green vegetation leading to the purple mountain backdrop and cloudless blue sky. A raucous call from a Stellar Blue Jay pierced through the peaceful sound of the wind blowing through the leaves

"This must be what heaven looks like," Sophia said on a sigh.

"Yep."

Gunner cleared his throat and began to speak at exactly the same time as she did. They both laughed then she said, "I'll go first."

He nodded, his expression becoming somber.

"Gunner, I'm so embarrassed and afraid you'll think less of me after I confess, so I'm going to dive right in."

"I'm afraid of the same."

"Remember when you got back from Nashville and you got drunk at the cantina?"

"Yeah."

"While you were in the bathroom your cell phone pinged . . . and I . . . um . . . because I was worried about you and . . . I didn't know why you were in such a bad place and . . ." her words tumbled out in a rush, "I looked at your messages and saw the photos." Her cheeks were on fire and she wrapped her arms around her knees and buried her face.

"So, you know." He said it as a statement rather than a question.

Her voice muffled, she said, "I only know that you have some compromising photos floating around, not why."

"The burning question yet to be answered . . . why. I don't have a clue."

Sophia peeked at him through her tousled mane of hair. "Really?"

His eyes burned with anger. "What I do know is that I was set up. Someone slipped something in my drink and I blacked out and woke up in bed with the woman in the picture. Nothing happened I'm sure of that much. Randy said I couldn't even walk myself to my room . . . I had to be carried. Pretty sure that ruled out any wild unbridled sex. When he and Jimmy left me, I was all by my lonesome. When I woke up, she was in my bed."

"Why didn't you report it?"

"Before I could even recover from the hangover, I got a text with photo attachments telling me to leave Nashville. It was the excuse I needed to throw in the towel. I'd been thinking about it for a while anyhow."

"Gunner, I'm so sorry."

He squeezed his eyes closed and blew out a breath. "You believe me?" The emotion behind the softly spoken words dissolved her own embarrassment. He looked so unsure of himself. She reached up and cupped his face, stroking his cheek with her thumb.

"Yes. I was shocked when I first saw them, but I knew there had to be a reason. Plus, you were both passed out in the pictures so someone else had to have taken them."

"Soph, I'm sorry I couldn't bring myself to tell you sooner."

"I'm sorry too. I should have told you about my

snooping. I have to confess something else. Amelia is doing a story."

"I know she told me, one about Nashville and Austin . . . comparing the two music scenes."

"No, I mean she is doing that story too, but she is also doing a story about you."

His eyes widened. "Me?"

"Yes. She has been trying to get to the bottom of why you up and quit so suddenly. I initially tried to talk her out of it, but she is a journalist at heart. Please don't be mad at her. She really likes you. She got the idea stuck in her head way before she got to know you. Now she's on a mission to find out about the pictures." Gunner was silent. "Gunner, you're not mad at her, are you?"

"Honestly, I do feel a bit surprised and maybe a little betrayed. I really liked Amelia. I feel duped."

Sophia grabbed his arm, "It's not like that I swear. She would never print anything without your final approval. And she won't release anything that could hurt you. She cares about you and she knows how much you mean to me."

He pinned her with his warm gaze. "How much do I mean to you?"

"I like you Gunner Cane. Much more than I had intended . . . my heart flutters every time I look at you. My knees get weak thinking about lying in bed next to you. I can't picture our lives together, but I can't picture my life without you in it either. Does that give you an idea?"

He leaned in close and kissed her softly. She could feel his warm breath against her cheeks. He pulled her onto his lap and she wrapped her arms around his neck and kissed him back. The heat of his hard body against hers was doing a number on her libido. He buried his fingers in her hair and groaned as her tongue darted between his lips.

He lifted his head, eyes blazing with desire. "Red, I knew I was in trouble the minute I laid eyes on you at the airport. Nothing since then has convinced me otherwise. Come to Nashville with me. I'm leaving in the next day or so to get to the bottom of things. I have to get out from under this cloud . . . I don't want to live with regrets. It'll only be for a couple of nights."

"Okay. I'm in. We can catch up with Amelia there too."

His eyes narrowed as he thought about that. Grinning he said, "I reckon I can forgive her. Can't take the hunt out of a bloodhound."

Sophia laughed. "That's for sure. She was born nosy."

"Let's head back. I need to make reservations for us. You'll get to meet my good buddy Randy and his wife and kids."

Sophia scrambled off his lap and stood, offering Gunner a hand up. Once standing, he interlaced their fingers and they strolled back to her cabin. He walked her to the door and kissed her forehead before leaving. "See ya at supper."

"Okay." She floated to her bedroom and sat on the edge of the bed her fingertips drifting to her lips. She could still taste him and was unsettled by how much she wanted him. Thinking ahead of their trip to Nashville, and of waking up next to him, she smiled.

37

*S*ophia liked Randy immediately. He was a big teddy bear of a man with a warm smile and playful countenance.

"Thanks for picking us up," Gunner said.

"No problem. It'd be stupid to rent a car when we have a spare sitting in our garage not being used much. How'd this loser talk you into coming as his plus one?" Randy said, winking at her.

"He can be quite charming when he puts his mind to it," she replied.

"Ha—so my wife tells me."

As they reached the exit a woman and her two teenage daughters approached them and the mother called out to Gunner. "I'm so sorry to bother you, but aren't you Gunner Cane?"

Gunner smiled wide and said, "Yes ma'am. How ya doing on this fine day?"

The young girls looked like they were about to

burst with excitement, eyes bright, cheeks flushed, the younger one bouncing up and down on the balls of her feet as she stared up at him.

"My daughters and I are huge fans. We've been to lots of your shows."

"Thank you."

"Um . . . can we have an autograph?"

Gunner gave a half shrug and said, "Sure, ya got a pen and something to write on?"

The mom quickly whipped out a pen from her purse and offered it to Gunner along with a paperback romance novel. The daughters shoved their magazines towards him.

Sophia stood several feet away from Gunner watching his adoring fans swoon as he asked for their names and scrawled messages for each of them. It was unsettling to witness this part of Gunner's life. Even though she was aware he'd made a name for himself here in Nashville, it was one thing to imagine it and quite another to experience it in real time. And this was just the beginning. If he did return to music and hit it big, his life would be under the prying eyes of the public all of the time.

Gunner glanced up and met her eyes then flashed a wide grin. Suddenly shy, Sophia looked down at the ground. *What is wrong with me? This is the same Gunner you woke up next to this morning. The only thing that's changed is the location.*

As if sensing her discomfort, he took a step towards her and reached for her hand, pulling her next to him. Gunner returned the last autographed magazine then slung his arm across her shoulders. The fans were now looking at Sophia with undisguised curiosity and something else. It almost felt as if she'd become a star just by association, as if Gunner's stardust was spilling over to her. *Weird.*

"Thank you so much," the teenagers gushed, wide eyed and adorable.

"You're welcome. Thanks for your support. It means a lot." Randy caught Sophia's eye and rolled his heavenward. She put a hand over her mouth stifling a giggle feeling her tension ease.

"Let's head to the parking lot," Randy said.

They stepped outside into the hot July heat and Gunner leaned down and whispered, "Sorry about that."

38

*G*unner had splurged and booked a luxury suite in the iconic Hermitage Hotel in the heart of downtown Nashville. He heard Sophia gasp when they entered the lobby. It was like stepping back in time. Luxurious, ornate . . . grand by any standards. It was almost like a Roman cathedral, following the classical Italian and French Renaissance architecture.

The lighting from the chandeliers and sconces reflected off the marble pillars and floors and the warm colors used in the massive room created a rich sumptuous ambience. The curves and arches . . . the painted glass skylight, the gold trim and gold crown molding . . . the grand staircase, it was no wonder it was a must-see destination. He could only guess that their suite would be just as lush.

"Pinch me," Sophia said, wide eyed with her head tilted back, staring at the ceiling. "This is breathtaking!

It's a work of art. It feels alive . . . like if these walls could talk . . . you know what I mean? It holds secrets and memories and history."

"It's got quite the history. A hot spot for celebrities. Lots of famous people have stayed here. Even presidents. I made dinner reservations tonight at the restaurant here. It's top notch."

"I can't wait to see our room."

"Phillip pulled some strings and reserved the City Suite for us. As the name implies, it's got great views of the city."

Sophia was so busy gawking that she stumbled and Gunner quickly grabbed her to keep her from falling. "Careful, Red."

"Oops."

"You and your heels. Here, give me your bag," he said. "You can hang on to me."

"My sexy knight . . ." she said, sliding her hand through his crooked elbow. Her cell phone rang and she withdrew her arm to search for her phone. Glancing at the caller ID she said, "Let me get this. It's Amelia."

They continued walking to their room as she listened to her friend. "I see. That's great Em. Okay. We just checked in and we're heading to our room now. I'll call you once we get settled in. Thanks. Bye. Yes, I'll tell him." The call ended and she said, "Amelia says hi. We're going to meet up with her tomorrow. She found your fangirl Harper and she's meeting her at a bar tonight."

Blowing out his breath he said, "Things just got real."

Slipping her arm through his again she said, "It's going to work out. Amelia is a pro. She'll get to the bottom of it."

"I hope so. This has been weighing me down for too long. I thought I'd buried it along with my career, but now I realize that it was always there, niggling at the back of my mind."

They reached their suite; Gunner swiped the card and they entered.

"Oh my God! I love it." He smiled indulgently as Soph kicked off her heels then ran to the windows to peer out at the cityscape. "It's fabulous! This must have cost you a fortune." Turning she ran over to the bed. "I'm going to need a step ladder to climb onto the bed," she said, giggling. She dove on top of the king-sized duvet and rolled onto her back, patting the space beside her invitingly.

He jumped on then climbed on top of her nibbling her neck.

"That tickles," Sophia said, squirming beneath him. He was already aroused.

"Kiss me," he commanded. Finding her lips soft, willing and parted, he swooped down, covering her mouth with his. Slow, sensual . . . he took his time using his lips and tongue to explore, leaving her panting. He pulled off her top then hooked his fingers under her bra straps, dragging them down her arms. Tugging on the cups, he released her breasts from their confinement. His breath hitched at the sight of her pale pink nipples and milky white mounds.

"Gunner," she said breathlessly.

"Ah Sophia, you're an enchantress without even

trying. You taste so good, your smell drives me insane. . . your body so incredibly fine." His breath was ragged as he trailed kisses along her jaw . . . under her chin, the hollow of her throat, below her collarbone. He unlatched her bra and ripped it off, thoroughly exploring her luscious mounds, kissing the tender swell below her breasts leading down to her belly. He roughly hiked her tube skirt up around her waist and nuzzled between her thighs, probing. She grabbed his hair and moaned his name.

He kissed her through the sheer silk panties and licked her inner thighs as he slid a finger beneath the elastic band and slipped it inside her. She writhed under his skillful attention and when he felt her body trembling, he tugged her underwear down her smooth silky thighs and kissed his way back up.

Kneeling, he unzipped his Levi's then pulled them down below his hips and rolled on a condom. Bending her knees, he spread her thighs wide as he positioned himself at her center and plunged inside. She was slick and snug around him and it felt like heaven. He closed his eyes for a moment and paused until she urged him on. When she rocked against him and wrapped her thighs around his waist, he lost it. He rode her hard, thrusting as she gripped him tight inside of her.

When he was near climax he said, "Look at me." His voice was hoarse with emotion.

She opened her eyes, dark bottomless pools of lust, and he went over the edge, falling into the depths of his passion, his body shuddering in release. His hands framed her face as he kissed her, lost in a swirl of sensation as her body began to tremble under him.

"Gunner," she cried out, her hands gripping his shoulders.

As his tremors subsided, he watched her ride the waves of her orgasm . . . so beautiful, so wild, so free. He kissed her eyelids and cheeks, the tip of her nose then landed back on her lips, savoring the taste of her, the feel of her soft body under him. He let his torso sink into hers and lay spent and content. He could feel her rapid breath against his cheek and smiled. As sure as he was of anything, he knew he'd never be able to let her go.

When Sophia woke up it took her a minute to figure out where she was. She felt the weight of Gunner's thigh on top of hers and his arm slung around her waist. His breathing was even and steady. *Oh yeah, we must have fallen asleep after we made love.* She had to use the bathroom, so she tried to slide out from under him without waking him up, but he gripped her and held on tight.

"Don't leave me."

She glanced at her watch. "We'd better get up. We have reservations for seven thirty and it's seven now."

"I don't want to let you go. You feel so good."

"We could cancel the reservation and get room service."

"Really? Are you sure? I wanted to take you out somewhere special."

"I'm positive. We can do that another night. But I have to go to the bathroom now then I think I'll take a shower. I feel gritty from traveling." He released her and she pulled her skirt down from around her waist and raced to the bathroom. Gunners throaty chuckle followed her.

Sophia took a quick shower then tucked a big fluffy towel around her body. She was towel drying her hair when Gunner walked in looking at a menu. He closed the toilet seat and sat down. "How does truffled parmesan frites and cider glazed crispy brussels sprouts sound for starters?"

"Yummy."

"They have beet salad or Caesar."

"Beet."

"Short ribs, filet, chicken confit, salmon or a burger."

"Hm . . . how's the salmon prepared?"

"Pan seared with broccolini sweet potato puree and black truffle honey."

"Sold."

"I'll call it in."

"Thanks," she said, smiling.

He stood and came up behind her, hugging her to him. Their eyes met in the mirror. "I'll never get enough of you," he said, kissing the nape of her neck. "You have a tiny little mole right behind your left ear. Did you know that?" He murmured planting a kiss there. Her eyes were heavy lidded as she shook her head. He dipped his tongue in her ear. "It matches the one on your hip. How am I going to keep you all to myself, hmm?" She leaned her head back on his shoulder and covered his hands with hers.

"Look who's talking, Mr. Nashville. How am I supposed to compete with every other woman on the planet?"

"There's no contest . . . you are the prettiest little filly I've ever laid eyes on . . . and that's no lie."

Sophia hardly recognized herself in the mirror. Her cheeks were flushed and her eyes heavy-lidded and shimmering, almost black. "I'll have to take your word on that."

"That creamy skin, those wonderfully expressive dark eyes, wild red hair, perfect body . . . adorably clumsy at times . . . intelligent . . ."

"You saved that for last I notice. Good catch."

His hands coasted down her arms as he leaned in and bit her shoulder before leaving to place their dinner order.

39

The following morning, Sophia was looking out the window when Gunner whooped out loud after reading a text message that had just arrived. "Red, it's our lucky day! Phillip Krauss nabbed four front row seats to see Vince Gill at the Grand Ole Opry for tomorrow night!"

"Fun. Are you going to invite Randy and his wife . . . Cindy, right?"

"Yeah, Cindy. That's what I was thinking. I know you two will hit it off. She's great. Alright with you?"

"Absolutely. Oh, and I forgot to tell you, we're meeting Amelia for coffee in about a half hour. She wants to fill us in on her conversation with Harper."

"Sweet. I'll jump through the shower."

Sophia pouted. "What, no kiss?"

"My poor baby. Let Gunner give you some loving."

Her chin lifted. "Never mind. If I have to ask . . ."

She didn't get the sentence out before he pounced on

her and covered her face with kisses until she was hysterical with laughter. "Okay, I give. Get going." She swatted his butt as he walked away.

Sophia sighed and hugged herself. She was afraid to admit how deeply attached she already was to this man. Not only did he make her libido go from zero to eighty with just a glance, she felt a cozy warmth and comfort when she was with him. *As her wise friend Amelia would say . . . Rot-Roh.*

*S*ophia immediately spotted Amelia sitting at a corner booth and ran to greet her, overjoyed at seeing her bestie. Amelia jumped up and hugged Sophia tightly. "Where's Mr. Wonderful?"

"He's parking the car. He'll be right in."

"You're sparkling from the inside out. You've got the glow," Amelia said studying her friend closely. "Love suits you."

Sophia's voice came out in a squeak, "Love?"

"Yes. L-O-V-E. You've heard of it."

"Amelia!" Gunner's greeting interrupted Amelia and Sophia was thankful.

"Hey, Gunner. I was just telling Sophia . . . ouch!" She rubbed her side where Sophia had elbowed her.

"What?" Gunner asked, his curiosity piqued.

"Nothing!" Sophia said quickly, her face hot.

"We'll talk later," Amelia said, winking at Gunner.

"Deal."

"What's everyone having? I'll go order." He took their orders, then left Sophia and Amelia alone again.

Sophia crossed her arms and glared. "I will literally

kill you if you go anywhere near that topic of conversation with Gunner. I mean it."

"Lighten up. I see love hasn't doused that temper of yours." She grinned wickedly.

"You're so bad. I don't know why I'm still your friend."

Using all of her charm, Amelia said, "Because you love me?"

Sophia softened. She could never stay irritated with Em for long. As rotten as she was, she was the best friend anyone could ask for. Never a dull moment, that was for sure.

"Here you go," Gunner said, handing them their coffees. He plopped down in the booth next to Sophia and stared across at Amelia expectantly.

"So, here's the scoop. As you know, I met with Harper yesterday and she claims that when she and her friends got back to their hotel room, admittedly drunk on their asses, an envelope had been slipped under her door. Inside was a room card and a note from you, Gunner, inviting her to your room with the number supplied. She figured you had delivered it before the show and before you got trashed."

Gunner looked stunned. "What the hell?"

"She said she was so wasted that she went to your room and undressed and crawled in bed with you. She tried to wake you up, but she couldn't. Then she passed out. She was confused and hurt the following morning when you were so furious with her. Later on, she figured out it must have been a set up."

Sophia raised one brow. "You believe her? I thought maybe she was in on it."

"I don't think she was. I showed her one of the photos you'd sent me. She seemed totally stunned and embarrassed . . . she even cried. She wasn't faking it."

"That wound up being a dead end then," Gunner said.

"Not really. We can cross her off the list at least. That's something," Amelia said.

Sophia said, "Okay, let's look at it this way, who else had both motive and opportunity?"

Amelia held up her fingers and ticked off a list. "One, we have your manager Greg, who gave Harper and her friends the free tickets to the show and invited them to the after party. Two, Greg was in deep financial doo doo . . . on the brink of bankruptcy and you were his main meal ticket. Three, Randy and Jimmy had opportunity since they took you back to your hotel room and put you to bed. Four, your contract was about to expire with your record label, and I heard there were rumors floating around at the time that you weren't staying with them . . . there's motive. Am I missing anything?" She asked Gunner.

He frowned. "I'm not sure if this is important. I dated Greg's sister Amber for about a month. She had a big crush on me and kept asking him to fix us up. It was after Natalie. I knew it was a mistake but I let Greg pressure me. She fixated on me right away . . . clingy, needy, she told me she'd been raped when she was in high school and had PTSD. I felt sorry for her so I let it go on longer than I should have. Big mistake."

Amelia's brow furrowed. "Then what happened?"

"I broke it off as gently as I could. I couldn't stay with someone out of pity. She didn't take it well . . . had a mental breakdown and started stalking me. It got pretty intense."

"How did Greg handle that?"

"He told me I was paranoid and Amber meant no harm. He wanted me to keep seeing her and gradually break up. I told him I couldn't do that. Initially, he had hard feelings. It changed things between us but not to the extent he'd sabotage my career. At least I hope not."

"So, Amber had motive but what about opportunity? She and Greg together could have set you up."

Gunner shook his head, "Naw, I can't see her doing that. She was broken but mostly a sweet girl. She was super sensitive. She wouldn't hurt me intentionally."

"Who else would have motive? After you left Nashville all was quiet again. It wasn't until you met with the new label that you received another threat. What's up with that?" Amelia said.

"Not to state the obvious but someone doesn't want you back in Nashville," Sophia said.

"What about Natalie? Or any rivals?" Amelia added.

"Not Natalie, she's been hounding me to get our band back together. As for Randy and Jimmy, same. They have no motive unless I'm missing something. Plus, Randy's like my brother."

"It could be a personal ax to grind or a professional hit job," Amelia said.

Gunner pinched the bridge of his nose deep in thought. "I think I need to have a conversation with Greg. He's got the most reason to want to see me fail."

"I agree, "Amelia said.

"Me too," Sophia concurred.

"That's where I'll start then," Gunner said.

Amelia pulled out her phone. "I'll text you his contact information if you need it. He was on my list."

"Do that in case it's changed. I'll see if he can meet me tomorrow."

Amelia held up her hands for high fives, "We've got a plan. Gunner you're going to get your life back. I won't give up until we get to the bottom of it."

"I appreciate it Amelia, but you know I can't let you do a story. In the end, this will be a waste of your time professionally."

"You can give me an exclusive interview when you make your big comeback. How's that sound?"

"Deal." Gunner reached his hand across the table and they shook on it.

40

*G*unner tapped his foot impatiently as he glanced at his watch. *Fifteen minutes late. How like Greg.* He signaled to the waitress and she came over to take his order. "I'll have a brisket barbeque sandwich with slaw and an order of fries."

She didn't bother writing it down. "Still sticking with water?"

"Yep. I may have been stood up . . . we'll see."

"I'll keep an eye out."

"Thanks."

He glanced through the plate glass window and saw Greg rush by on his way inside. He entered looking flustered and Gunner stood up motioning him over.

"Sorry I'm late."

"Some things never change . . . still a day late and a dollar short."

"How ya been?" Greg asked as he took a seat across from Gunner.

"Some good, some not so good."

"Doing any music?"

"Nope . . . nothing besides singing around a campfire."

"That's a waste. I hate to hear it."

Gunner narrowed his eyes. "You sure about that?"

"What's that supposed to mean?"

"Just how it sounds. I already ordered my food since I was beginning to think I'd been ditched. You might want to put your order in."

Greg turned in his seat and waved to the server. After she left, he turned to face Gunner and said, "I'm guessing this isn't a cozy kumbaya reunion."

Gunner's lips twisted. "You're still quick on the uptake I see."

"Spit it out then."

Gunner pulled out his cell and brought up a photo and thrust it in Greg's face. "I'll cut right to the chase. Know anything about this?"

Greg's eyes opened wide in shock. "Whoa! Dude, what are you accusing me of here?"

Gunner gritted his teeth. "Take a good hard look . . . you sure nothings ringing a bell?"

"I recognize the girl. That was your number one fan. She came to one of your last shows. I got her and her friends' tickets."

"Yeah, I know you did. And invited her to the after party even though I specifically told you not to. I needed that like I needed a hole in my head."

"That was part of my job Gunner. You know, promote my rising star. I might have been trying to get a dig in, but that's it."

"Someone set me up and chased me out of Nashville with these photographs and I think it was you. You had the motive and the opportunity. Nobody else did."

"What motive? Are you nuts?"

"You knew I was thinking about moving to a different label and different management. You were pissed about your sister . . . you invited Harper and her friends to Atlanta and forced her on me."

Greg looked panicked. He held up his hand. "Stop right there. You have the wrong guy. Did I think you were a self-centered bastard? Yes. I'd given you ten years of my life and blood to help you succeed . . . then you were going to dump me just when you were about to hit the big time. I hated you back then. You dumped my sister like she was some groupie. I definitely had the motive. But it wasn't me."

Gunner drummed his fingers against the table frowning. Greg sounded sincere. His bullshit detector stayed silent. Still . . . *Who else could it be? It had to be an inside job. Someone who had access to my personal information, my room key, my schedule.*

Greg pulled at his collar a sheen of sweat on his brow. "I swear, I'd never do something this dirty. I have a family to feed. I'm not about to sabotage my career over losing one musician."

"Revenge for your sister then?"

Greg shook his head slowly. "When I think back on it, it was Jimmy who told me to give those girls the tickets. I assumed he had the hots for one of them."

"Yeah right. Deflect and distract. Jimmy has no ax to grind with me."

"You know he was in love with my sister, right?"

"What?"

"You heard me. You were probably so involved with yourself and Natalie that you didn't even notice. While Amber was fixated on you, Jimmy was all about Amber. You were hitting the booze pretty hard back then. I'm not surprised you missed it."

"I don't believe you."

"Whether you do or don't doesn't change the fact that it's the truth."

The server arrived with their food and they took a short break from the conversation to eat. Gunner squirted a gallon of ketchup over his fries then shoved a handful into his mouth. Chewing he said, "Did anything ever happen between Jimmy and Amber?"

"They went out a few times. Early on. Jimmy busted my balls until I convinced Amber to go out with him. It was nothing serious on her part. She said he was okay, but not her type. Like most women, she preferred the bad boys, like you."

"I'm hardly a bad boy, but that's beside the point. I guess you didn't learn from that to stay out of the match-making business."

"I'm a slow learner."

Gunner took a bite of his sandwich and shook his head slowly. "I don't see it. When Natalie flew out to my ranch to convince me to return to Nashville, everyone was on board. Jimmy and Randy are excited as hell to go on tour together and cut a new album. Before I even touched down back in Wyoming those miserable photos resurfaced with a warning to stay out of Nashville."

Greg shrugged. "I don't know what to tell you. All I know for sure is that it wasn't me. I'd grill Jimmy. Whether you want to believe it or not, Jimmy had motive and opportunity. He took it hard when you dated then dumped my sister. People are capable of just about anything. I've learned in this business not to trust anyone as far as you can throw 'em. I hate that I've become so cynical, but there you have it."

They finished their lunch and settled up the bill.

"Gunner, I mean it when I say I'm really sorry this is happening to you. Look, the shit that went down before, that's all in the past. I don't have any hard feelings and Amber is happily in love . . . and it's with a pharmacist, not a freakin' musician. Thank God! I managed to wrangle a couple of promising musicians to sign on with me as their manager. My future is looking brighter than it was a year ago. I got no complaints."

"I'm glad to hear it. Shouldn't have ever mixed business with family. I never meant to hurt Amber . . . but you know that."

"You're a decent guy Gunner. I wish you the best and if you return to Nashville, I'll be rooting for ya."

"Thanks Greg. Take care."

"You do the same. I'll keep my ear to the ground. If I pick up on anything, I'll let ya know."

After Greg left, Gunner texted Sophia that he was on his way to pick her up. He froze for a moment before pressing send. *I'm getting used to this. It's nice to have someone to share stuff with. Someone on the other end that gives a damn . . . someone like Sophia. I'll be alright no matter how this all goes down. Nashville or not.* Smiling he pushed send, got into his car and left to get the woman who held his heart in her hands.

41

Gunner and Sophia stood under the Grand Ole Opry sign and took a selfie. Cindy held her palm out and said, "Let me take one of you guys then you can take a picture of Randy and me." Sophia handed her the phone and Gunner hugged her tightly to his side, putting his lips against her cheek for the shot.

"Now face the camera, Gun." She took several more photos, then they switched places with Randy and Cindy and snapped a few of them. Gunner flagged down a passerby and asked if they'd take one of all four of them. Gunner, clowning around, jumped on Randy's back for the group shot. They were all laughing in the picture and it was Sophia's favorite one of all.

They had a half hour to kill before the show started and Randy and Gunner headed straight to the bar in the lobby to order their cocktails. Cindy and Sophia went to the ladies' room. Sophia touched up her bright red lipstick with slightly unsteady hands. Cindy dried her hands and studied Sophia as their eyes met in the mirror.

Smiling kindly, Cindy said, "I've known Gunner for over ten years and I've never seen him this crazy about anyone. He's really into you Sophia."

"Really?"

"Cross my heart."

"It scares me to feel this much again. Just when I think I've got my emotions under control he looks at me and I'm a puddle of feels. I'm trying to give up on managing it and just go with the flow." She laughed softly. "Sometimes I even succeed at it . . . I was afraid to care too much . . . now I guess I'm getting used to sweaty palms and my insides quivering all the damn time." She held out her hand to prove the point.

Cindy laughed. "Full disclosure, I still get butterflies when Randy gives me his smoldering look." Cindy linked her arm through Sophia's and they went to find their hot dates.

Gunner and Randy were in a deep discussion when she spotted them, but that didn't stop Gunner's covetous eyes from watching her approach. He handed her a drink then slipped his arm around her waist holding her to him. "You girls are a sight for sore eyes."

Randy continued. "Listen bro, I just can't wrap my brain around Jimmy being behind it all. There has to be something else . . . something we're not seeing."

Gunner's brow furrowed. "I don't want to believe it either but I've got to confront him about it."

"We'll do it together. He might take it a little better."

"I know you have more history with him. I'd really appreciate that Randy."

"I'll set it up for tomorrow. We'll meet at our favorite watering hole, grab a burger and some beer. Loosen him up a little first."

Sophia rubbed her cheek against Gunner's arm, *mm*, soft cotton, solid muscle and the smell of freshly laundered shirt. He leaned down and kissed the top of her head. She looked up and her heart melted.

"It's going to be okay," she said softly.

"With you by my side babe, how can it be anything but."

Randy rolled his eyes, "I can't take all this; you're making it hard for me bro, now my wife is going to be putting the pressure on." Cindy elbowed him and he clutched his side, doubling over comically.

"Let's go find our seats and catch us some Vince Gill," Gunner said, taking Sophia's hand leading the way.

"I can't wait. I love him so much!" Cindy said.

Randy glared at her, "He's already taken and so are you."

"I love when my man gets possessive," she said grinning.

"Well I'll be. Phillip really scored big with these seats," Randy said, as they took their front row center seats.

"Yeah. Pretty highfalutin," Gunner said.

The lights dimmed and Gunner intertwined his

fingers with hers. She smiled up at him and something flickered in his eyes. He half-turned in his seat and tilted her chin up with his knuckles then tucked a lock of hair behind her ear. Kissing her softly on the lips he whispered, "I'm never going to let you go. Consider yourself warned." Her belly did a somersault as the rest of the world disappeared and it was only the two of them. Then the opening act took the stage and the music carried them away for the next several hours.

*R*andy and Cindy dropped them off at the hotel entrance and the minute they entered their room, Gunner gathered Sophia into his arms, burying his nose in her hair. A thrill raced through her body . . . *He doesn't even have to lift a finger, I'm so easy.*

He held her for a moment then led her over to the bed. Cupping her face in his palms, he stared into her eyes. "I want you Sophia Russo. All of you."

She responded by slipping her hands under his shirt, her palms sliding up over his toned belly and chest coming to rest on his shoulders. They kissed deeply until her knees were weak . . . her body quivering. He lifted his head, his eyes pinning her as he slowly began to undress her. When she was standing with only her silk underwear between them, he kneeled at her feet and looked up, his eyes glittering as he hooked his thumbs under the elastic band of her panties and slid them, torturously slow, down the length of her thighs. He stood and reached around to unfasten her bra, the soft hair on his forearms brushing against her sensitive skin. As her breasts spilled out, she heard his sharp intake of breath then his tongue flicked against her nipple.

At first, she felt vulnerable standing naked before him, especially with him fully clothed, but his tongue quickly made her forget about everything but his mouth on her body. She dissolved into a million sensations . . . softening . . . liquefied.

She desperately needed to feel his skin against hers. Dragging his shirt over his head she peppered his bare chest with kisses as she reached down to unzip his jeans. It was her turn to kneel, trailing her mouth down his toned body, lingering when she reached his flat belly. She rubbed her cheek against his soft fuzz. She pulled his pants and underwear down his muscular thighs. He stepped out of them then reached for her hand and tugged her up to her feet. He lifted her into his arms and cradled her for a moment before he gently lay her on the bed. He laid down on his side facing her.

He covered her mouth with his. As he cupped her bottom, she could feel his arousal pressing against her. After slipping on a condom, he pushed her onto her back, spreading her open with his knees he slid inside her.

They made passionate love, both climaxing hard and quickly. Afterwards, they lay motionless, their bodies melted together, both languid and spent. Half asleep, she felt his lips in her hair as he tenderly brushed it away from her brow. Just as she was drifting off, she thought she heard him whisper "I love you."

They woke up in the middle of the night and made

love again. This time Gunner was slow and thorough, leaving her feeling like a warm puddle. She didn't think she'd ever move again. They lay facing each other. "Gunner?"

"Hm?"

She rubbed her thumb over his bottom lip. "Do you think we have a chance at this? I mean us . . . with the distance and our careers . . . I . . . I'm scared. I'm beginning to feel too attached."

In an exaggerated drawl Gunner said, "Babe, I can't promise you it will always be easy, but like I said before, if you think for a second that I'm gonna let you get away, you got another thang comin'!"

"Promise?"

"Promise. We'll figure it out. Life's full of risks, we never know what's around the corner. I mean look at us . . . never in a million years did I think I'd meet a sassy pastry chef and be swept off my feet. Life's funny like that." His slow drawl was both sexy and endearing. "I'm just now beginning to realize how much I've been burying my head in the sand this past year."

She rubbed the tip of her nose back and forth across his. "I love you, Gunner Cane."

"Excuse me ma'am, what did you just say?"

She looked at him innocently, "What?"

He crawled on top of her pinning her arms over her head. She bit her bottom lip to keep from laughing as he stared down at her. "Say it again."

"I'm not sure what you mean."

He nuzzled her neck, tickling her until she cried out. "Alright, I give. I love you. Are you happy now?"

He released her hands and gathered her up in his arms. "Dang straight I'm happy."

"Can I go back to sleep now?"

"Yes. I love you too, Red."

She fell back to sleep wrapped in her lover's embrace.

42

*G*unner and Randy headed to their meeting with Jimmy.

"What's the plan?" Randy asked, buckling himself in.

"Totally winging it."

"That's how we roll."

"I won't beat around the bush for too long. Feel free to jump in any time."

"Sure thing."

Gunner turned on the radio and Thomas Rhett's "Makes Me Wanna" filled the airwaves, reminding Gunner of his and Sophia's first date.

Randy gave Gunner a sideways look and said, "You can tell me to mind my own business, but you and Sophia seem pretty tight."

"Yeah. She's it for me. Honestly Randy, it makes me question if I even knew what love was before her."

Randy's eyes lit up. "Lovesick. I knew it!" He jokingly stuck his palm against Gunner's forehead. "Yep, you've got it bad. How'd that old classic go? He belted out a few bars of a tune. "Got a fever of one hundred and three . . . hot blooded."

"You're an ass, you know that, right?"

They pulled into the corner parking lot and Gunner killed the engine. They hopped out and walked the half block to the bar. The door creaked loudly as they entered the dimly lit saloon. Gunner's boots clomped on the old wooden floor. The back bar was a dark and ornate mahogany; mirror-backed shelves were lined with bottle after bottle of liquor. The antique sconces cast a golden light which reflected off the glasses lined up. Jimmy was already sitting there nursing a mug of draft beer, flirting with the pretty young bartender. There were a few other patrons but business was slow this time of day. A little early for the happy hour crowd.

"Hey Jimmy," Gunner said.

"What're ya drinking? It's on me," Jimmy said.

"I'll have whatever you're drinkin'," Gunner replied, nodding hello at the bartender whose eyes sparked with interest.

"Bourbon and coke for me," Randy said.

Gunner grabbed his frosty mug and took a slug then said, "Let's move to a booth."

Jimmy settled up while Randy and Gunner claimed the booth off in the farthest back corner.

Sliding in across from them, Jimmy said, "This is great! Just like old times." He had his long dark hair pulled back in a ponytail and he pushed his dark framed glasses up. He looked like he hadn't shaved in several days, his thin face dark with stubble.

Gunner narrowed his eyes. "Before we go any further, there's something I need to check out with you."

Jimmy's expression turned wary. "What, this isn't a social call?"

Randy jumped in. "Jimmy, this has to stay right here."

"Course it will. Shoot."

"When Gunner quit Nashville and the band last year, there was more to it than we knew about back then."

"O-k-a-y," he drawled out slowly. "Y'all going to fill me in now?"

Gunner jumped in. "I'm going to be straight with you. I was set up that last night we played in Atlanta. Someone drugged me then made sure I was passed out and took pictures of me in bed with one of my fans. Harper to be exact." He pulled out his phone and found the graphic photographs and showed them to Jimmy. "The message along with it told me to get out of Nashville or they'd be released to the tabloids." Gunner carefully watched for Jimmy's reaction.

Jimmy's eyes widened in shock. "What the hell! Why didn't ya say so? We could've helped."

"I'm going to ask ya point blank. Was it you?"

"Are you fucking kidding me? Why would I shoot myself in the foot?"

"Look, I'm only asking because there were very few people that could have pulled it off. We've pretty much ruled everyone else out but you. Understand that I have to ask."

His face reddened. "I guess we aren't as good of friends as I thought we were."

"It's not that. Don't take it that way. Listen, it was someone that had access to my room number, Harper's room number and a spare key to my room. Also, someone who was close enough to me that night to slip dope in my drink."

"Did you check with the fangirl? She was obsessed with you. How about Greg? He was pissed as hell at you."

"I talked to Greg already. His story checked out to me."

Randy piped in. "I didn't know you'd dated his sister."

"Yeah, so what?"

"It must have stuck in your craw when Gunner started dating her after she dumped you."

"Why would it? He's free to date anyone he wants."

"Is it true that you were the one that suggested inviting the fans to the Atlanta show?" Randy asked.

"Hell, I can't remember that far back. I could've. So what?"

"You always knew Gunner didn't want to mix it up with the fans."

"Yeah, so it probably wasn't me that invited them. Sounds like something Greg would've done. He was always pushing the fans on us. You guys know that."

"Yes, except he says it wasn't him."

"He can say anything he wants but he had an ax to grind with you Gunner. Starting with Amber and ending with you dumping him."

"That's why I questioned him first."

Jimmy rubbed the back of his neck, looking frustrated. "Look, I was excited as hell when I heard Gunner was considering getting the band back together. Why would I go and fuck it up now? I have as much to lose as anyone."

Gunner looked over at Randy and he gave a half shrug. Jimmy seemed to be telling the truth. *WTF where do I go from here? We're leaving Nashville tomorrow.* "I hope you understand we had to ask. No hard feelings, I hope."

Jimmy looked relieved. "No bro, I understand you had to ask. No hard feelings." They finished their drinks and agreed to stay in touch. Gunner promised to let him know after he made his final decision about reuniting with the band.

On the way home they were both quiet until Gunner said, "I may never know who did it but I believe Jimmy. What'd you think?"

"I'd have a hard time thinking he was capable of doing something like that. We'd played together for so long."

"I'm relieved. I didn't want it to be him," Gunner admitted.

"Me either."

. . .

*W*hen they reached Randy's place the racket that greeted them made Gunner feel wistful. Sophia was sitting on the floor with a squealing JJ on her lap. The toddler's fit of giggles was joyful and contagious. Pete was running around the room in a superman costume, his cape flowing dramatically behind him. Amelia and Cindy were huddled together on the loveseat, feet curled up beneath them sipping coffee.

Randy had a wide grin on his face. "Welcome to my world."

"Pretty nice world, my friend. I'm envious."

Sophia looked up and caught Gunner's eye and smiled shyly. "Hi, handsome."

"Did ya miss me?" he asked, joining her on the floor. She nodded.

"Hey little feller, come to Uncle Gunner." He reached out his arms and JJ reached back.

"Uncle Gunner, I'm superman!" Pete said, vying for Gunner's attention.

"I see that. Are you keeping these beautiful ladies safe?"

He tilted his head and stared at Gunner in confusion. Gunner said, "Your ma and Soph and Amelia."

"Oh them. Yeah. Didn't I, Mom?"

"Yes. Thank goodness you were here."

Pete gave his mom a thumbs up and charged out of the room bellowing, "Don't be afraid. I'm superman!" They all chuckled.

"You about ready to go?" Gunner asked Sophia.

"Whenever you are."

"Amelia?"

"Anytime you are."

He hopped agilely to his feet and handed JJ to Cindy then gave Sophia a hand up.

"I don't want you to go," Cindy said. "I hope you take the offer, Gunner. I miss you."

"I miss y'all too. We'll see what happens. Meantime, thanks for everything. You guys are the best."

Amelia set her mug down and stood. "I guess it's that time. Thanks for having me Cindy. I feel like I've known you forever."

"You'll be in Nashville for a few more days. Let's have lunch before you go."

"I'll call you."

Randy gave Gunner a big bear hug. His voice gruff he said, "Let's go for it. I feel like it's our time."

"You'll be the first to know. I need a few days to think about it and to see if anything else turns up with those threats."

"You may have to go for it despite them and see where it takes you. We've got your back one hundred percent. Even if the photos surface, so what. You're an adult and at least we know now that she was legal age. We also know it wasn't her that set you up, so she's not trying to get anything out of it. She's as much a victim as you are."

"There is that. Thanks bud. I'll be in touch."

Sophia hugged everyone and said her goodbyes. She felt the sting of tears. Who knew when she'd see these new friends again . . . if ever? She hated to leave but she also felt the pull of Wyoming. It had gotten under her skin. The vastness, the beauty, the horses . . .

the peace it brought her . . . and one particular cowboy. Her heart felt light just thinking about returning. Glancing over at Gunner, she caught him watching her and she smiled. He winked as if he'd been reading her mind.

43

*S*ophia was leaning against the kitchen counter chatting with Gunner's mom when Gunner came in from the barn. He spotted her and his eyes lit up. "Sophia, I didn't expect you to be here. Hey Mom." He slung his arm across Sophia's shoulders and squeezed.

"How did the branding go?" Abby asked.

"Smooth as a pig's ear except I missed Elijah. We could've used him. His roping skills would've come in handy."

"That boy. I don't know what I'm going to do with him. He can't ride broncos for the rest of his life. It's too hard on the ole bod."

"Don't worry Ma. He'll figure it out," Gunner said reassuringly.

"I would've thought after his last injury it would have penetrated that thick skull of his. He's not in his twenties anymore. It's about time you two settled down and thought about having a family." Sophia felt her cheeks heat and looked down.

"Think so?" he drawled. "What do you think about that Soph?" He grinned and she knew he had noticed her flushed face.

"Gunner Cane you're embarrassing the poor dear. Quit your teasing and do something about it before this one gets away."

"I intend to," Gunner said. Sophia gasped and covered her mouth. Gunner laughed and Abby shook her head.

"I don't know what I'm to do about you, son. Sophia don't pay him any mind. Ya hear?"

Sophia nodded.

"Back to the branding. We're definitely going to have to hire a couple more ranch hands. Especially if I take up touring again," Gunner said.

"Luke and your father have already interviewed a couple of people. They've narrowed it down and three are coming in for a second interview this week."

Gunner's eyes widened. "Wow that was fast work."

"You know your brother."

"Speaking of Luke, besides interviews where's big brother been hiding out anyway? I haven't seen hide nor hair of him since I got back."

"He's been working on revamping our website and in talks with that new outdoor adventure group to see if we can help each other out. Being neighborly and all."

"Yeah, my anti-social brother being neighborly. That's a good one."

"Don't say things ya don't mean. You know how

hard it's been on him since Lauren died." Abby looked at Sophia. "He and Lauren were together since middle school. They were best friends their whole lives. True soul mates. I was afraid that we were going to lose Luke for a while after she passed. It was only because of Clayton that he pulled himself out."

"That's heartbreaking," Sophia said.

"Indeed, it was. Lauren was such a lovely person. Quiet and kind, she loved little Clay so much." Abby's eyes grew misty. "That was the hardest part for her. Knowing she'd never see her baby grow up. She never complained though. She was taking care of all of us until the end. She made Luke promise that he'd remarry someday. He said he would to pacify her, but he has no interest."

Sophia nodded. "Grief is different for everyone. It takes as long as it takes. I think my dad would've been lost without my mom, too. They're best friends, like Lauren and Luke, I imagine."

"I guess you're right, but I worry about him. He keeps to himself far too much."

Gunner interjected. "I was hoping maybe you'd like to join me. I'm taking Amitola out for a ride."

"Sure. Who will I ride?"

"We'll ride tandem. You don't weigh more than a bale of hay soaking wet. We'll hop on together and ride her bareback."

He tugged her hand, pulling her behind him as he called over his shoulder to his mom, "See ya Ma."

· · ·

*T*hey passed Beau on their way to the tack room and he looked up from stacking hay bales. He brushed his sweat soaked hair back from his brow then plunked his cowboy hat back on. By the looks of things, he'd been working for quite some time. The truck bed was almost empty and the bales were stacked neatly about six foot high.

Beau flashed a huge grin. "Hey Soph, been a while. You guys going for a ride?"

"Yes. Working hard I see."

"My helper made a run to the feed store to pick up grain so I'm on my own. I didn't do all this by my lonesome."

"I'm glad." Sophia smiled.

"We're taking Amitola out for a short one," Gunner said.

"Perfect day fer it."

Gunner grabbed what he needed and they went to fetch Amitola. They stood by the gate and Gunner whistled then called her name and she came galloping in from the pasture. He haltered her and tied her to a hitching post while Sophia watched.

"She's such a beauty," Sophia said, enjoying the view of Gunner's fine body bent over the horse's hooves. He had taken his shirt off and he looked so good. His muscular back was tanned and lean. Her stomach fluttered just thinking about their lovemaking the night before.

"She has a soul to match. I love this filly. I can be in the darkest place and she lifts me out of it every time."

He slipped her bridle on. "I'll climb on first and help you up. Just stand on the middle fence rung there."

He jumped up then held out his hand and gripped hers, hauling her onto Amitola's back behind him. She slipped her arms around his waist and hugged him tight. Her sleeveless shirt allowed for maximum skin contact. "Are you sure we aren't too heavy for her?"

"No way. She's fine."

Sophia rubbed her cheek against Gunner's back and took in his heady male scent. A little bit of sweat, a bit of horse and some cedar. *Mm . . .* she flattened her palms on his ripped abs, just below his navel. It was all she could do to not slip her hands into the waist band of his jeans.

He smoothed his rough palm over her arm. "How can skin be so damn soft? Yours feels like silk. Hold on tight now ya hear?" He reached down to squeeze her thigh before taking up the reins. "Giddy up," he said, then clicked his tongue urging Amitola forward. They took the trail head towards the river. The trust between horse and rider was obvious, his confidence instilled calm in his horse and was sexy as hell.

*T*he scenery was breathtaking and the mountains beckoned. Sitting on Amitola, nestled so close behind Gunner was exhilarating. There wasn't a cloud to be seen in the big blue sky. *I don't know when I've ever felt this alive.* They were quiet for some time, both lost in the moment. Gunner's body straightened and he pointed ahead. Off in the distance a small herd of elk grazed. He gently reined Amitola to a stop and they watched until the elk became aware of them and bolted off.

"Oh my! That was magical," Sophia said.

"It's such a contrast to the city life," he said quietly. "When I came back after being away, it took me some time to appreciate what I had. I was so disillusioned that I couldn't see the miracles right in front of my face."

"That just makes you human," Sophia said softly.

"I've been thinking real hard about things, taking inventory of myself. It came to me this morning that I didn't have to choose one over the other. What if I make Wyoming my home base between touring and recording?"

"I don't see why you couldn't."

"That leads me to a proposition I have for you. What if you stay on here . . . work as our pastry chef, Mom still doing most of the cooking? When I'm on tour, if I'm lucky enough to continue, you go with me."

She drew in a sharp breath. "What are you saying?"

"I'm saying . . . move here with me. Make Wyoming your home . . . or more to my liking . . . make me your home."

"I . . . I . . . you caught me off guard. I'm sorry . . . I . . ."

"Let me start again. I've been going about this all wrong. Instead of cowering waiting for the other shoe to drop, why not take the bull by the horns and say to hell with it. I never used to be a yellow belly, but lately I've been makin' decisions out of fear and embarrass-ment. If they release the photos, so what? I'll make a statement and let the chips fall wherever they will. If it's meant to be, I'll make music. As long as you're by my side, that's the most important thing."

"It's a lot to take in. I . . . you know I . . . my home has always been Chicago. I'm a city girl. My parents are there. Amelia lives there, I don't know."

"I don't expect an answer immediately. Think about it. You can visit your folks whenever you want. Becca will still be here helping Ma and we have the assistants too, so you won't feel locked down. Sophia, we can make this work. I can't imagine my life without you in it."

Sophia sighed and hugged him. "I've got to admit that when I got on that plane in Nashville and thought about returning here, it's like I was coming home. This place, the people, the land, the ranch, has all snuck up on me and seeped into my bones. Not to mention some smooth-talking cowboy."

He covered her hands with his. "I won't keep bugging you about it. Just let your imagination run with it. Dream big. You can always try it and if it doesn't work you can change your mind."

"I need time to think . . . it's got nothing to do with my feeling for you . . . you know that right? It's just hard for me to imagine our future together. It'd be such a big change. But when I stay put in the present everything's perfect."

"I've learned most of my limits are the ones I make up in my own head. I used to believe that I could do anything I put my mind to . . . then I lost my way for a bit. Had to get back to it, I reckon. You're starting over, too. Now's good a time as any—why not take a leap of faith, I won't let you fall."

She sighed. "You make it sound so simple . . . at least you've come to a decision about getting the band back together."

"An opportunity like this doesn't come knocking every day. I wouldn't want to blow it for the rest of the group either."

"I think you should go for it. And I still haven't given up hope that Amelia will get to the bottom of who sent those threats. It would be nice if you could lay that to rest permanently."

"It'd be nice, but I don't have to let it dictate how I live my life anymore. I keep thinking I'm missing something that's right in front of my face. It started when I was in Nashville. I can't get to it though." He shook his head.

They both got quiet again. The horse plodded along; the rhythm of the gait, the fresh air and sunshine lulled Sophia into a dreamlike state. She felt like she was melting into Gunner, feeling his movements, the subtle rise and fall of his hips between her thighs with the easy gait of Amitola. *I could fall asleep right now.*

"Soph?"

"Mm?"

"I can see it."

"See what?"

"Our future together." She hugged him then slipped her hand under the waist of his jeans. He gently took ahold of it and placed it back on his belly. He chuckled softly. "You trying to get us thrown off the horse?"

"That scenario hadn't occurred to me." She bit his shoulder and said, "Spoilsport."

"Just wait until I get you back home. You'll see who the spoilsport is."

"Winning," she smiled as he turned to head back, nudging Amitola into a fast canter.

44

*I*n the middle of the night, Sophia was startled awake as Gunner sat bolt upright in bed. They'd arrived back in Nashville that afternoon, a day before the band was scheduled to play their first concert in almost a year. It took her several seconds to recall where they were. *Oh yeah . . . hotel room.* She opened one eye and looked at him. "You okay? Bad dream?"

"It just came to me."

"What?"

"What's been bugging me since the last time we were in Nashville."

Sophia sat up next to him and touched his shoulder. "I'm not sure I'm following."

"Remember when I told you that there was something teasing the back of my mind?"

"Vaguely."

"I remember what it was now. When me and Randy

met with Jimmy, he said something off the cuff . . . he knew I'd been threatened again . . . not from the time before but recently."

"What did he say?"

"It was something like 'Why would I shoot myself in the foot now? I'm excited about the band getting back together.' He wasn't referring to the past—it was said about the present. Problem is we never told him about the recent threats, only about the one from a year ago."

"Are you sure? To me that statement is ambiguous."

"I reckon that could be said, but it was the way he said it. It was like he wouldn't derail us now that we had this new opportunity."

"It's a little late to confront him now. You've got a show tonight. You can ask Jimmy about it later. Right now, your focus needs to be on your performance. It's your big launch. Plus, it's hardly proof that it was Jimmy."

"I know, but it's a gut feeling."

Sophia cradled his head against her shoulder and rubbed his back soothingly. "Go back to sleep. You need your rest; you've got a big day tomorrow." She glanced at the red glow of the bedside clock. "Or should I say today?"

He kissed her neck and within minutes Sophia could hear his soft steady breath and knew he'd drifted off to sleep. She on the other hand, was wide awake and plotting how she and Amelia could prove whether or not Jimmy was behind the setup.

.   .   .

"We'd better hightail it outta here," Gunner said, looking at his watch for the umpteenth time.

"I guess we'd better leave now or Gunner's gonna wear a groove into our hardwood floors," Randy said. They'd watched him nervously pace back and forth between the living room and dining room for the last half-hour.

"I want to check out the setup and we've got to do a short rehearsal and our sound check. You know as well as anyone, anything can go wrong," Gunner said.

Sophia stepped in front of him and put her hands on his shoulders and looked him in the eye. "No 'what ifs' remember? You'll handle whatever comes up. Now get out of here before you drive us all crazy. I'll see you at the show."

Gunner leaned down and kissed her thoroughly. Randy's son Pete groaned dramatically holding his belly, then loudly proclaimed, "I'm going to barf." Which made everyone laugh, distracting them from their pre-performance jitters.

Cindy closed the door behind them and said, "I think I'm more nervous than they are."

"I know, right?" Sophia agreed. "I wish Amelia would get here. We need to get our plans laid out."

"I know you couldn't say anything with the guys here, but are you sure you want to go through with this?"

"Yes. It was Amelia's idea and I have to agree. It seems like our best shot at getting to the bottom of things."

"But what if you get caught? It's breaking and entering. You could go to jail."

"That's why we can't get caught."

There was a knock at the door and Cindy got up to let Amelia in. She was dressed non-descriptively with sunglasses on and her hair tucked up in a ball cap.

"Cindy, do you have a hat for Sophia? Her red hair would really stand out."

"Yeah, let me get it. I also have a pair of sunglasses if you need them."

"I've got a pair, thanks."

Cindy returned and they huddled together going over their loose plan. They knew Jimmy lived alone and that he had to be at the rehearsal and sound check by five. The show started at eight. Cindy was very familiar with the layout of Jimmy's house and she mapped out the floor plan.

Cindy said, "You guys won't stand out much anyway because of his bohemian lifestyle. There are always people coming and going . . . jam sessions, people crashing there overnight. I wouldn't be surprised if the door was unlocked and you can walk right in."

"That would be a blessing," Sophia said. Her palms were sweaty and her heart raced. Cindy had the bright idea to wrap Sophia's hair in a scarf before adding the hat over it. She stood behind her and wound it around her head, tying it off at the nape of her neck before placing the bolo hat over the fabric. Stepping back to admire her handywork she said, "Perfect."

Amelia stood and patted Sophia on the back and said, "Let's do this thing. Get it over with."

"Go team!" Cindy said.

A half hour later they set up surveillance from their car a few doors down from Jimmy's place. All appeared to be quiet.

"We'll give it a half hour, if there's no action we'll knock on the front door, then if there's no answer we'll try the door like Cindy suggested. If it's locked, on to plan B," Amelia said.

"My stomach is in knots. I hope I don't have to suddenly use the bathroom," Sophia said.

"You'd better not."

They waited and waited until Sophia wanted to crawl out of her skin. She glanced over at Amelia and said, "How can you be this calm?"

"I'm an adrenalin junkie. Goes with my profession. Sometimes you have to go way outside of the box for a scoop. To me, this seems like a three on a scale of one to ten."

"That's good to hear."

"Are you ready?"

"Not really, but the longer we sit here the less ready I'm becoming."

"Follow my lead. Remember to act like we belong here. Jimmy invited us."

"Got it."

They stepped out of their rental and marched up to the front door. Amelia knocked and waited several seconds before trying again. When she was sure nobody was on the other side, she tried the door. "It's locked," she said keeping her voice low.

"Figures," Soph said.

"Let's go around to the back. Thank God he has a privacy fence."

They let themselves into the back yard and walked around the perimeter of the back house. "Looks like the basement window is our best bet. I'll go in first," Amelia said, squatting down. She pried off the outer screen and pushed against the glass. "We might have to break it."

Sophia wrung her hands. "Are you sure?"

"I'll try the other two windows, but if they're all locked that's the only way."

While Amelia checked that out, Sophia tried the back door. Her eyes widened in shock when the knob turned and she was able to push it open.

"Amelia," she hissed, jumping up and down, waving to her friend trying to get her attention.

Amelia looked up and her jaw dropped, then a big smile spread across her face. She straightened and ran to Sophia and they went inside.

"I'll go through his bedroom and you start going through the kitchen drawers. We know he used a burner and I'm sure he has his personal phone on him. If you find anything come and get me." Just as Amelia was turning towards the hallway, they both heard the front door open. Amelia grabbed Sophia by the arm and pulled her along. She opened the first door she saw which happened to be a hall closet and they dove in, quickly shutting themselves inside.

Sophia had landed right on top of Amelia; their limbs were entangled with little room to maneuver. Not to mention that they couldn't make a sound because the voices were very close by . . . in fact they were right outside their hiding spot.

"Jimmy said his black boots were in the bedroom closet," a female voice said.

"He'd forget his head if it wasn't attached," a second female replied.

"He needs his wallet too. Top drawer of his desk."

"I'll get that then."

Sophia was between a fit of giggles and a full-blown panic attack. *What the hell am I doing here?* She was afraid to breathe for fear of them hearing her. The closet was small, stuffy and dark. She was sure she was crushing Amelia but if they moved, they'd be caught. *Poor Amelia.* Amelia shifted slightly under her and something banged against the closet wall. They both froze . . . waiting . . . *nothing . . . we didn't give ourselves away.*

After what felt like hours, they heard the women leave. Still afraid to come out of hiding they didn't make a move to get out for several minutes. Amelia whispered, "I'm not sure I'll be able to move. Both my legs are asleep."

"My left foot is completely numb," Soph said softly. She pressed the stem of her watch and it glowed revealing the time. "We're going to miss the show if we don't get out of here."

Sophia reached for the knob and opened the door. They fell out into the hallway and lay sprawled there. Amelia disentangled herself and shook out her legs. "I'm not sure I'll ever get feeling back."

Sophia grimaced, massaging her calf. "What were we thinking? We must be crazy!"

"We're already here. Let's get cracking."

Amelia stood up and stomped her feet and

stretched then headed for Jimmy's bedroom. Sophia returned to the kitchen and started going through drawers. Minutes later Amelia came up behind her and said, "Score." She held up a cell phone, her cheeks flushed with excitement.

"Can you access it?"

"Yep. The photos are there."

"Wow! I can't believe it. I mean I thought it was him but I'm still shocked. Could it really be this easy?"

Amelia laughed. "Easy? Let's get the hell out of here." They left through the front door.

45

*G*unner tried phoning Sophia for the fourth
time and it went straight to voicemail again.
He was beginning to get worried. They were
about to take the stage and he hadn't talked to her since
he'd left the house. He turned his phone off and
handed it to one of the roadies. Randy caught his eye
and jerked his thumb towards the stage. Gunner
nodded.

Natalie came up behind him and said, "Ya ready to
take Nashville by storm?" She was decked out with her
usual dramatic flair. Long flowing peasant dress, tattoos
displayed, cowboy boots and wild hair . . . the stunning
bad girl of country music.

Randy joined them. Per usual he and Dirk had kept
it simple . . . black tees, hats and jeans along with their
cowboy boots. Jimmy wore his hair in a man bun and
had on tan cargo shorts and a Trailers tee shirt. Gunner
looked down at his own attire, Miranda Lambert tee

shirt tucked into his faded Levi's, his trusty cowboy hat and scuffed up boots. He looked back up at Natalie.

"Yeah, how 'bout you?" he asked.

"Beyond ready. You boys look as gorgeous as ever. You'll have the women climbing onto the stage. And, by the way Gunner, you sounded amazing during sound check."

"Thanks. So did you."

"Where's Sophia?" Randy asked.

Gunner frowned. "I have no idea. I can't reach her."

"I'm sure you heard that Phillip rented the entire rooftop restaurant for our after party," Natalie said.

"Yep. Will your new guy friend be there?"

"Yes. You'll like him. He's a keeper."

The announcer took the stage to introduce them and the crowd cheered. "We're pleased to have the one and only Gunner Cane and The Trailers back . . . playing here for the first time after taking some time off. Let's give them a warm welcome."

Jimmy walked on first to take a seat behind his drums, followed by Randy, Dirk, Natalie, then Gunner. Natalie picked up her fiddle from the stand, placed it under her chin and began playing a rousing hoe down melody that had the crowd on their feet. Drums were added, then bass and guitar, finally Gunner joined in with his guitar. They slowed the intro tune and Gunner stepped up to the mic. He looked out at the crowd of expectant faces and felt momentarily choked up. *I'm really here. This is happening.*

Taking one last glance backstage, his heart skipped a beat when he saw Sophia smiling at him, making a heart shape with her hands over her chest. He nodded and winked, now at ease, he began to sing.

*S*ophia hung on to Gunner's arm as they took the elevator up to the rooftop, where the celebratory afterparty was being held. Her dark eyes sparkled like jewels; her hair was swept up in a chignon with escaped tendrils framing her delicate face and tear-drop ruby earrings dangled from each ear. His eyes swept up and down her body, lingering on the hint of cleavage her short strapless black dress provided before meeting her gaze.

"You look good enough to eat," Gunner said. "Those red lips . . . mm."

"Glad you approve." Her cheeks flushed under his intense stare.

"Approve? Darlin I'm ready to lasso you, ditch this party and take you back to our hotel and ravish you."

Amelia cleared her throat. "Excuse me guys, but remember me . . . good ole Amelia?"

Gunner chuckled. "Yeah, our very own Miss Marple."

"I take offense to that! I'm way to young and sexy to be compared to Miss Marple. How about Dana Scully from X-files? Besides, I had a sidekick . . . maybe we could be Cagney and Lacey."

"Keep my innocent girlfriend out of this. She was corrupted plain and simple."

Amelia sputtered. "She is the one who came to me!"

"But I'm sure it was your idea to trespass."

"It's obvious you have a lot to learn about my friend.

She might seem all sweet and innocent, but she's got a wild streak a mile long."

Gunner raised a teasing eyebrow at Sophia. "Is that true? I'll have to hear more later."

The elevator doors opened and they stepped right out to the roof top terrace with the party in full swing. In late September the Tennessee nights were still warm. Twinkle lights were strung around the perimeter of the patio area as well as over the arbor covering the outdoor bar. There were huge planters with bright colorful flowers and potted trees everywhere. Tall café tables and stools dotted the area and loud country music streamed through overhead speakers. Drinks were flowing and laughter filled the air. Gunner spotted Randy with his arm around Cindy, who waved excitedly when she spied them.

"There's Cindy! Let's go over there." Sophia tugged on his arm.

"Looks like the wait staff are walking around with trays of appetizers. I'll go round us up some drinks. What's your pleasure Miss Marple?" He couldn't resist ribbing Amelia. She was so easy.

Ignoring him, Amelia said, "Tell your boyfriend I'll have a glass of Chardonnay."

Sophia laughed. "I swear you two are like siblings. I'll have the same."

"I'll meet you over there."

*A*fter handing them their drinks, Gunner pulled Randy aside to fill him in on what Soph and Amelia had discovered. "I think I'm going to get him alone and confront him about it. Care to join me?"

"Tonight?" Randy asked.

"Why not? I can't work with him after this anyway. I just want to know why . . . give him a chance to explain and make sure it stops right here and now."

Randy hung his head. "Whatever you think's best."

"No time like the present. Speaking of the devil, look who just arrived." Gunner nodded towards the elevator as Jimmy stepped out with a woman on each arm.

"Honestly, it's like a fist in the gut. It tears me up that it was him," Gunner said.

Randy patted him on the back. "I know, me too. We've been through so much together. The fat and the lean times . . . everything in between. I'll never get it."

After he and Sophia had made the rounds, Gunner caught Randy's attention and jerked his head in Jimmy's direction. Randy nodded and he and Cindy joined them at their table.

"We're going to have a chat with Jimmy," Gunner announced. "Shouldn't take too long." Sophia fidgeted nervously with her wine glass. He hadn't been able to convince her that this was the right time to confront Jimmy. He tilted her chin up and kissed her nose. "Don't look so worried, Red."

She gave a half shrug and said, "I can't help it. I wish you'd wait."

"I'm sorry Soph. I want to get it over with. It's eating me up."

"I know it is. It's your call. Good luck."

He and Randy went to find Jimmy.

. . .

"*M*an, what a show tonight! I'm higher than a kite," Jimmy said as Gunner and Randy approached.

Gunner's throat tightened. "Jimmy, can we have a word in private with ya?"

Jimmy jammed his hands in his front pockets and faced Gunner, his body in a defensive stance. "Sure man, but what's this about? You've been acting strange all day."

"Let's go off in that corner and chat a bit."

Jimmy's eyes darted around and landed on Randy. "What's going on Randy? You're both looking mighty serious." Randy looked away.

Gunner turned and headed for the far corner away from the rest of the partiers. Jimmy and Randy followed. Gunner kept his back to them. Slapping his palms on the cinderblock wall, he stared out at the city lights and the river view below.

He slowly turned to face them and said the only thing he could think to say.

"Why Jimmy?"

Jimmy's hands balled into fists. "What are ya talking about?"

A muscle in Gunner's jaw twitched. "We know it was you. All I want to know is why. Why'd ya do it Jimmy?"

The color drained out of his face. "I don't know what the hell yer talking about."

Gunner grabbed Jimmy by the shoulders and shook him hard. "Why?"

Randy reached into his pocket and pulled out the burner phone Gunner had slipped to him, waving the screen with a photo in front of Jimmy's face. Panicked, Jimmy shoved them aside and ran. Looking around wildly he suddenly jumped onto the wall, balancing on the ledge facing the river. "Leave me alone! I . . . it wasn't me. I don't know where you got that, but it's not my phone." He frantically dug into his back pocket, teetering on the block wall. Turning he said, "See? Here's my phone." Seeing their expressions his shoulders slumped. He looked down at the dark waters of the rushing river. Voice anguished he said, "I ain't going to no prison."

"Jimmy!" Gunner sprang forward. "Get down. Nothins' worth your life."

"Really? What do you know about my life?"

"We played together, worked together, ten years man." Gunner's voice broke. "I thought we were friends."

He looked down at Gunner, lips twisted. "Friends?"

Gunner's eyes narrowed. "Weren't we?"

"Let's see . . . oh yeah, being friends with Gunner Cane . . . the wonder boy. Born with a silver spoon in his mouth. Had everything handed to him. All the women love him . . . a real star. A friend who stole my girl right out from under me." Jimmy's voice choked up. "Stole her and then dumped her like a piece of trash. I loved her. How could ya do that to me? Huh?"

"You're talking about Amber?"

"Duh, ya catchin on yet? Course it was Amber. You were so into yourself I bet you didn't even know I was dating her, did ya?" Jimmy's face scrunched up and he choked back a sob. "You didn't even give a shit when she had a breakdown did ya? Life was your bowl of fuckin' cherries wasn't it? Do ya know what it's like to always be second fiddle? Course ya don't." Bitterly, he continued. "Nashville's rising star. The golden boy."

Gunner rubbed his temples. "About Amber . . . Greg set that up. I didn't have any interest in her. I only went out with her because she was pressuring Greg to fix us up. I had no idea you were dating her."

"Like I said, if ya didn't know, it was because it wasn't about you." He swayed on the edge for a second and Gunner held his breath.

"I don't know what to say. You could have confronted me. Punched me out . . . something . . . anything . . . but blackmail?"

"Blackmail? It wasn't no blackmail. I was trying to get you to leave Nashville. I couldn't stand the sight of ya anymore. You were unhappy anyways . . . I just gave you the excuse ya needed to leave."

Gunner shook his head in disbelief. "Do you even hear yourself?"

Randy jumped in. "Jimmy, come down. Let's talk about this. Gunner won't press charges. Right Gunner? Think of your parents . . . your new girl."

Jimmy hung his head, looking back down at the dark waters below.

Gunner moved to Jimmy's left side trying to distract him while Randy flanked him on his right. "Jimmy, I don't believe you when ya say we weren't friends. We had some good times together. It might not have seemed like it to you, but I was torn up when Amber broke down. I beat myself up that I ever let Greg twist my arm. I'm so sorry. If I'd have known you liked her, I'd never have agreed to take her out in the first place. I swear to you."

He looked down at Gunner and it was the moment Randy had been waiting for. He lunged quickly and wrapped his arms around Jimmy's waist and pulled him down from the ledge. They both tumbled to the ground, Randy using his weight to keep Jimmy pinned down.

Gunner's heart was racing so fast he felt dizzy. He crouched down and bent over his knees, taking in big gulps of air. The world had stood still when Jimmy teetered on that ledge. Hands down the scariest moment of Gunner's life. Randy was now sitting with his arm wrapped around Jimmy while he sobbed.

Gunner sat down beside them, his body still shaking. "Jimmy, I was half out of my mind after Natalie left. I'm sorry I let ya down. Please forgive me. You got to let this bitterness go or it'll eat ya alive. You're the most talented drummer I know. Don't waste your time comparing yourself or thinking something's missing from your life."

"I swear I didn't think it was blackmail. I knew ya had family and the ranch to go back to . . . that you was a cowboy at heart. You hadn't been happy in Nashville for a long time . . . since you and Natalie split. That's how I justified it I reckon. I swear I've got nothing more besides what's on that phone. I'm sorry."

"I believe ya and I forgive ya Jimmy. I'll destroy the phone and be done with it."

Gunner stood and brushed himself off and turned and walked away, leaving Jimmy in Randy's capable hands. His steps leaden, he headed back to the party. Just at the edge of the lights he stopped and watched Sophia laughing at something Amelia had said. He stood frozen to the spot, unable to move. Just then, Sophia looked up and saw him standing there. She rose and walked slowly towards him. When she reached him, sadness clouded her eyes as she gathered him to her and held on tight. "It's going to be alright," she said. He buried his face in her neck and breathed deep.

46

*S*ophia sprinkled more flour onto the dough and continued kneading. She had the kitchen to herself and the radio tuned into a country station. *I'm learning.* She smiled. *Hard to believe it's been three weeks since we got back from Nashville.* She was settling into her routine nicely. She'd made a promise to herself to let go and dive into life on the ranch for a while . . . see how it fit. She missed her parents like crazy, but she talked to them almost every day.

Gunner wouldn't have to return to Nashville until early spring to rehearse for the tour with Miranda. Until then, the band could practice and do some sound mixing for their new CD virtually. She rubbed her itchy nose; too late she realized she'd just added another layer of flour to her face. She wiped her palms down her apron and swiped at her nose again. Clayton came running in. "Sophia! Come quick. I have to show you something."

"Can it wait one minute? I have to make this dough up into loaves."

"No. I promise it can't wait."

Sighing she took his proffered hand and let him lead her out. "Hurry," he said tugging her along.

"I'm coming."

He headed towards the main lodge foyer. When they got close, he said, "Close your eyes and don't peek."

"What are you up too?"

"Please. And you got to promise you won't open them till I tell ya."

She smiled indulgently. "Okay, I promise." She closed her eyes. *What is this little buck snort up too?* He held her hand and pulled her forward then stopped.

"Okay, you can open them."

She opened one eye, half afraid of what Clay had in store for her.

"Surprise!"

Her mouth gaped open. "Mom! Dad! Amelia! What in the world?"

She ran to her parents and hugged them. "What are you guys doing here?"

"We were invited by that good looking cowboy standing over there," her mom said. She looked over and Gunner was practically beaming. He looked so pleased with himself that she had to laugh.

"Now how did you manage to keep this a secret?"

"Thanks to Amelia's help we carried it off." He walked over to her and slung his arm across her shoulders, looking smug. Sophia looked around curiously at the rest of the group. Eli was home; Becca, Luke, and

Gunner's parents were all there. So was Hank, standing very close to Amelia as a matter of fact. Beau stood off to the side playing with the rim of his cowboy hat, and of course Lenny and Clifford were happily in the middle of the fray, tails wagging.

Her eyes narrowed. "Is it somebody's birthday or something?"

"Guess again," Gunner said.

"I can't." With everyone staring at her she remembered that she was a hot mess. Covered in flour and hair piled randomly on top of her head, no makeup . . . *crap.*

Gunner stepped in front of her and when she met his twinkling eyes she suddenly knew. Her hands shook and her heart leapt into her throat as he knelt on one knee before her. He was hers. And she was his. *That's all that matters.*

"Sophia, the day I met you, I knew I'd never be the same. You had the prettiest smile I'd ever seen and the sassiest mouth I'd ever wanted to kiss. I want you by my side for the rest of my life. You're it for me. I can't remember my life before you and I never want to know it without you. I promise to do my best to make you feel loved and cherished every single day. I'm asking . . . no . . . truthfully I'm begging, will you marry me?"

The emotion behind his earnest words tugged at her heart and her voice wavered when she answered him. "Gunner Cane, you had me at 'the prettiest smile.' It's a big fat yes!" She leaned down and kissed him softly on the lips as everyone cheered. He stood and picked her up, swinging her around.

"You just made this cowboy's dreams come true. I love you Sophia Russo."

"I love you Gunner Cane. I guess a cowboy can be tamed after all."

He covered her mouth with his and kissed her senseless as their closest family and friends hooted and hollered and the hounds bayed with joyful abandon.

The End for Now

Thanks for reading Cowboy Magic, Book One of The Triple C Ranch Series. I so loved these characters and hope you did too! If you haven't read my Billionaire series there's the link below for Book One. Happy Reading!

~Jill Downey

∩

Please Consider leaving a Review on Amazon.com

I hope you will consider leaving a review on Amazon.com. A rating or even a even a brief comment would be very much appreciated.

Facebook page: search for Author Jill Downey

Here's the universal link to **Book One**, *Seduced by a Billionaire*:
mybook.to/SeducedbyaBillionaire

Here's the universal link to **The Heartland Series complete box set:**

mybook.to/BoxSetHeartlandSeries

Please join my **Facebook readers group**, where I have giveaways, teasers and pre-release excerpts: https://www.facebook.com/groups/179183050062278/

BOOKS BY JILL DOWNEY

The Heartland Series:

More Than A Boss

More Than A Memory

More Than A Fling

The Heartland Series Box Set

The Carolina Series:

Seduced by a Billionaire

Secret Billionaire

Playboy Billionaire

A Billionaire's Christmas

The Carolina Series Box Set

The Triple C Ranch Series

Cowboy Magic

Cowboy Surprise

Printed in Great Britain
by Amazon

21466591R00195